LAXDAELA SAGA

Anonymous

Organized and designed by Lu Evans

Translated from Icelandic by Muriel A.C. Press

Cover image: Pixabay

Printed in the United States of America, 2017

Authorship

As is the case with the other Icelanders' sagas, the author of Laxdœla saga is unknown. Since the saga has often been regarded as an unusually feminine saga, it has been speculated that it was composed by a woman.

The extensive knowledge the author shows of locations and conditions in the Breiðafjörður area show that the author must have lived in Western Iceland. Internal evidence shows that the saga must have been composed sometime in the period 1230-1260.

On several occasions, Laxdœla saga explicitly cites what appear to be written sources. It twice refers to the writings of Ari Þorgilsson, once to a lost Þorgils saga Höllusonar and once to a Njarðvíkinga saga, perhaps an alternative name for Gunnars þáttr Þiðrandabana. The author was also likely familiar with a number of other written historical sources. Nevertheless, the main sources of the author must have been oral traditions, which he or she fleshed out and shaped according to his or her tastes.

Laxdœla saga is preserved in numerous manuscripts. The oldest manuscript to contain the saga in its entirety is Möðruvallabók dating to the mid-14th century. There are also five vellum fragments, the oldest dating to ca. 1250, and numerous young paper manuscripts, some of which are valuable for textual criticism of the saga.

Scholars have divided the manuscripts into two groups, the Y group, which includes Möðruvallabók, and the Z group, which includes the oldest fragment. The greatest divergence between the groups is that the Y group contains an addition of ten chapters to the saga. These chapters were not written by the original author and are regarded by scholars as a separate work, Bolla þáttr Bollasonar. Another difference between the groups is that the theft of Kjartan's sword is narrated in two different ways. Most other differences between the manuscripts are minor variations in wording.

LAXDAELA SAGA

CHAPTER I
Of Ketill Flatnose and his
Descendants, 9th Century A.D.

Ketill Flatnose was the name of a man. He was the son of Bjorn the Ungartered. Ketill was a mighty and high-born chieftain (hersir) in Norway. He abode in Raumsdale, within the folkland of the Raumsdale people, which lies between Southmere and Northmere. Ketill Flatnose had for wife Yngvild, daughter of Ketill Wether, who was a man of exceeding great worth. They had five children; one was named Bjorn the Eastman, and another Helgi Bjolan. Thorunn the Horned was the name of one of Ketill's daughters, who was the wife of Helgi the Lean, son of Eyvind Eastman, and Rafarta, daughter of Kjarval, the Irish king. Unn "the Deep-minded" was another of Ketill's daughters, and was the wife of Olaf the White, son of Ingjald, who was son of Frodi the Valiant, who was slain by the Svertlings. Jorunn, "Men's Wit-breaker," was the name of yet another of Ketill'sdaughters. She was the mother of Ketill the Finn, who settled on land at Kirkby. His son was Asbjorn, father of Thorstein, father of Surt, the father of Sighat the Speaker-at-Law.

CHAPTER II
Ketill and his Sons
prepare to leave Norway

In the latter days of Ketill arose the power of King Harald the Fairhaired, in such a way that no folkland king or other great men could thrive in the land unless he alone ruled what title should be theirs. When Ketill heard that King Harald was minded to put to him the same choice as to other men of might—namely, not only to put up with his kinsmen being left unatoned, but to be made himself a hireling to boot—he calls together a meeting of his kinsmen, and began his speech in this wise: "You all know what dealings there have been between me and King Harald, the which there is no need of setting forth; for a greater need besets us, to wit, to take counsel as to the troubles that now are in store for us. I have true news of King Harald's enmity towards us, and to me it seems that we may abide no trust from that quarter. It seems to me that there are two choices left us, either to fly the land or to be slaughtered each in his own seat. Now, as for me, my will is rather to abide the same death that my kinsmen suffer, but I would not lead you by my wilfulness into so great a trouble, for I know the temper of my kinsmen and friends, that ye would not desert me, even though it would be some trial of manhood to follow me." Bjorn, the son of Ketill, answered: "I will make known my wishes at once. I will follow the example of noble men, and fly this land. For I deem myself no greater a man by abiding at home the thralls of King Harald, that they may chase me away from my own possessions, or that else I may have to come by utter death at their hands." At this there was made a good cheer, and they all thought it was spoken bravely. This counsel then was settled, that they should leave the country, for the sons of Ketill urged it much, and no one spoke against it. Bjorn and Helgi wished to go to Iceland, for they said they had heard many pleasing news thereof. They had been told that there was good land to be had there, and no need to pay money for it; they said there was plenty of whale and salmon and other fishing all the year round there. But Ketill said, "Into that fishing place I shall never come in my old age." So Ketill then told his mind, saying his desire was rather to go west over the sea, for there was a chance of getting a good livelihood. He knew lands there wide about, for there he had harried far and wide.

CHAPTER III

Ketill's Sons go to Iceland

After that Ketill made a great feast, and at it he married his daughter Thorunn the Horned to Helgi the Lean, as has been said before. After that Ketill arrayed his journey west over the sea. Unn, his daughter, and many others of his relations went with him. That same summer Ketill's sons went to Iceland with Helgi, their brother-in-law. Bjorn, Ketill's son, brought his ship to the west coast of Iceland, to Broadfirth, and sailed up the firth along the southern shore, till he came to where a bay cuts into the land, and a high mountain stood on the ness on the inner side of the bay, but an island lay a little way off the land. Bjorn said that they should stay there for a while. Bjorn then went on land with a few men, and wandered along the coast, and but a narrow strip of land was there between fell and foreshore. This spot he thought suitable for habitation. Bjorn found the pillars of his temple washed up in a certain creek, and he thought that showed where he ought to build his house. Afterwards Bjorn took for himself all the land between Staff-river and Lavafirth, and abode in the place that ever after was called Bjornhaven. He was called Bjorn the Eastman. His wife, Gjaflaug, was the daughter of Kjallak the Old. Their sons were Ottar and Kjallak, whose son was Thorgrim, the father of Fight-Styr and Vemund, but the daughter of Kjallak was named Helga, who was the wife of Vestar of Eyr, son of Thorolf "Bladder-skull," who settled Eyr. Their son was Thorlak, father of Steinthor of Eyr. Helgi Bjolan brought his ship to the south of the land, and took all Keelness, between

Kollafirth and Whalefirth, and lived at Esjuberg to old age. Helgi the Lean brought his ship to the north of the land, and took Islefirth, all along between Mastness and Rowanness, and lived at Kristness. From Helgi and Thornunn all the Islefirthers are sprung.

CHAPTER IV
Ketill goes to Scotland, A.D. 890

Ketill Flatnose brought his ship to Scotland, and was well received by the great men there; for he was a renowned man, and of high birth. They offered him there such station as he would like to take, and Ketill and his company of kinsfolk settled down there—all except Thorstein, his daughter's son, who forthwith betook himself to warring, and harried Scotland far and wide, and was always victorious. Later on he made peace with the Scotch, and got for his own one-half of Scotland. He had for wife Thurid, daughter of Eyvind, and sister of Helgi the Lean. The Scotch did not keep the peace long, but treacherously murdered him. Ari, Thorgil's son, the Wise, writing of his death, says that he fell in Caithness. Unn the Deep-minded was in Caithness when her son Thorstein fell. When she heard that Thorstein was dead, and her father had breathed his last, she deemed she would have no prospering in store there. So she had a ship built secretly in a wood, and when it was ready built she arrayed it, and had great wealth withal; and she took with her all her kinsfolk who were left alive; and men deem that scarce may an example be found that any one, a woman only, has ever got out of such a state of war with so much wealth and so great a following. From this it may be seen how peerless among women she was. Unn had with her many men of great worth and high birth. A man named Koll was one of the worthiest amongst her followers, chiefly owing to his descent, he being by title a "Hersir." There was also in the journey with Unn a man named Hord, and he too was also a man of high birth and of great worth. When she was ready, Unn took her ship to the Orkneys; there she stayed a little while, and there she married off Gro, the daughter of Thorstein the Red. She was the mother of Greilad, who married Earl Thorfinn, the son of Earl Turf-Einar, son of Rognvald Mere-Earl. Their son was Hlodvir, the father of Earl Sigurd, the father of Earl Thorfinn, and from them come all the kin of the Orkney Earls. After that Unn steered her ship to the Faroe Isles, and stayed there for some time. There she married off another daughter of Thorstein, named Olof, and from her sprung the noblest race of that land, who are called the Gate-Beards.

CHAPTER V

Unn goes to Iceland, A.D. 895

Unn now got ready to go away from the Faroe Isles, and made it known to her shipmates that she was going to Iceland. She had with her Olaf "Feilan," the son of Thorstein, and those of his sisters who were unmarried. After that she put to sea, and, the weather being favourable, she came with her ship to the south of Iceland to Pumice-Course (Vikrarskeid). There they had their ship broken into splinters, but all the men and goods were saved. After that she went to find Helgi, her brother, followed by twenty men; and when she came there he went out to meet her, and bade her come stay with him with ten of her folk. She answered in anger, and said she had not known that he was such a churl; and she went away, being minded to find Bjorn, her brother in Broadfirth, and when he heard she was coming, he went to meet her with many followers, and greeted her warmly, and invited her and all her followers to stay with him, for he knew his sister's high-mindedness. She liked that right well, and thanked him for his lordly behaviour. She stayed there all the winter, and was entertained in the grandest manner, for there was no lack of means, and money was not spared. In the spring she went across Broadfirth, and came to a certain ness, where they ate their mid-day meal, and since that it has been called Daymealness, from whence Middlefell-strand stretches (eastward). Then she steered her ship up Hvammsfirth and came to a certain ness, and stayed there a little while. There Unn lost her comb, so it was afterwards called Combness. Then she went about all the Broadfirth-Dales, and took to her lands as wide as she wanted. After that Unn steered her ship to the head of the bay, and there her high-seat pillars were washed ashore, and then she deemed it was easy to know where she was to take up her abode. She had a house built there: it was afterwards called Hvamm, and she lived there. The same spring as Unn set up household at Hvamm, Koll married Thorgerd, daughter of Thorstein the Red. Unn gave, at her own cost, the bridal-feast, and let Thorgerd have for her dowry all Salmonriver-Dale; and Koll set up a household there on the south side of the Salmon-river. Koll was a man of the greatest mettle: their son was named Hoskuld.

CHAPTER VI
Unn Divides her Land

After that Unn gave to more men parts of her land-take. To Hord she gave all Hord-Dale as far as Skramuhlaups River. He lived at Hordabolstad (Hord-Lair-Stead), and was a man of the greatest mark, and blessed with noble offspring. His son was Asbjorn the Wealthy,

Anonymous

who lived in Ornolfsdale, at Asbjornstead, and had to wife Thorbjorg, daughter of Midfirth-Skeggi. Their daughter was Ingibjorg, who married Illugi the Black, and their sons were Hermund and Gunnlaug Worm-tongue. They are called the Gilsbecking-race. Unn spoke to her men and said: "Now you shall be rewarded for all your work, for now I do not lack means with which to pay each one of you for your toil and good-will. You all know that I have given the man named Erp, son of Earl Meldun, his freedom, for far away was it from my wish that so high-born a man should bear the name of thrall." Afterwards Unn gave him the lands of Sheepfell, between Tongue River and Mid River. His children were Orm and Asgeir, Gunbjorn, and Halldis, whom Alf o' Dales had for wife. To Sokkolf Unn gave Sokkolfsdale, where he abode to old age. Hundi was the name of one of her freedmen. He was of Scottish kin. To him she gave Hundidale. Osk was the name of the fourth daughter of Thorstein the Red. She was the mother of Thorstein Swart, the Wise, who found the "Summer eeke." Thorhild was the name of a fifth daughter of Thorstein. She was the mother of Alf o' Dales, and many great men trace back their line of descent to him. His daughter was Thorgerd, wife of Ari Marson of Reekness, the son of Atli, the son of Ulf the Squinter and Bjorg, Eyvond's daughter, the sister of Helgi the Lean. From them come all the Reeknessings. Vigdis was the name of the sixth daughter of Thorstein the Red. From her come the men of Headland of Islefirth.

CHAPTER VII
Of the Wedding of Olaf "Feilan," A.D. 920

Olaf "Feilan" was the youngest of Thorstein's children. He was a tall man and strong, goodly to look at, and a man of the greatest mettle. Unn loved him above all men, and made it known to people that she was minded to settle on Olaf all her belongings at Hvamm after her day. Unn now became very weary with old age, and she called Olaf "Feilan" to her and said: "It is on my mind, kinsman, that you should settle down and marry." Olaf took this well, and said he would lean on her foresight in that matter. Unn said: "It is chiefly in my mind that your wedding-feast should be held at the end of the summer, for that is the easiest time to get in all the means needed, for to me it seems a near guess that our friends will come hither in great numbers, and I have made up my mind that this shall be the last bridal feast arrayed by me." Olaf answered: "That is well spoken; but such a woman alone I mean to take to wife who shall rob thee neither of wealth nor rule (over thine own)." That same summer Olaf "Feilan" married Alfdis. Their wedding was at Hvamm. Unn spent much money on this feast, for she let be bidden thereto men of high degree wide about from other parts. She invited Bjorn and Helgi "Bjolan," her brothers, and they came with many followers. There came Koll o' Dales, her kinsman-in-law, and Hord of Hord-Dale, and many other great men. The wedding feast was very crowded; yet there did not come nearly so many as Unn had asked, because the Islefirth people had such a long way to come. Old age fell now fast upon Unn, so that she did not get up till mid-day, and went early to bed. No one did she allow to come to her for advice between the time she went to sleep at night and the time she was aroused, and she was very angry if any one asked how it fared with her strength. On this day Unn slept somewhat late; yet she was on foot when the guests came, and went to meet them and greeted her kinsfolk and friends with great courtesy, and said they had shown their affection to her in "coming hither from so far, and I specially name for this Bjorn and Helgi, but I wish to thank you all who are here assembled." After that Unn went into the hall and a great company with her, and when all seats were taken in the hall, every one was much struck by the lordliness of the feast. Then Unn said: "Bjorn and Helgi, my brothers, and all my other kindred and friends, I call witnesses to this, that this dwelling with all its belongings that you now see before you, I give into the hands of my kinsman, Olaf, to own and to manage." After that Unn stood up and said she would go to the bower where she was wont to sleep, but bade every one have for pastime whatever was most to his mind, and that ale should be the cheer of the common folk. So the tale goes, that Unn was a woman both tall and portly. She walked at a quick step out along the hall, and people could not help saying to each other how stately the lady was yet. They feasted that evening till they thought it time to go to bed. But the day after Olaf went to the sleeping bower of Unn, his grandmother, and when he came into the chamber there was Unn sitting up against her pillow, and she was dead. Olaf went into the hall after that and told these tidings. Every one thought it a wonderful thing, how Unn had upheld her dignity to the day of her death. So they now drank together Olaf's wedding and Unn's funeral honours, and the last day of the feast Unn was carried to the howe (burial mound) that was made for her. She was laid in a ship in the cairn, and much treasure with her, and after that the cairn was closed up. Then Olaf "Feilan" took over the household of Hvamm and all charge of the wealth there, by the advice of his kinsmen who were there. When the feast came to an end Olaf gave lordly gifts to the men most held in honour before they went away. Olaf became a mighty man and a great chieftain. He lived at Hvamm to old age. The children of Olaf and Alfdis were Thord Yeller, who married Hrodny, daughter of Midfirth Skeggi; and their sons were, Eyjolf the Grey, Thorarin Fylsenni, and Thorkell Kuggi. One daughter of Olaf Feilan was Thora, whom Thorstein Cod-biter, son of Thorolf Most-Beard, had for wife; their sons were Bork the Stout, and Thorgrim, father of Snori the Priest. Helga was another daughter of Olaf; she was the wife of Gunnar Hlifarson; their daughter was Jofrid, whom Thorodd, son of Tongue-Odd, had for wife, and afterwards Thorstein, Egil's son. Thorunn was the name of yet one of his daughters. She was the wife of Herstein, son of Thorkell Blund-Ketill's son. Thordis was the name of a third daughter of Olaf: she was the wife of Thorarin, the Speaker-at-Law, brother of Ragi. At that time, when Olaf was living at Hvamm, Koll o' Dales, his brother-in-law, fell ill and died. Hoskuld, the son of Koll, was young at the time of his father's death: he was fulfilled of wits before the tale of his years. Hoskuld was a hopeful man, and well made of body. He took over his father's goods and household. The homestead where Koll lived was named after him, being afterwards called Hoskuldstead. Hoskuld was soon in his householding blessed with friends, for that many supports stood thereunder, both kinsmen and friends whom Koll had gathered round him. Thorgerd, Thorstein's daughter, the mother of Hoskuld, was still a young woman and most goodly; she did not care for Iceland after the death of Koll. She told Hoskuld her son that she wished to go abroad, and take with her that share of goods which fell to her lot. Hoskuld said he took it much to heart that they should part, but he would not go against her in this any more than in

Anonymous

anything else. After that Hoskuld bought the half-part in a ship that was standing beached off Daymealness, on behalf of his mother. Thorgerd betook herself on board there, taking with her a great deal of goods. After that Thorgerd put to sea and had a very good voyage, and arrived in Norway. Thorgerd had much kindred and many noble kinsmen there. They greeted her warmly, and gave her the choice of whatever she liked to take at their hands. Thorgerd was pleased at this, and said it was her wish to settle down in that land. She had not been a widow long before a man came forward to woo her. His name was Herjolf; he was a "landed man" as to title, rich, and of much account. Herjolf was a tall and strong man, but he was not fair of feature; yet the most high-mettled of men, and was of all men the best skilled at arms. Now as they sat taking counsel on this matter, it was Thorgerd's place to reply to it herself, as she was a widow; and, with the advice of her relations, she said she would not refuse the offer. So Thorgerd married Herjolf, and went with him to his home, and they loved each other dearly. Thorgerd soon showed by her ways that she was a woman of the greatest mettle, and Herjolf's manner of life was deemed much better and more highly to be honoured now that he had got such an one as she was for his wife.

CHAPTER VIII
The Birth of Hrut and Thorgerd's
Second Widowhood, A.D. 923

Herjolf and Thorgerd had not long been together before they had a son. The boy was sprinkled with water, and was given the name of Hrut. He was at an early age both big and strong as he grew up; and as to growth of body, he was goodlier than any man, tall and broad-shouldered, slender of waist, with fine limbs and well-made hands and feet. Hrut was of all men the fairest of feature, and like what Thorstein, his mother's father, had been, or like Ketill Flatnose. And all things taken together, he was a man of the greatest mettle. Herjolf now fell ill and died, and men deemed that a great loss. After that Thorgerd wished to go to Iceland to visit Hoskuld her son, for she still loved him best of all men, and Hrut was left behind well placed with his relations. Thorgerd arrayed her journey to Iceland, and went to find Hoskuld in his home in Salmonriver-Dale. He received his mother with honour. She was possessed of great wealth, and remained with Hoskuld to the day of her death. A few winters after Thorgerd came to Iceland she fell sick and died. Hoskuld took to himself all her money, but Hrut his brother owned one-half thereof.

CHAPTER IX
Hoskuld's Marriage, A.D. 935

At this time Norway was ruled by Hakon, Athelstan's fosterling. Hoskuld was one of his bodyguard, and stayed each year, turn and turn about, at Hakon's court, or at his own home, and was a very renowned man both in Norway and in Iceland. Bjorn was the name of a man who lived at Bjornfirth, where he had taken land, the firth being named after him. This firth cuts into the land north from Steingrim's firth, and a neck of land runs out between them. Bjorn was a man of high birth, with a great deal of money: Ljufa was the name of his wife. Their daughter was Jorunn: she was a most beautiful woman, and very proud and extremely clever, and so was thought the best match in all the firths of the West. Of this woman Hoskuld had heard, and he had heard besides that Bjorn was the wealthiest yeoman throughout all the Strands. Hoskuld rode from home with ten men, and went to Bjorn's house at Bjornfirth. He was well received, for to Bjorn his ways were well known. Then Hoskuld made his proposal, and Bjorn said he was pleased, for his daughter could not be better married, yet turned the matter over to her decision. And when the proposal was set before Jorunn, she answered in this way: "From all the reports I have heard of you, Hoskuld, I cannot but answer your proposal well, for I think that the woman would be well cared for who should marry you; yet my father must have most to say in this matter, and I will agree in this with his wishes." And the long and short of it was, that Jorunn was promised to Hoskuld with much money, and the wedding was to be at Hoskuldstead. Hoskuld now went away with matters thus settled, and home to his abode, and stays now at home until this wedding feast was to be held. Bjorn came from the north for the wedding with a brave company of followers. Hoskuld had also asked many guests, both friends and relations, and the feast was of the grandest. Now, when the feast was over each one returned to his home in good friendship and with seemly gifts. Jorunn Bjorn's daughter sits behind at Hoskuldstead, and takes over the care of the household with Hoskuld. It was very soon seen that she was wise and well up in things, and of manifold knowledge, though rather high-tempered at most times. Hoskuld and she loved each other well, though in their daily ways they made no show thereof. Hoskuld became a great chieftain; he was mighty and pushing, and had no lack of money, and was thought to be nowise less of his ways than his father, Koll. Hoskuld and Jorunn had not been married long before they came to have children. A son of theirs was named Thorliek. He was the eldest of their children. Bard was another son of theirs. One of their daughters was called Hallgerd, afterwards surnamed "Long-Breeks." Another daughter was called Thurid. All their children were most hopeful. Thorliek was a very tall man, strong and handsome, though silent and rough; and men thought that such was the turn of his temper, as that he would be no man of fair dealings, and Hoskuld often would say, that he would take very much after the race of the men of the Strands. Bard, Hoskuld's son, was most manly to look at, and of goodly strength, and from his appearance it was easy to see that he would take more after his father's people. Bard was of quiet ways while he was growing up, and a man lucky in friends, and Hoskuld loved him best of all his children. The house of Hoskuld now stood in great honour and renown. About this time Hoskuld gave his sister Groa in marriage to Velief the Old, and their son was "Holmgang"-Bersi.

CHAPTER X
Of Viga Hrapp

Hrapp was the name of a man who lived in Salmon-river-Dale, on the north bank of the river on the opposite side to Hoskuldstead, at the place that was called later on Hrappstead, where there is now waste land. Hrapp was the son of Sumarlid, and was called Fight-Hrapp. He was Scotch on his father's side, and his mother's kin came from Sodor, where he was brought up. He was a very big,strong man, and one not willing to give in even in face of some odds; and for the reason that was most overbearing, and would never make good what he had misdone, he had had to fly from West-over-the-sea, and had bought the land on which he afterwards lived. His wife was named Vigdis, and was

Hallstein's daughter; and their son was named Sumarlid. Her brother was named Thorstein Surt; he lived at Thorsness, as has been written before. Sumarlid was brought up there, and was a most promising young man. Thorstein had been married, but by this time his wife was dead. He had two daughters, one named Gudrid, and the other Osk. Thorkell trefill married Gudrid, and they lived in Svignaskard. He was a great chieftain, and a sage of wits; he was the son of Raudabjorn. Osk, Thorstein's daughter, was given in marriage to a man of Broadfirth named Thorarin. He was a valiant man, and very popular, and lived with Thorstein, his father-in-law, who was sunk in age and much in need of their care. Hrapp was disliked by most people, being overbearing to his neighbours; and at times he would hint to them that theirs would be a heavy lot as neighbours, if they held any other man for better than himself. All the goodmen took one counsel, and went to Hoskuld and told him their trouble. Hoskuld bade them tell him if Hrapp did any one any harm, "For he shall not plunder me of men or money."

CHAPTER XI
About Thord Goddi and Thorbjorn Skrjup

Thord Goddi was the name of a man who lived in Salmon-river-Dale on the northern side of the river, and his house was Vigdis called Goddistead. He was a very wealthy man; he had no children, and had bought the land he lived on. He was a neighbour of Hrapp's, and was very often badly treated by him. Hoskuld looked after him, so that he kept his dwelling in peace. Vigdis was the name of his wife. She was daughter of Ingjald, son of Olaf Feilan, and brother's daughter of Thord Yeller, and sister's daughter of Thorolf Rednose of Sheepfell. This

Thorolf was a great hero, and in a very good position, and his kinsmen often went to him for protection. Vigdis had married more for money than high station. Thord had a thrall who had come to Iceland with him, named Asgaut. He was a big man, and shapely of body; and though he was called a thrall, yet few could be found his equal amongst those called freemen, and he knew well how to serve his master. Thord had many other thralls, though this one is the only one mentioned here. Thorbjorn was the name of a man. He lived in Salmon-river-Dale, next to Thord, up valley away from his homestead, and was called Skrjup. He was very rich in chattels, mostly in gold and silver.

He was an huge man and of great strength. No squanderer of money on common folk was he. Hoskuld, Dalakoll's son, deemed it a drawback to his state that his house was worse built than he wished it should be; so he bought a ship from a Shetland man. The ship lay up in the mouth of the river Blanda. That ship he gets ready, and makes it known that he is going abroad, leaving Jorunn to take care of house and children. They now put out to sea, and all went well with them; and they hove somewhat southwardly into Norway, making Hordaland, where the market-town called Biorgvin was afterwards built. Hoskuld put up his ship, and had there great strength of kinsmen, though here they be not named. Hakon, the king, had then his seat in the Wick. Hoskuld did not go to the king, as his kinsfolk welcomed him with open arms. That winter all was quiet (in Norway).

CHAPTER XII
Hoskuld Buys a Slave Woman
There were tidings at the beginning of the summer that the king went with his fleet eastward to a

tryst in Brenn-isles, to settle peace for his land, even as the law laid down should be done every third summer. This meeting was held between rulers with a view to settling such matters as kings had to adjudge—matters of international policy between Norway, Sweden, and Denmark. It was deemed a pleasure trip to go to this meeting, for thither came men from well-nigh all such lands as we know of. Hoskuld ran out his ship, being desirous also to go to the meeting; moreover, he had not been to see the king all the winter through. There was also a fair to be made for. At the meeting there were great crowds of people, and much amusement to be got—drinking, and games, and all sorts of entertainment. Nought, however, of great interest happened there. Hoskuld met many of his kinsfolk there who were come from Denmark. Now, one day as Hoskuld went out to disport himself with some other men, he saw a stately tent far away from the other booths. Hoskuld went thither, and into the tent, and there sat a man before him in costly raiment, and a Russian hat on his head. Hoskuld asked him his name. He said he was called Gilli: "But many call to mind the man if they hear my nickname—I am called Gilli the Russian." Hoskuld said he had often heard talk of him, and that he held him to be the richest of men that had ever belonged to the guild of merchants. Still Hoskuld spoke: "You must have things to sell such as we should wish to buy." Gilli asked what he and his companions wished to buy. Hoskuld said he should like to buy some bonds-woman, "if you have one to sell." Gilli answers: "There, you mean to give me trouble by this, in asking for things you don't expect me to have in stock; but it is not sure that follows." Hoskuld then saw that right across the booth there was drawn a curtain; and Gilli then lifted the curtain, and Hoskuld saw that there were twelve women seated behind the curtain. So Gilli said that Hoskuld should come on and have a look, if he would care to buy any of these women. Hoskuld did so. They sat all together across the booth. Hoskuld looks carefully at these women. He saw a woman sitting out by the skirt of the tent, and she was very ill-clad. Hoskuld thought, as far as he could see, this woman was fair to look upon. Then said Hoskuld, "What is the price of that woman if I should wish to buy her?" Gilli replied, "Three silver pieces is what you must weigh me out for her." "It seems to me," said Hoskuld, "that you charge very highly for this bonds-woman, for that is the price of three (such)." Then Gilli said, "You speak truly, that I value her worth more than the others. Choose any of the other eleven, and pay one mark of silver for her, this one being left in my possession." Hoskuld said, "I must first see how much silver there is in the purse I have on my belt," and he asked Gilli to take the scales while he searched the purse. Gilli then said, "On my side there shall be no guile in this matter; for, as to the ways of this woman, there is a great drawback which I wish, Hoskuld, that you know before we strike this bargain." Hoskuld asked what it was. Gilli replied, "The woman is dumb. I have tried in many ways to get her to talk, but have never got a word out of her, and I feel quite sure that this woman knows not how to speak." Then, said Hoskuld, "Bring out the scales, and let us see how much the purse I have got here may weigh." Gilli did so, and now they weigh the silver, and there were just three marks weighed. Then said Hoskuld, "Now the matter stands so that we can close our bargain. You take the money for yourself, and I will take the woman. I take it that you have behaved honestly in this affair, for, to be sure, you had no mind to

Anonymous

deceive me herein." Hoskuld then went home to his booth. That same night Hoskuld went into bed with her. The next morning when men got dressed, spake Hoskuld, "The clothes Gilli the Rich gave you do not appear to be very grand, though it is true that to him it is more of a task to dress twelve women than it is to me to dress only one." After that Hoskuld opened a chest, and took out some fine women's clothes and gave them to her; and it was the saying of every one that she looked very well when she was dressed. But when the rulers had there talked matters over according as the law provided, this meeting was broken up. Then Hoskuld went to see King Hakon, and greeted him worthily, according to custom. The king cast a side glance at him, and said, "We should have taken well your greeting, Hoskuld, even if you had saluted us sooner; but so shall it be even now."

CHAPTER XIII
Hoskuld Returns to Iceland, A.D. 948

After that the king received Hoskuld most graciously, and bade him come on board his own ship, and "be with us so long as you care to remain in Norway." Hoskuld answered: "Thank you for your offer; but now, this summer, I have much to be busy about, and that is mostly the reason I was so long before I came to see you, for I wanted to get for myself house-timber." The king bade him bring his ship in to the Wick, and Hoskuld tarried with the king for a while. The king got house-timber for him, and had his ship laden for him. Then the king said to Hoskuld, "You shall not be delayed here longer than you like, though we shall find it difficult to find a man to take your place." After that the king saw Hoskuld off to his ship, and said: "I have found you an honourable man, and now my mind misgives me that you are sailing for the last time from Norway, whilst I am lord over that land." The king drew a gold ring off his arm that weighed a mark, and gave it to Hoskuld; and he gave him for another gift a sword on which there was half a mark of gold. Hoskuld thanked the king for his gifts, and for all the honour he had done him. After that Hoskuld went on board his ship, and put to sea. They had a fair wind, and hove in to the south of Iceland; and after that sailed west by Reekness, and so by Snowfellness in to Broadfirth. Hoskuld landed at Salmon-river-Mouth. He had the cargo taken out of his ship, which he took into the river and beached, having a shed built for it. A ruin is to be seen now where he built the shed. There he set up his booths, and that place is called Booths'-Dale. After that Hoskuld had the timber taken home, which was very easy, as it was not far off. Hoskuld rode home after that with a few men, and was warmly greeted, as was to be looked for. He found that all his belongings had been kept well since he left. Jorunn asked, "What woman that was who journeyed with him?" Hoskuld answered, "You will think I am giving you a mocking answer when I tell you that I do not know her name." Jorunn said, "One of two things there must be: either the talk is a lie that has come to my ears, or you must have spoken to her so much as to have asked her her name." Hoskuld said he could not gainsay that, and so told her the truth, and bade that the woman should be kindly treated, and said it was his wish she should stay in service with them. Jorunn said, "I am not going to wrangle with the mistress you have brought out of Norway, should she find living near me no pleasure; least of all should I think of it if she is both deaf and dumb." Hoskuld slept with his wife every night after he came

Anonymous

home, and had very little to say to the mistress. Every one clearly saw that there was something betokening high birth in the way she bore herself, and that she was no fool. Towards the end of the winter Hoskuld's mistress gave birth to a male child. Hoskuld was called, and was shown the child, and he thought, as others did, that he had never seen a goodlier or a more noble-looking child. Hoskuld was asked what the boy should be called. He said it should be named Olaf, for Olaf Feilan had died a little time before, who was his mother's brother. Olaf was far before other children, and Hoskuld bestowed great love on the boy. The next summer Jorunn said, "That the woman must do some work or other, or else go away." Hoskuld said she should wait on him and his wife, and take care of her boy besides. When the boy was two years old he had got full speech, and ran about like children of four years old. Early one morning, as Hoskuld had gone out to look about his manor, the weather being fine, and the sun, as yet little risen in the sky, shining brightly, it happened that he heard some voices of people talking; so he went down to where a little brook ran past the home-field slope, and he saw two people there whom he recognised as his son Olaf and his mother, and he discovered she was not speechless, for she was talking a great deal to the boy. Then Hoskuld went to her and asked her her name, and said it was useless for her to hide it any longer. She said so it should be, and they sat down on the brink of the field. Then she said, "If you want to know my name, I am called Melkorka." Hoskuld bade her tell him more of her kindred. She answered, "Myr Kjartan is the name of my father, and he is a king in Ireland; and I was taken a prisoner of war from there when I was fifteen winters old." Hoskuld said she had kept silence far too long about so noble a descent. After that Hoskuld went on, and told Jorunn what he had just found out during his walk. Jorunn said that she "could not tell if this were true," and said she had no fondness for any manner of wizards; and so the matter dropped. Jorunn was no kinder to her than before, but Hoskuld had somewhat more to say to her. A little while after this, when Jorunn was going to bed, Melkorka was undressing her, and put her shoes on the floor, when Jorunn took the stockings and smote her with them about the head. Melkorka got angry, and struck Jorunn on the nose with her fist, so that the blood flowed. Hoskuld came in and parted them. After that he let Melkorka go away, and got a dwelling ready for her up in Salmon-river-Dale, at the place that was afterwards called Melkorkastad, which is now waste land on the south of the Salmon river. Melkorka now set up household there, and Hoskuld had everything brought there that she needed; and Olaf, their son, went with her. It was soon seen that Olaf, as he grew up, was far superior to other men, both on account of his beauty and courtesy.

CHAPTER XIV
The Murder of Hall, Ingjald's Brother

Ingjald was the name of a man. He lived in Sheepisles, that lie out in Broadfirth. He was called Sheepisles' Priest. He was rich, and a mighty man of his hand. Hall was the name of his brother. He was big, and had the makings of a man in him; he was, however, a man of small means, and looked upon by most people as an unprofitable sort of man. The brothers did not usually agree very well together. Ingjald thought Hall did not shape himself after the fashion of doughty men, and Hall thought Ingjald was but little minded to lend furtherance to his affairs. There is a fishing place in Broadfirth called Bjorn isles. These islands lie many together, and were profitable in many ways. At that time men went there a great deal for the fishing, and at all seasons there were a great many men there. Wise men set great store by people in outlying fishing-stations living peacefully together, and said that it would be unlucky for the fishing if there was any quarrelling; and most men gave good heed to this. It is told how one summer Hall, the brother of Ingjald, the Sheepisles' Priest, came to Bjorn isles for fishing. He took ship as one of the crew with a man called Thorolf. He was a Broadfirth man, and was well-nigh a penniless vagrant, and yet a brisk sort of a man. Hall was there for some time, and palmed himself off as being much above other men. It happened one evening when they were come to land, Hall and Thorolf, and began to divide the catch, that Hall wished both to choose and to divide, for he thought himself the greater man of the two. Thorolf would not give in, and there were some high words, and sharp things were said on both sides, as each stuck to his own way of thinking. So Hall seized up a chopper that lay by him, and was about to heave it at Thorolf's head, but men leapt between them and stopped Hall; but he was of the maddest, and yet unable to have his way as at this time. The catch of fish remained undivided. Thorolf betook himself away that evening, and Hall took possession of the catch that belonged to them both, for then the odds of might carried the day. Hall now got another man in Thorolf's place in the boat, and went on fishing as before. Thorolf was ill-contented with his lot, for he felt he had come to shame in their dealings together; yet he remained in the islands with the determination to set straight the humble plight to which he had been made to bow against his will. Hall, in the meantime, did not fear any danger, and thought that no one would dare to try to get even with him in his own country. So one fair-weather day it happened that Hall rowed out, and there were three of them together in the boat. The fish bit well through the day, and as they rowed home in the evening they were very merry. Thorolf kept spying about Hall's doings during the day, and is standing in the landing-place when Hall came to land. Hall rowed in the forehold of the boat, and leapt overboard, intending to steady the boat; and as he jumped to land Thorolf happens to be standing near, and forthwith hews at him, and the blow caught him on his neck against the shoulder, and off flew his head. Thorolf fled away after that, and Hall's followers were all in a flurried bustle about him. The story of Hall's murder was told all over the islands, and every one thought it was indeed great news; for the man was of high birth, although he had had little good luck. Thorolf now fled from the islands, for he knew no man there who would shelter him after such a deed, and he had no kinsmen he could expect help from; while in the neighbourhood were men from whom it might be surely looked for that they would beset his life, being moreover men of much power, such as was Ingjald, the Sheepisles' Priest, the brother of Hall. Thorolf got himself ferried across to the mainland. He went with great secrecy. Nothing is told of his journey, until one evening he came to Goddistead. Vigdis, the wife of Thord Goddi, was some sort of relation to Thorolf, and on that account he turned towards that house. Thorolf had also heard before how matters stood there, and how Vigdis was endowed with a good deal more courage than Thord, her husband. And forthwith the same evening that Thorolf came to Goddistead he went to Vigdis to tell her his trouble, and to beg her help. Vigdis answered his pleading in this way: "I do not deny our relationship, and in this way alone I can look upon the deed you have done, that I deem you in no way the worser man for it. Yet this I see, that those who shelter you will thereby have at stake their lives and means, seeing what great men they are who will be taking up the blood-suit. And Thord," she said, "my husband, is not much of a warrior; but the counsels of us women are mostly guided by little foresight if anything is wanted. Yet I am loath to keep aloof from you altogether, seeing that, though I am but a woman, you have set your heart on finding some shelter here." After that Vigdis led him to an outhouse, and told him to wait for her there, and put a lock on the door. Then she went to Thord, and said, "A man has come here as a guest, named Thorolf. He is some sort of relation of mine, and I think he will need to dwell here some long time if you will allow it." Thord said he could not away with men coming to put up at his house, but bade him rest there over the next day if he had no trouble on hand, but otherwise he should be off at his swiftest. Vigdis answered, "I have offered him already to stay on, and I cannot take back my word, though he be not in even friendship with all men." After that she told Thord of the slaying of Hall, and that Thorolf who was come there was the man who had killed him. Thord was very cross-grained at this, and said he well knew how that Ingjald would take a great deal of money from him for the sheltering that had been given him already, seeing that doors here have been locked after this man. Vigdis answered, "Ingjald shall take none of your money for giving one night's shelter to Thorolf, and he shall remain here all this winter through." Thord said, "In this manner you can checkmate me most thoroughly, but it is against my wish that a man of such evil luck should stay here." Still Thorolf stayed there all the winter. Ingjald, who had to take up the blood-suit for his brother, heard this, and so arrayed him for a journey into the Dales at the end of the winter, and ran out a ferry of his whereon they went twelve together. They sailed from the west with a sharp north-west wind, and landed in Salmon-river-Mouth in the evening. They put up their ferry-boat, and came to Goddistead in the evening, arriving there not unawares, and were cheerfully welcomed. Ingjald took Thord aside for a talk with him, and told him his errand, and said he had heard of Thorolf, the slayer of his brother, being there. Thord said there was no truth in that. Ingjald bade him not to deny it. "Let us rather come to a bargain together: you give up the man, and put me to no toil in the matter of getting at him. I have three marks of silver that you shall have, and I will overlook the offences you have brought on your hands for the shelter given to Thorolf." Thord thought the money fair, and had now a promise of acquittal of the offences for which he had hitherto most dreaded and for which he would have to abide sore loss of money. So he said, "I shall no doubt hear people speak ill of me for this, none the less this will have to be our bargain." They slept until it wore towards the latter end of the night, when it lacked an hour of day.

CHAPTER XV
Thorolf's Escape with Asgaut the Thrall

Ingjald and his men got up and dressed. Vigdis asked Thord what his talk with Ingjald had been about the evening before. Thord said they had talked about many things, amongst others how the place was to be ransacked, and how they should be clear of the case if

Thorolf was not found there. "So I let Asgaut, my thrall, take the man away." Vigdis said she had no fondness for lies, and said she should be very loath to have Ingjald sniffing about her house, but bade him, however, do as he liked. After that Ingjald ransacked the place, and did not hit upon the man there. At that moment Asgaut came back, and Vigdis asked him where he had parted with Thorolf. Asgaut replied, "I took him to our sheephouses as Thord told me to." Vigdis replied, "Can anything be more exactly in Ingjald's way as he returns to his ship? nor shall any risk be run, lest they should have made this plan up between them last night. I wish you to go at once, and take him away as soon as possible. You shall take him to Sheepfell to Thorolf; and if you do as I tell you, you shall get something for it. I will give you your freedom and money, that you may go where you will." Asgaut agreed to this, and went to the sheephouse to find Thorolf, and bade him get ready to go at once. At this time Ingjald rode out of Goddistead, for he was now anxious to get his money's worth. As he was come down from the farmstead (into the plain) he saw two men coming to meet him; they were Thorolf and Asgaut. This was early in the morning, and there was yet but little daylight. Asgaut and Thorolf now found themselves in a hole, for Ingjald was on one side of them and the Salmon River on the other. The river was terribly swollen, and there were great masses of ice on either bank, while in the middle it had burst open, and it was an ill-looking river to try to ford. Thorolf said to Asgaut, "It seems to me we have two choices before us. One is to remain here and fight as well as valour and manhood will serve us, and yet the thing most likely is that Ingjald and his men will take our lives without delay; and the other is to tackle the river, and yet that, I think, is still a somewhat dangerous one." Asgaut said that Thorolf should have his way, and he would not desert him, "whatever plan you are minded to follow in this matter." Thorolf said, "We will make for the river, then," and so they did, and arrayed themselves as light as possible. After this they got over the main ice, and plunged into the water. And because the men were brave, and Fate had ordained them longer lives, they got across the river and upon the ice on the other side. Directly after they had got across, Ingjald with his followers came to the spot opposite to them on the other side of the river. Ingjald spoke out, and said to his companions, "What plan shall we follow now? Shall we tackle the river or not?" They said he should choose, and they would rely on his foresight, though they thought the river looked impassable. Ingjald said that so it was, and "we will turn away from the river;" and when Thorolf and Asgaut saw that Ingjald had made up his mind not to cross the river, they first wring their clothes and then make ready to go on. They went on all that day, and came in the evening to Sheepfell. They were well received there, for it was an open house for all guests; and forthwith that same evening Asgaut went to see Thorolf Rednose, and told him all the matters concerning their errand, "how Vigdis, his kinswoman, had sent him this man to keep in safety." Asgaut also told him all that had happened between Ingjald and Thord Goddi; therewithal he took forth the tokens Vigdis had sent. Thorolf replied thus, "I cannot doubt these tokens. I shall indeed take this man in at her request. I think, too, that Vigdis has dealt most bravely with this matter and it is a great pity that such a woman should have so feeble a husband. And you, Asgaut, shall dwell here as long as you like." Asgaut said he would tarry there for no length of time. Thorolf now takes unto him his namesake, and made him one of his followers; and Asgaut and they parted good friends, and he went on his homeward journey. And now to tell of Ingjald. He turned back to Goddistead when he and Thorolf parted. By that time men had come there from the nearest farmsteads at the summons of Vigdis, and no fewer than twenty men had gathered there already. But when Ingjald and his men came to the place, he called Thord to him, "You have dealt in a most cowardly way with me, Thord," says he, "for I take it to be the truth that you have got the man off." Thord said this had not happened with his knowledge; and now all the plotting that had been between Ingjald and Thord came out. Ingjald now claimed to have back his money that he had given to Thord. Vigdis was standing near during this talk, and said it had fared with them as was meet, and prayed Thord by no means to hold back this money, "For you, Thord," she said, "have got this money in a most cowardly way." Thord said she must needs have her will herein. After that Vigdis went inside, and to a chest that belonged to Thord, and found at the bottom a large purse. She took out the purse, and went outside with it up to where Ingjald was, and bade him take the money. Ingjald's brow cleared at that, and he stretched out his hand to take the purse. Vigdis raised the purse, and struck him on the nose with it, so that forthwith blood fell on the earth. Therewith she overwhelmed him with mocking words, ending by telling him that henceforth he should never have the money, and bidding him go his way. Ingjald saw that his best choice was to be off, and the sooner the better, which indeed he did, nor stopped in his journey until he got home, and was mightily ill at ease over his travel.

CHAPTER XVI

Thord becomes Olaf's Foster Father, A.D. 950

About this time Asgaut came home. Vigdis greeted him, and asked him what sort of reception they had had at Sheepfell. He gave a good account of it, and told her the words wherewith Thorolf had spoken out his mind. She was very pleased at that. "And you, Asgaut," she said, "have done your part well and faithfully, and you shall now know speedily what wages you have worked for. I give you your freedom, so that from this day forth you shall bear the title of a freeman. Therewith you shall take the money that Thord took as the price for the head of Thorolf, my kinsman, and now that money will be better bestowed." Asgaut thanked her for her gift with fair words. The next summer Asgaut took a berth in Day-Meal-Ness, and the ship put to sea, and they came in for heavy gales, but not a long sea-voyage, and made Norway. After that Asgaut went to Denmark and settled there, and was thought a valiant and true man. And herewith comes to an end the tale of him. But after the plot Thord Goddi had made up with Ingjald, the Sheepisles priest, when they made up their minds to compass the death of Thorolf, Vigdis' kinsman, she returned that deed with hatred, and divorced herself from Thord Goddi, and went to her kinsfolk and told them the tale. Thord Yeller was not pleased at this; yet matters went off quietly. Vigdis did not take away with her from Goddistead any more goods than her own heirlooms. The men of Hvamm let it out that they meant to have for themselves one-half of the wealth that Thord was possessed of. And on hearing this he becomes exceeding faint-hearted, and rides forthwith to see Hoskuld to tell him of his troubles. Hoskuld said, "Times

Anonymous

have been that you have been terror-struck, through not having with such overwhelming odds to deal." Then Thord offered Hoskuld money for his help, and said he would not look at the matter with a niggard's eye. Hoskuld said, "This is clear, that you will not by peaceful consent allow any man to have the enjoyment of your wealth." Answers Thord, "No, not quite that though; for I fain would that you should take over all my goods. That being settled, I will ask to foster your son Olaf, and leave him all my wealth after my days are done; for I have no heir here in this land, and I think my means would be better bestowed then, than that the kinsmen of Vigdis should grab it." To this Hoskuld agreed, and had it bound by witnesses. This Melkorka took heavily, deeming the fostering too low. Hoskuld said she ought not to think that, "for Thord is an old man, and childless, and I wish Olaf to have all his money after his day, but you can always go to see him at any time you like." Thereupon Thord took Olaf to him, seven years old, and loved him very dearly. Hearing this, the men who had on hand the case against Thord Goddi thought that now it would be even more difficult than before to lay claim to the money. Hoskuld sent some handsome presents to Thord Yeller, and bade him not be angry over this, seeing that in law they had no claim on Thord's money, inasmuch as Vigdis had brought no true charges against Thord, or any such as justified desertion by her. "Moreover, Thord was no worse a man for casting about for counsel to rid himself of a man that had been thrust upon his means, and was as beset with guilt as a juniper bush is with prickles." But when these words came to Thord from Hoskuld, and with them large gifts of money, then Thord allowed himself to be pacified, and said he thought the money was well placed that Hoskuld looked after, and took the gifts; and all was quiet after that, but their friendship was rather less warm than formerly. Olaf grew up with Thord, and became a great man and strong. He was so handsome that his equal was not to be found, and when he was twelve years old he rode to the Thing meeting, and men in other countrysides looked upon it as a great errand to go, and to wonder at the splendid way he was made. In keeping herewith was the manner of Olaf's war-gear and raiment, and therefore he was easily distinguished from all other men. Thord got on much better after Olaf came to live with him. Hoskuld gave Olaf a nickname, and called him Peacock, and the name stuck to him.

CHAPTER XVII
About Viga Hrapp's Ghost, A.D. 950

The tale is told of Hrapp that he became most violent in his behaviour, and did his neighbours such harm that they could hardly hold their own against him. But from the time that Olaf grew up Hrapp got no hold of Thord. Hrapp had the same temper, but his powers waned, in that old age was fast coming upon him, so that he had to lie in bed. Hrapp called Vigdis, his wife, to him, and said, "I have never been of ailing health in life," said he, "and it is therefore most likely that this illness will put an end to our life together. Now, when I am dead, I wish my grave to be dug in the doorway of my fire hall, and that I be put: thereinto, standing there in the doorway; then I shall be able to keep a more searching eye on my dwelling." After that Hrapp died, and all was done as he said, for Vigdis did not dare do otherwise. And as evil as he had been to deal with in his life, just so he was by a great deal more when he was dead, for he walked again a great deal after he was dead. People said that he killed most of his servants in his ghostly appearances. He caused a great deal of trouble to those who lived near, and the house of Hrappstead became deserted. Vigdis, Hrapp's wife, betook herself west to Thorstein Swart, her brother. He took her and her goods in. And now things went as before, in that men went to find Hoskuld, and told him all the troubles that Hrapp was doing to them, and asked him to do something to put an end to this. Hoskuld said this should be done, and he went with some men to Hrappstead, and has Hrapp dug up, and taken away to a place near to which cattle were least likely to roam or men to go about. After that Hrapp's walkings-again abated somewhat. Sumarlid, Hrapp's son, inherited all Hrapp's wealth, which was both great and goodly. Sumarlid set up household at Hrappstead the next spring; but after he had kept house there for a little time he was seized of frenzy, and died shortly afterwards. Now it was the turn of his mother, Vigdis, to take there alone all this wealth; but as she would not go to the estate of Hrappstead, Thorstein Swart took all the wealth to himself to take care of. Thorstein was by then rather old, though still one of the most healthy and hearty of men.

CHAPTER XVIII
Of the Drowning of Thorstein Swart

At that time there rose to honour among men in Thorness, the kinsmen of Thorstein, named Bork the Stout and his brother, Thorgrim. It was soon found out how these brothers would fain be the greatest men there, and were most highly accounted of. And when Thorstein found that out, he would not elbow them aside, and so made it known to people that he wished to change his abode, and take his household to Hrappstead, in Salmon-river-Dale. Thorstein Swart got ready to start after the spring Thing, but his cattle were driven round along the shore. Thorstein got on board a ferry-boat, and took twelve men with him; and Thorarin, his brother-in-law, and Osk, Thorstein's daughter, and Hild, her daughter, who was three years old, went with them too. Thorstein fell in with a high south-westerly gale, and they sailed up towards the roosts, and into that roost which is called Coal-chest-Roost, which is the biggest of the currents in Broadfirth. They made little way sailing, chiefly because the tide was ebbing, and the wind was not favourable, the weather being squally, with high wind when the squalls broke over, but with little wind between whiles. Thorstein steered, and had the braces of the sail round his shoulders, because the boat was blocked up with goods, chiefly piled-up chests, and the cargo was heaped up very high; but land was near about, while on the boat there was but little way, because of the raging current against them. Then they sailed on to a hidden rock, but were not wrecked. Thorstein bade them let down the sail as quickly as possible, and take punt poles to push off the ship. This shift was tried to no avail, because on either board the sea was so deep that the poles struck no bottom; so they were obliged to wait for the incoming tide, and now the water ebbs away under the ship. Throughout the day they saw a seal in the current larger by much than any others, and through the day it would be swimming round about the ship, with flappers none of the shortest, and to all of them it seemed that in him there were human eyes. Thorstein bade them shoot the seal, and they tried, but it came to nought. Now the tide rose; and just as the ship was getting afloat there broke upon them a violent squall, and the boat heeled over, and every one on board the boat was drowned, save one man, named Gudmund, who drifted ashore with some timber. The place where he was washed up was afterwards called Gudmund's Isles. Gudrid, whom Thorkell Trefill had for wife, was entitled to the inheritance left by Thorstein, her father. These tidings spread far and near of the drowning of Thorstein Swart, and the men who were lost there. Thorkell sent straightway for the man Gudmund, who had been washed ashore, and when he came and met Thorkell, he (Thorkell) struck a bargain with him, to the end that he should tell the story of the loss of lives even as he (Thorkell) was going to dictate it to him. Gudmund agreed. Thorkell now asked him to tell the story of this mishap in the hearing of a good many people. Then Gudmund spake on this wise: "Thorstein was drowned first, and then his son-in-law, Thorarin"—so that then it was the turn of Hild to come in for the money, as she was the daughter of Thorarin. Then he said the maiden was drowned, because the next in inheritance to her was Osk, her mother, and she lost her life the last of them, so that all the money thus came to Thorkell Trefill, in that his wife Gudrid must take inheritance after her sister. Now this tale is spread abroad by Thorkell and his men; but Gudmund ere this had told the tale in somewhat another way. Now the kinsmen of Thorarin misdoubted this tale somewhat, and said they would not believe it unproved, and claimed one-half of the heritage against Thorkell; but Thorkell maintained it belonged to him alone, and bade that ordeal should be taken on the matter, according to their custom. This was the ordeal at that time, that men had had to pass under "earth-chain," which was a slip of sward cut loose from the soil, but both ends thereof were left adhering to the earth, and the man who should go through with the ordeal should walk thereunder. Thorkell Trefill now had some misgivings himself as to whether the deaths of the people had indeed taken place as he and Gudmund had said the second time. Heathen men deemed that on them rested no less responsibility when ceremonies of this kind had to be gone through than Christian men do when ordeals are decreed. He who passed under "earth-chain" cleared himself if the sward-slip did not fall down upon him. Thorkell made an arrangement with two men that they should feign quarrelling over something or another, and be close to the spot when the ordeal was being gone through with, and touch the sward-slip so unmistakably that all men might see that it was they who knocked it down. After this comes forward he who was to go through with the ordeal, and at the nick of time when he had got under the "earth-chain," these men who had been put up to it fall on each other with weapons, meeting close to the arch of the sward-slip, and lie there fallen, and down tumbles the "earth-chain", as was likely enough. Then men rush up between them and part them, which was easy enough, for they fought with no mind to do any harm. Thorkell Trefill then asked people as to what they thought about the ordeal, and all his men now said that it would have turned out all right if no one had spoilt it. Then Thorkell took all the chattels to himself, but the land at Hrapstead was left to lie fallow.

CHAPTER XIX
Hrut Comes to Iceland

Now of Hoskuld it is to be told that his state is one of great honour, and that he is a great chieftain. He had in his keep a great deal of money that belonged to his (half) brother, Hrut, Herjolf's son. Many men would have it that Hoskuld's means would be heavily cut into if he should be made to pay to the full the heritage of his (Hrut's) mother. Hrut was of the bodyguard of King Harald, Gunnhild's son, and was much honoured by him, chiefly for the reason that he approved himself the best man in all deeds of manly trials, while, on the other hand, Gunnhild, the Queen, loved him so much that she held there was not his equal within the guard, either in talking or in anything else. Even when men were compared, and noblemen therein were pointed to, all men easily saw that Gunnhild thought that at the bottom there must be sheer thoughtlessness, or else envy, if any man was said to be Hrut's equal. Now, inasmuch as Hrut had in Iceland much money to look after, and many noble kinsfolk to go and see, he desired to go there, and now arrays his journey for Iceland. The king gave him a ship at parting and said he had proved a brave man and true. Gunnhild saw Hrut off to his ship, and said, "Not in a hushed voice shall this be spoken, that I have proved you to be a most noble man, in that you have prowess equal to the best man here in this land, but are in wits a long way before them". Then she gave him a gold ring and bade him farewell. Whereupon she drew her mantle over her head and went swiftly home. Hrut went on board his ship, and put to sea. He had a good breeze, and came to Broadfirth. He sailed up the bay, up to the island, and, steering in through Broadsound, he landed at Combness, where he put his gangways to land. The news of the coming of this ship spread about, as also that Hrut, Herjolf's son, was the captain. Hoskuld gave no good cheer to these tidings, and did not go to meet Hrut. Hrut put up his ship, and made her snug. He built himself a dwelling, which since has been called Combness. Then he rode to see Hoskuld, to get his share of his mother's inheritance. Hoskuld said he had no money to pay him, and said his mother had not gone without means out of Iceland when she met with Herjolf. Hrut liked this very ill, but rode away, and there the matter rested. All Hrut's kinsfolk, excepting Hoskuld, did honour to Hrut. Hrut now lived three winters at Combness, and was always demanding the money from Hoskuld at the Thing meetings and other law gatherings, and he spoke well on the matter. And most men held that Hrut had right on his side. Hoskuld said that Thorgerd had not married Herjolf by his counsel, and that he was her lawful guardian, and there the matter dropped. That same autumn Hoskuld went to a feast at Thord Goddi's, and hearing that, Hrut rode with twelve men to Hoskuldstead and took away twenty oxen, leaving as many behind. Then he sent some men to Hoskuld, telling them where he might search for the cattle. Hoskuld's house-carles sprang forthwith up, and seized their weapons, and words were sent to the nearest neighbours for help, so that they were a party of fifteen together, and they rode each one as fast as they possibly could. Hrut and his followers did not see the pursuit till they were a little way from the enclosure at Combness. And forthwith he and his men jumped off their horses, and tied them up, and went forward unto a certain sandhill. Hrut said that there they would make a stand, and added that though the money claim against Hoskuld sped slowly, never should that be said that he had run away before his thralls. Hrut's followers said that they had odds to deal with. Hrut said he would never heed that; said they should fare all the worse the more they were in number. The men of Salmon-river-Dale now jumped off their horses, and got ready to fight. Hrut bade his men not trouble themselves about the odds, and goes for them at a rush. Hrut had a helmet on his head, a drawn sword in one hand and a shield in the other. He was of all men the most skilled at arms. Hrut was then so wild that few could keep up with him. Both sides fought briskly for a while; but the men of Salmon-river-Dale very soon found that in Hrut they had to deal with one for whom they were no match, for now he slew two men at every onslaught. After that the men of Salmon-river-Dale begged for peace. Hrut replied that they should surely have peace. All the house-carles of Hoskuld who were yet alive were wounded, and four were killed. Hrut then went home, being somewhat wounded himself; but his followers only slightly or not at all, for he had been the foremost in the fight. The place has since been called Fight-Dale where they fought. After that Hrut had the cattle killed. Now it must be told how Hoskuld got men together in a hurry when he heard of the robbery and rode home. Much at the same time as he arrived his house-carles came home too, and told how their journey had gone anything but smoothly. Hoskuld was wild with wrath at this, and said he meant to take at Hrut's hand no robbery or loss of lives again, and gathered to him men all that day. Then Jorunn, his wife, went and talked to him, and asked him what he had made his mind up to. He said, "It is but little I have made up my mind to, but I fain would that men should oftener talk of something else than the slaying of my house-carles". Jorunn answered, "You are after a fearful deed if you mean to kill such a man as your brother, seeing that some men will have it that it would not have been without cause if Hrut had seized these goods even before this; and now he has shown that, taking after the race he comes from, he means no longer to be an outcast, kept from what is his own. Now, surely he cannot have made up his mind to try his strength with you till he knew that he might hope for some backing-up from the more powerful among men; for, indeed, I am told that messages have been passing in quiet between Hrut and Thord Yeller. And to me, at least, such matters seem worthy of heed being paid to them. No doubt Thord will be glad to back up matters of this kind, seeing how clear are the bearings of the case. Moreover you know, Hoskuld, that since the quarrel between Thord Goddi and Vigdis, there has not been the same fond friendship between you and Thord Yeller as before, although by means of gifts you staved off the enmity of him and his kinsmen in the beginning. I also think, Hoskuld," she said, "that in that matter, much to the trial of their temper, they feel they have come off worst at the hands of yourself and your son, Olaf. Now this seems to me the wiser counsel: to make your brother an honourable offer, for there a hard grip from greedy wolf may be looked for. I am sure that Hrut will take that matter in good part, for I am told he is a wise man, and he will see that that would be an honour to both of you." Hoskuld quieted down greatly at Jorunn's speech, and thought this was likely to be true. Then men went between them who were friends of both sides, bearing words of peace from Hoskuld to Hrut. Hrut also said he was ready to do honour to Hoskuld for what he on his side had misdone. So now these matters were shaped and settled between the brothers, who now take to living together in good brotherhood from this time forth. Hrut now looks after his homestead, and became mighty man of his ways. He did not mix himself up in general things, but in whatever matter he took a part he

Anonymous

would have his own way. Hrut now moved his dwelling, and abode to old age at a place which now is called Hrutstead. He made a temple in his home-field, of which the remains are still to be seen. It is called Trolls' walk now, and there is the high road. Hrut married a woman named Unn, daughter of Mord Fiddle. Unn left him, and thence sprang the quarrels between the men of Salmon-river-Dale and the men of Fleetlithe. Hrut's second wife was named Thorbjorg. She was Armod's daughter. Hrut married a third wife, but her we do not name. Hrut had sixteen sons and ten daughters by these two wives. And men say that one summer Hrut rode to the Thing meeting, and fourteen of his sons were with him. Of this mention is made, because it was thought a sign of greatness and might. All his sons were right goodly men.

CHAPTER XX
Melkorka's Marriage and Olaf the Peacock's Journey, A.D. 955 Of Thorliek Hoskuldson

Hoskuld now remained quietly at home, and began now to sink into old age, and his sons were now all grown up. Thorliek sets up household of his own at a place called Combness, and Hoskuld handed over to him his portion. After that he married a woman named Gjaflaug, daughter of Arnbjorn, son of Sleitu Bjorn, and Thordaug, the daughter of Thord of Headland. It was a noble match, Gjaflaug being a very beautiful and high-minded woman. Thorliek was not an easy man to get on with, but was most warlike. There was not much friendship between the kinsmen Hrut and Thorliek. Bard Hoskuld's son stayed at home with his father, looked after the household affairs no less than Hoskuld himself. The daughters of Hoskuld do not have much to do with this story, yet men are known who are descended from them. Olaf, Hoskuld's son, was now grown up, and was the handsomest of all men that people ever set eyes on. He arrayed himself always well, both as to clothes and weapons. Melkorka, Olaf's mother, lived at Melkorkastead, as has been told before. Hoskuld looked less after Melkorka's household ways than he used to do, saying that that matter concerned Olaf, her son. Olaf said he would give her such help as he had to offer her. Melkorka thought Hoskuld had done shamefully by her, and makes up her mind to do something to him at which he should not be over pleased. Thorbjorn Skrjup had chiefly had on hand the care of Melkorka's household affairs. He had made her an offer of marriage, after she had been an householder for but a little while, but Melkorka refused him flatly. There was a ship up by Board-Ere in Ramfirth, and Orn was the name of the captain. He was one of the bodyguard of King Harald, Gunnhild's son. Melkorka spoke to Olaf, her son, and said that she wished he should journey abroad to find his noble relations, "For I have told the truth that Myrkjartan is really my father, and he is king of the Irish and it would be easy for you betake you on board the ship that is now at Board-Ere." Olaf said, "I have spoken about it to my father, but he seemed to want to have but little to do with it; and as to the manner of my foster-father's money affairs, it so happens that his wealth is more in land or cattle than in stores of islandic market goods." Melkorka said, "I cannot bear your being called the son of a slave-woman any longer; and if it stands in the way of the journey, that you think you have not enough money, then I would rather go to the length even of marrying Thorbjorn, if then you should be more willing than before to betake yourself to the journey. For I think he will be willing to hand out to you as much

Anonymous

wares as you think you may need, if I give my consent to his marrying me. Above all I look to this, that then Hoskuld will like two things mightily ill when he comes to hear of them, namely, that you have gone out of the land, and that I am married." Olaf bade his mother follow her own counsel. After that Olaf talked to Thorbjorn as to how he wished to borrow wares of him, and a great deal thereof. Thorbjorn answered, "I will do it on one condition, and that is that I shall marry Melkorka for them; it seems to me, you will be as welcome to my money as to that which you have in your keep." Olaf said that this should then be settled; whereupon they talked between them of such matters as seemed needful, but all these things they agreed should be kept quiet. Hoskuld wished Olaf to ride with him to the Thing. Olaf said he could not do that on account of household affairs, as he also wanted to fence off a grazing paddock for lambs by Salmon River. Hoskuld was very pleased that he should busy himself with the homestead. Then Hoskuld rode to the Thing; but at Lambstead a wedding feast was arrayed, and Olaf settled the agreement alone. Olaf took out of the undivided estate thirty hundred ells' worth of wares, and should pay no money for them.[1] Bard, Hoskuld's son, was at the wedding, and was a party with them to all these doings. When the feast was ended Olaf rode off to the ship, and found Orn the captain, and took berth with him. Before Olaf and Melkorka parted she gave him a great gold finger-ring, and said, "This gift my father gave me for a teething gift, and I know he will recognise it when he sees it." She also put into his hands a knife and a belt, and bade him give them to her nurse: "I am sure she will not doubt these tokens." And still further Melkorka spake, "I have fitted you out from home as best I know how, and taught you to speak Irish, so that it will make no difference to you where you are brought to shore in Ireland." After that they parted. There arose forthwith a fair wind, when Olaf got on board, and they sailed straightway out to sea.

[1] *One hundred = 120 X 30 = 3600 x 120 = 432,000 ells altogether.*

CHAPTER XXI
Olaf the Peacock goes to Ireland, A.D. 955

Now Hoskuld came back from the Thing and heard these tidings, and was very much displeased. But seeing that his near akin were concerned in the matter, he quieted down and let things alone. Olaf and his companions had a good voyage, and came to Norway. Orn urges Olaf to go to the court of King Harald, who, he said, bestowed goodly honour on men of no better breeding than Olaf was. Olaf said he thought he would take that counsel. Olaf and Orn now went to the court, and were well received. The king at once recognised Olaf for the sake of his kindred, and forthwith bade him stay with him. Gunnhild paid great heed to Olaf when she knew he was Hrut's brother's son; but some men would have it, that she took pleasure in talking to Olaf without his needing other people's aid to introduce him. As the winter wore on, Olaf grew sadder of mood. Orn asked him what was the matter of his sorrow? Olaf answered, "I have on hand a journey to go west over the sea; and I set much store by it and that you should lend me your help, so that it may be undertaken in the course of next summer." Orn bade Olaf not set his heart on going, and said he did not know of any ships going west over the sea. Gunnhild joined in their talk, and said, "Now I hear you talk together in a manner that has not happened before, in that each of you wants to have his own way!" Olaf greeted Gunnhild well, without letting drop their talk. After that Orn went away, but Gunnhild and Olaf kept conversing together. Olaf told her of his wish, and how much store he set by carrying it out, saying he knew for certain that Myrkjartan, the king, was his mother's father. Then Gunnhild said, "I will lend you help for this voyage, so that you may go on it as richly furnished as you please." Olaf thanked her for her promise. Then Gunnhild had a ship prepared and a crew got together, and bade Olaf say how many men he would have to go west over the sea with him. Olaf fixed the number at sixty; but said that it was a matter of much concern to him, that such a company should be more like warriors than merchants. She said that so it should be; and Orn is the only man mentioned by name in company with Olaf on this journey. The company were well fitted out. King Harald and Gunnhild led Olaf to his ship, and they said they wished to bestow on him their good-luck over and above other friendship they had bestowed on him already. King Harald said that was an easy matter; for they must say that no goodlier a man had in their days come out of Iceland. Then Harald the king asked how old a man he was. Olaf answered, "I am now eighteen winters." The king replied, "Of exceeding worth, indeed, are such men as you are, for as yet you have left the age of child but a short way behind; and be sure to come and see us when you come back again." Then the king and Gunnhild bade Olaf farewell. Then Olaf and his men got on board, and sailed out to sea. They came in for unfavourable weather through the summer, had fogs plentiful, and little wind, and what there was was unfavourable; and wide about the main they drifted, and on most on board fell "sea-bewilderment." But at last the fog lifted over-head; and the wind rose, and they put up sail. Then they began to discuss in which direction Ireland was to be sought; and they did not agree on that. Orn said one thing, and most of the men went against him, and said that Orn was all bewildered: they should rule who were the greater in number. Then Olaf was asked to decide. He said, "I think we should follow the counsel of the wisest; for the counsels of foolish men I think will be of all the worse service for us in the greater number they gather together." And now they deemed the matter settled, since Olaf spake in this manner; and Orn took the steering from that time. They sailed for days and nights, but always with very little wind. One night the watchmen leapt up, and bade every one wake at once, and said they saw land so near that they had almost struck on it. The sail was up, but there was but little wind. Every one got up, and Orn bade them clear away from the land, if they could. Olaf said, "That is not the way out of our plight, for I see reefs all about astern; so let down the sail at once, and we will take our counsel when there is daylight, and we know what land this is." Then they cast anchors, and they caught bottom at once. There was much talk during the night as to where they could be come to; and when daylight was up they recognised that it was Ireland. Orn said, "I don't think we have come to a good place, for this is far away from the harbours or market-towns, whose strangers enjoy peace; and we are now left high and dry, like sticklebacks, and near enough, I think, I come to the laws of the Irish in saying that they will lay claim to the goods we have on board as their lawful prize, for as flotsam they put down ships even when sea has ebbed out shorter from the stern (than here)." Olaf said no harm would happen, "But I have seen that to-day there is a

Anonymous

gathering of men up inland; so the Irish think, no doubt, the arrival of this ship a great thing. During the ebb-tide to-day I noticed that there was a dip, and that out of the dip the sea fell without emptying it out; and if our ship has not been damaged, we can put out our boat and tow the ship into it." There was a bottom of loam where they had been riding at anchor, so that not a plank of the ship was damaged. So Olaf and his men tow their boat to the dip, cast anchor there. Now, as day drew on, crowds drifted down to the shore. At last two men rowed a boat out to the ship. They asked what men they were who had charge of that ship, and Olaf answered, speaking in Irish, to their inquiries. When the Irish knew they were Norwegians they pleaded their law, and bade them give up their goods; and if they did so, they would do them no harm till the king had sat in judgment on their case. Olaf said the law only held good when merchants had no interpreter with them. "But I can say with truth these are peaceful men, and we will not give ourselves up untried." The Irish then raised a great war-cry, and waded out into the sea, and wished to drag the ship, with them on board, to the shore, the water being no deeper than reaching up to their armpits, or to the belts of the tallest. But the pool was so deep where the ship was floating that they could not touch the bottom. Olaf bade the crew fetch out their weapons, and range in line of battle from stem to stern on the ship; and so thick they stood, that shield overlapped shield all round the ship, and a spear-point stood out at the lower end of every shield. Olaf walked fore to the prow, and was thus arrayed: he had a coat of mail, and a gold-reddened helmet on his head; girt with a sword with gold-inlaid hilt, and in his hand a barbed spear chased and well engraved. A red shield he had before him, on which was drawn a lion in gold. When the Irish saw this array fear shot through their hearts, and they thought it would not be so easy a matter as they had thought to master the booty. So now the Irish break their journey, and run all together to a village near. Then there arose great murmur in the crowd, as they deemed that, sure enough, this must be a warship, and that they must expect many others; so they sent speedily word to the king, which was easy, as he was at that time a short way off, feasting. Straightway he rides with a company of men to where the ship was. Between the land and the place where the ship lay afloat the space was no greater than that one might well hear men talking together. Now Olaf stood forth in the same arrayal whereof is written before, and men marvelled much how noble was the appearance of the man who was the captain of the ship. But when the shipmates of Olaf see how a large company of knights rides towards them, looking a company of the bravest, they grow hushed, for they deemed here were great odds to deal with. But when Olaf heard the murmur which went round among his followers, he bade them take heart, "For now our affairs are in a fair way; the Irish are now greeting Myrkjartan, their king." Then they rode so near to the ship, that each could hear what the other said. The king asked who was the master of the ship. Olaf told his name, and asked who was the valiant-looking knight with whom he then was talking. He answered, "I am called Myrkjartan." Olaf asked, "Are you then a king of the Irish?" He said he was. Then the king asked Olaf for news commonly talked of, and Olaf gave good answers as to all news he was asked about. Then the king asked whence they had put to sea, and whose men they were. And still the king asked, more searchingly than before, about Olaf's kindred, for

Anonymous

the king found that this man was of haughty bearing, and would not answer any further than the king asked. Olaf said, "Let it be known to you that we ran our ship afloat from the coast of Norway, and these are of the bodyguard of King Harald, the son of Gunnhild, who are here on board. And as for my race, I have, sire, to tell you this, that my father lives in Iceland, and is named Hoskuld, a man of high birth; but of my mother's kindred, I think you must have seen many more than I have. For my mother is called Melkorka, and it has been told me as a truth that she is your daughter, king. Now, this has driven me upon this long journey, and to me it is a matter most weighty what answer you give in my case." The king then grew silent, and had a converse with his men. The wise men asked the king what might be the real truth of the story that this man was telling. The king answered, "This is clearly seen in this Olaf, that he is high-born man, whether he be a kinsman of mine or not, as well as this, that of all men he speaks the best of Irish." After that the king stood up, and said, "Now I will give answer to your speech, in so far as we grant to you and all your shipmates peace; but on the kinship you claim with us, we must talk more before I give answer to that." After that they put out their gangways to the shore, and Olaf and his followers went on land from the ship; and the Irish now marvel much how warrior-like these men are. Olaf greeted the king well, taking off his helmet and bowing to the king, who welcomes Olaf with all fondness. Thereupon they fall to talking together, Olaf pleading his case again in a speech long and frank; and at the end of his speech he said he had a ring on his hand that Melkorka had given him at parting in Iceland, saying "that you, king, gave it her as a tooth gift." The king took and looked at the ring, and his face grew wondrous red to look at; and then the king said, "True enough are the tokens, and become by no means less notable thereby that you have so many of your mother's family features, and that even by them you might be easily recognised; and because of these things I will in sooth acknowledge your kinship, Olaf, by the witnessing of these men that here are near and hear my speech. And this shall also follow that I will ask you to my court, with all your suite, but the honour of you all will depend thereon of what worth as a man I find you to be when I try you more." After that the king orders riding-horses to be given to them, and appoints men to look after their ship, and to guard the goods belonging to them. The King now rode to Dublin, and men thought this great tidings, that with the king should be journeying the son of his daughter, who had been carried off in war long ago when she was only fifteen winters old. But most startled of all at these tidings was the foster-mother of Melkorka, who was then bed-ridden, both from heavy sickness and old age; yet she walked with no staff even to support her, to meet Olaf. The king said to Olaf, "Here is come Melkorka's foster-mother, and she will wish to hear all the tidings you can tell about Melkorka's life." Olaf took her with open arms, and set the old woman on his knee, and said her foster-daughter was well settled and in a good position in Iceland. Then Olaf put in her hands the knife and the belt, and the old woman recognised the gifts, and wept for joy, and said it was easy to see that Melkorka's son was one of high mettle, and no wonder, seeing what stock he comes of. The old woman was strong and well, and in good spirits all that winter. The king was seldom at rest, for at that time the lands in the west were at all times raided by war-bands. The king drove from his land that winter both Vikings and raiders. Olaf was with his suite in the king's ship, and those who came against them thought his was indeed a grim company to deal with. The king talked over with Olaf and his followers all matters needing counsel Olaf proved himself to the king both wise and eager-minded in all deeds of prowess. But towards the latter end of the winter the king summoned a Thing, and great numbers came. The king stood up and spoke. He began his speech thus: "You all know that last autumn there came hither a man who is the son of my daughter, and high-born also on his father's side; and it seems to me that Olaf is a man of such prowess and courage that here such men are not to be found. Now I offer him my kingdom after my day is done, for Olaf is much more suitable for a ruler than my own sons." Olaf thanked him for this offer with many graceful and fair words, and said he would not run the risk as to how his sons might behave when Myrkjartan was no more; said it was better to gain swift honour than lasting shame; and added that he wished to go to Norway when ships could safely journey from land to land, and that his mother would have little delight in life if he did not return to her. The king bade Olaf do as he thought best. Then the Thing was broken up. When Olaf's ship was ready, the king saw him off on board; and gave him a spear chased with gold, and a gold-bedecked sword, and much money besides. Olaf begged that he might take Melkorka's foster-mother with him; but the king said there was no necessity for that, so she did not go. Then Olaf got on board his ship, and he and the king parted with the greatest friendship. Then Olaf sailed out to sea. They had a good voyage, and made land in Norway; and Olaf's journey became very famous. They set up their ship; and Olaf got horses for himself, and went, together with his followers, to find King Harald.

CHAPTER XXII

Olaf the Peacock comes Home to Iceland, A.D. 957

Olaf Hoskuldson then went to the court of King Harald. The king gave him a good welcome, but Gunnhild a much better. With many fair words they begged him to stay with them, and Olaf agreed to it, and both he and Orn entered the king's court. King Harald and Gunnhild set so great a store by Olaf that no foreigner had ever been held in such honour by them. Olaf gave to the king and Gunnhild many rare gifts, which he had got west in Ireland. King Harald gave Olaf at Yule a set of clothes made out of scarlet stuff. So now Olaf stayed there quietly all the winter. In the spring, as it was wearing on, Olaf and the king had a conversation together, and Olaf begged the king's leave to go to Iceland in the summer, "For I have noble kinsfolk there I want to go and see." The king answered, "It would be more to my mind that you should settle down with us, and take whatever position in our service you like best yourself." Olaf thanked the king for all the honour he was offering him, but said he wished very much to go to Iceland, if that was not against the king's will. The king answered, "Nothing shall be done in this in an unfriendly manner to you, Olaf. You shall go out to Iceland in the summer, for I see you have set your heart on it; but neither trouble nor toil shall you have over your preparations, for I will see after all that," and thereupon they part talking. King Harald had a ship launched in the spring; it was a merchant ship, both great and good. This ship the king ordered to be laden with wood, and fitted out with full rigging. When the ship was ready the king had Olaf called to him, and said, "This ship shall be your own, Olaf, for I should not like you to start from Norway this

Anonymous

summer as a passenger in any one else's ship." Olaf thanked the king in fair words for his generosity. After that Olaf got ready for his journey; and when he was ready and a fair wind arose, Olaf sailed out to sea, and King Harald and he parted with the greatest affection. That summer Olaf had a good voyage. He brought his ship into Ramfirth, to Board-Ere. The arrival of the ship was soon heard of, and also who the captain was. Hoskuld heard of the arrival of Olaf, his son, and was very much pleased, and rode forthwith north to Hrutafjord with some men, and there was a joyful meeting between the father and son. Hoskuld invited Olaf to come to him, and Olaf said he would agree to that; so he set up his ship, but his goods were brought (on horseback) from the north. And when this business was over Olaf himself rode with twelve men home to Hoskuldstead, and Hoskuld greeted his son joyfully, and his brothers also received him fondly, as well as all his kinsfolk; but between Olaf and Bard was love the fondest. Olaf became very renowned for this journey; and now was proclaimed the descent of Olaf, that he was the daughter's son of Myrkjartan, king of Ireland. The news of this spread over the land, as well as of the honour that mighty men, whom he had gone to see, had bestowed on him. Melkorka came soon to see Olaf, her son, and Olaf greeted her with great joy. She asked about many things in Ireland, first of her father and then of her other relations. Olaf replied to everything she asked. Then she asked if her foster-mother still lived. Olaf said she was still alive. Melkorka asked why he had not tried to give her the pleasure of bringing her over to Iceland. Olaf replied, "They would not allow me to bring your foster-mother out of Ireland, mother." "That may be so," she replied, and it could be seen that this she took much to heart. Melkorka and Thorbjorn had one son, who was named Lambi. He was a tall man and strong, like his father in looks as well as in temper. When Olaf had been in Iceland a month, and spring came on, father and son took counsel together. "I will, Olaf," said Hoskuld, "that a match should be sought for you, and that then you should take over the house of your foster-father at Goddistead, where still there are great means stored up, and that then you should look after the affairs of that household under my guidance." Olaf answered, "Little have I set my mind on that sort of thing hitherto; besides, I do not know where that woman lives whom to marry would mean any great good luck to me. You must know I shall look high for a wife. But I see clearly that you would not have broached this matter till you had made up your mind as to where it was to end." Hoskuld said, "You guess that right. There is a man named Egil. He is Skallagrim's son. He lives at Borg, in Borgarfjord. This Egil has a daughter who is called Thorgerd, and she is the woman I have made up my mind to woo on your behalf, for she is the very best match in all Borgarfjord, and even if one went further afield. Moreover, it is to be looked for, that an alliance with the Mere-men would mean more power to you." Olaf answered, "Herein I shall trust to your foresight, for if this match were to come off it would be altogether to my liking. But this you must bear in mind, father, that should this matter be set forth, and not come off, I should take it very ill." Hoskuld answered, "I think I shall venture to bring the matter about." Olaf bade him do as he liked. Now time wears on towards **Olaf's proposal** the Thing. Hoskuld prepares his journey from home with a crowded company, and Olaf, his son, also accompanies him on the journey. They set up their booth. A great many people were there. Egil

Skallagrim's son was at the Thing. Every one who saw Olaf remarked what a handsome man he was, and how noble his bearing, well arrayed as he was as to weapons and clothes.

CHAPTER XXIII

The Marriage of Olaf Peacock and Thorgerd, the Daughter of Egil, A.D. 959

It is told how one day the father and son, Hoskuld and Olaf, went forth from their booth to find Egil. Egil greeted them well, for he and Hoskuld knew each other very well by word of mouth. Hoskuld now broaches the wooing on behalf of Olaf, and asks for the hand of Thorgerd. She was also at the Thing. Egil took the matter well, and said he had always heard both father and son well spoken of, "and I also know, Hoskuld," said Egil, "that you are a high-born man and of great worth, and Olaf is much renowned on account of his journey, and it is no wonder that such men should look high for a match, for he lacks neither family nor good looks; but yet this must be talked over with Thorgerd, for it is no man's task to get Thorgerd for wife against her will." Hoskuld said, "I wish, Egil, that you would talk this over with your daughter." Egil said that that should be done. Egil now went away to find his daughter, and they talked together. Egil said, "There is here a ma named Olaf, who is Hoskuld's son, and he is now one of the most renowned of men. Hoskuld, his father, has broached a wooing on behalf of Olaf, and has sued for your hand; and I have left that matter mostly for you to deal with. Now I want to know your answer. But it seems to me that it behoves you to give a good answer to such a matter, for this match is a noble one." Thorgerd answered, "I have often heard you say that you love me best of all your children, but now it seems to me you make that a falsehood if you wish me to marry the son of a bonds-woman, however goodly and great a dandy he may be." Egil said, "In this matter you are not so well up, as in others. Have you not heard that he is the son of the daughter of Myrkjartan, king of Ireland? so that he is much higher born on his mother's side than on his father's, which, however, would be quite good enough for us." Thorgerd would not see this; and so they dropped the talk, each being somewhat of a different mind. The next day Egil went to Hoskuld's booth. Hoskuld gave him a good welcome, and so they fell a-talking together. Hoskuld asked how this wooing matter had sped. Egil held out but little hope, and told him all that had come to pass. Hoskuld said it looked like a closed matter, "Yet I think you have behaved well." Olaf did not hear this talk of theirs. After that Egil went away. Olaf now asks, "How speeds the wooing?" Hoskuld said, "It pointed to slow speed on her side." Olaf said, "It is now as I told you, father, that I should take it very ill if in answer (to the wooing) I should have to take shaming words, seeing that the broaching of the wooing gives undue right to the wooed. And now I shall have my way so far, that this shall not drop here. For true is the saw, that 'others' errands eat the wolves'; and now I shall go straightway to Egil's booth." Hoskuld bade him have his own way. Olaf now dressed himself in this way, that he had on the scarlet clothes King Harald had given him, and a golden helmet on his head, and the gold-adorned sword in his hand that King Myrkjartan had given him. Then Hoskuld and Olaf went to Egil's booth. Hoskuld went first, and Olaf followed close on his heels. Egil greeted him well, and Hoskuld sat down by him, but Olaf stood up and looked about him. He saw a woman sitting on the dais in the booth, she was goodly and had the looks of one of high degree, and very well dressed. He thought to himself this must be Thorgerd, Egil's daughter. Olaf went up to the dais and sat down by her. Thorgerd greeted the man, and asked who he was. Olaf told his own and his father's name, and "You must think it very bold that the son of a slave should dare to sit down by you and presume to talk to you!" She said, "You cannot but mean that you must be thinking you have done deeds of greater daring than that of talking to women." Then they began to talk together, and they talked all day. But nobody heard their conversation. And before they parted Egil and Hoskuld were called to them; and the matter of Olaf's wooing was now talked over again, and Thorgerd came round to her father's wish. Now the affair was all easily settled and the betrothal took place. The honour was conceded to the Salmon-river-Dale men that the bride should be brought home to them, for by law the bride-groom should have gone to the bride's home to be married. The wedding was to take place at Hoskuldstead when seven weeks summer had passed. After that Egil and Hoskuld separated. The father and son rode home to Hoskuldstead, and all was quiet the rest of the summer. After that things were got ready for the wedding at Hoskuldstead, and nothing was spared, for means were plentiful. The guests came at the time settled, and the Burgfirthmen mustered in a great company. Egil was there, and Thorstein, his son. The bride was in the journey too, and with her a chosen company out of all the countryside. Hoskuld had also a great company awaiting them. The feast was a brave one, and the guests were seen off with good gifts on leaving. Olaf gave to Egil the sword, Myrkjartan's gift, and Egil's brow brightened greatly at the gift. Nothing in the way of tidings befell, and every one went home.

CHAPTER XXIV

The Building of Herdholt, A. D. 960

Olaf and Thorgerd lived at Hoskuldstead and loved each other very dearly; it was easily seen by every one that she was a woman of very high mettle, though she meddled little with every-day things, but whatever Thorgerd put her hand to must be carried through as she wished. Olaf and Thorgerd spent that winter turn and turn about at Hoskuldstead, or with Olaf's foster-father. In the spring Olaf took over the household business at Goddistead. The following summer Thord fell ill, and the illness ended in his death. Olaf had a cairn raised over him on the ness that runs out into the Salmon-river and is called Drafn-ness, with a wall round which is called Howes-garth. After that liegemen crowded to Olaf and he became a great chieftain. Hoskuld was not envious of this, for he always wished that Olaf should be consulted in all great matters. The place Olaf owned was the stateliest in Salmon-river-Dale. There were two brothers with Olaf, both named An. One was called An the White and the other An the Black. They had a third brother who was named Beiner the Strong. These were Olaf's smiths, and very valiant men. Thorgerd and Olaf had a daughter who was named Thurid. The land that Hrapp had owned all lay waste, as has been told before. Olaf thought that it lay well and set before his father his wishes on the matter; how they should send down to Trefill with this errand, that Olaf wished to buy the land and other things thereto belonging at Hrappstead. It was soon arranged and the bargain settled, for Trefill saw that better was one crow in the hand than two in the wood. The bargain arranged was that Olaf should give three marks of silver for the land; yet that was not fair price, for the lands were wide and fair and very rich in useful produce, such as good salmon fishing and seal catching. There were wide woods too, a little further up than Hoskuldstead, north of the Salmon-river, in which was a space cleared, and it was well-nigh a matter of certainty that the flocks of Olaf would gather together there whether the weather was hard or mild. One autumn it befell that on that same hill Olaf had built a dwelling of the timber that was cut out of the forest, though some he got together from drift-wood strands. This was a very lofty dwelling. The buildings stood empty through the winter. The next spring Olaf went thither and first gathered together all his flocks which had grown to be a great multitude; for, indeed, no man was richer in live stock in all Broadfirth. Olaf now sent word to his father that he should be standing out of doors and have a look at his train as he was moving to his new home, and should give him his good wishes. Hoskuld said so it should be. Olaf now arranged how it should be done. He ordered that all the shiest of his cattle should be driven first and then the milking live stock, then came the dry cattle, and the pack horses came in the last place; and men were ranged with the animals to keep them from straying out of straight line. When the van of the train had got to the new homestead, Olaf was just riding out of Goddistead and there was nowhere a gap breaking the line. Hoskuld stood outside his door together with those of his household. Then Hoskuld spake, bidding Olaf his son welcome and abide all honour to this new dwelling of his, "And somehow my mind forebodes me that this will follow, that for a long time his name will be remembered." Jorunn his wife said, "Wealth enough the slave's son has got for his name to be long remembered." At the moment that the house-carles had unloaded the pack horses Olaf rode into the place. Then he said, "Now you shall have your curiosity satisfied with regard to what you have been talking about all the winter, as to what this place shall be called; it shall be called Herdholt." Every one thought this a very happy name, in view of what used to happen there.[2] Olaf now sets up his household at Herdholt, and a stately one it soon became, and nothing was lacking there. And now the honour of Olaf greatly increased, there being many causes to bring it about: Olaf was the most beloved of men, for whatever he had to do with affairs of men, he did so that all were well contented with their lot. His father backed him up very much towards being a widely honoured man, and Olaf gained much in power from his alliance with the Mere-men. Olaf was considered the noblest of all Hoskuld's sons. The first winter that Olaf kept house at Herdholt, he had many servants and workmen, and work was divided amongst the house-carles; one looked after the dry cattle and another after the cows. The fold was out in the wood, some way from the homestead. One evening the man who looked after the dry cattle came to Olaf and asked him to make some other man look after the neat and "set apart for me some other work." Olaf answered, "I wish you to go on with this same work of yours." The man said he would sooner go away. "Then you think there is something wrong," said Olaf. "I will go this evening with you when you do up the cattle, and if I think there is any excuse for you in this I will say nothing about it, but otherwise you will find that your lot will take some turn for the worse." Olaf took his gold-set spear, the king's gift, in his hand, and left home, and with him the house-carle. There was some snow on the ground. They came to the fold, which was open, and Olaf bade the house-carle go in. "I will drive up the cattle and you tie them up as they come in." The house-carle went to the fold-door. And all unawares Olaf finds him leaping into his open arms. Olaf asked why he went on so terrified? He replied, "Hrapp stands in the doorway of the fold, and felt after me, but I have had my fill of wrestling with him." Olaf went to the fold door and struck at him with his spear. Hrapp took the socket of the spear in both hands and wrenched it aside, so that forthwith the spear shaft broke. Olaf was about to run at Hrapp but he disappeared there where he stood, and there they parted, Olaf having the shaft and Hrapp the spear-head. After that Olaf and the house-carle tied up the cattle and went home. Olaf saw the house-carle was not to blame for his grumbling. The next morning Olaf went to where Hrapp was buried and had him dug up. Hrapp was found undecayed, and there Olaf also found his spear-head. After that he had a pyre made and had Hrapp burnt on it, and his ashes were flung out to sea. After that no one had any more trouble with Hrapp's ghost.

[2] i.e., in view of the fact stated above that Olaf's flocks would always be gathering there.

CHAPTER XXV
About Hoskuld's Sons

Now Hoskuld's sons shall be told about. Thorliek, Hoskuld's son, had been a great seafarer, and taken service with men in lordly station when he was on his merchant voyages before he settled down as a householder, and a man of mark he was thought to be. He had also been on Viking raids, and given good account of himself by reason of his courage. Bard, Hoskuld's son, had also been a seafarer, and was well accounted of wherever he went, for he was the best of brave men and true, and a man of moderation in all things. Bard married a Broadfirth woman, named Astrid, who came of a good stock. Bard's son was named Thorarin, and his daughter Gudney, who married Hall, the son of Fight Styr, and from them are descended many great families. Hrut, Herjolf's son, gave a thrall of his, named Hrolf, his freedom, and with it a certain amount of money, and a dwelling-place where his land joined with Hoskuld's. And it lay so near the landmark that Hrut's people had made a mistake in the matter, and settled the freedman down on the land belonging to Hoskuld. He soon gained there much wealth. Hoskuld took it very much to heart that Hrut should have placed his freedman right up against his ear, and bade the freedman pay him money for the lands he lived on "for it is mine own." The freedman went to Hrut and told him all they had spoken together. Hrut bade him give no heed, and pay no money to Hoskuld. "For I do not know," he said, "to which of us the land belonged." So the freedman went home, and goes on with his household just as before. A little later, Thorliek, Hoskuld's son, went at the advice of his father to the dwelling of the freedman and took him and killed him, and Thorliek claimed as his and his father's own all the money the freedman had made. Hrut heard this, and he and his sons liked it very ill. They were most of them grown up, and the band of kinsmen was deemed a most forbidding one to grapple with. Hrut fell back on the law as to how this ought to turn out, and when the matter was searched into by lawyers, Hrut and his son stood at but little advantage, for it was held a matter of great weight that Hrut had set the freedman down without leave on Hoskuld's land, where he had made money, Thorliek having slain the man within his and his father's own lands. Hrut took his lot very much to heart; but things remained quiet. After that Thorliek had a homestead built on the boundary of Hrut and Hoskuld's lands, and it was called Combness. There Thorliek lived for a while, as has been told before. Thorliek begat a son of his wife. The boy was sprinkled with water and called Bolli. He was at an early age a very promising man.

CHAPTER XXVI
The Death of Hoskuld, A.D. 985

Hoskuld, Koll o' Dales' son, fell ill in his old age, and he sent for his sons and other kinsfolk, and when they were come Hoskuld spoke to the brothers Bard and Thorliek, and said, "I have taken some sickness, and as I have not been much in the way of falling ill before, I think this may bring me to death; and now, as you know, you are both begotten in wedlock, and are entitled to all inheritance left by me. But there is a third son of mine, one who is not born in wedlock, and I will ask you brothers to allow him, Olaf to wit, to be adopted, so that he take of my means one-third with you." Bard answered first, and said that he would do as his father wished, "for I look for honour from Olaf in every way, the more so the wealthier he becomes." Then Thorliek said, "It is far from my wish that Olaf be adopted; he has plenty of money already; and you, father, have for a long time given him a great deal, and for a very long time dealt unevenly with us. I will not freely give up the honour to which I am born." Hoskuld said, "Surely you will not rob me of the law that allows me to give twelve ounces to my son, seeing how high-born Olaf is on his mother's side." To this Thorliek now agreed. Then Hoskuld took the gold ring, Hakon's gift, that weighed a mark, and the sword, King's gift whereon was half a mark of gold, and gave them to Olaf, his son, and therewith his good luck and that of the family, saying he did not speak in this way because he did not know well enough that the luck had already come to him. Olaf took his gifts, and said he would risk how Thorliek would like it. Thorliek liked it very ill, and thought that Hoskuld had behaved in a very underhand way to him. Olaf said, "I shall not give up the gifts, Thorliek, for you agreed to the gift in the face of witnesses; and I shall run the risk to keep it." Bard said he would obey his father's wishes. After that Hoskuld died, and his death was very much grieved for, in the first place by his sons, and next by all his relations and friends. His sons had a worthy cairn made for him; but little money was put into it with him. And when this was over, the brothers began to talk over the matter of preparing an "arvale" (burial feast) after their father, for at that time such was the custom. Olaf said, "It seems to me that we should not be in a hurry about preparing this feast, if it is to be as noble as we should think right; now the autumn is very far worn, and the ingathering of means for it is no longer easy; most people who have to come a long way would find that a hard matter in the autumn days; so that it is certain that many would not come of the men we most should like to see. So I will now make the offer, next summer at the Thing, to bid men to the feast, and I will bear one-third of the cost of the wassail." The brothers agreed to that, and Olaf now went home. Thorliek and Bard now share the goods between them. Bard had the estate and lands, which was what most men held to, as he was the most popular; but Thorliek got for his share more of the chattels. Olaf and Bard got on well together, but Olaf and Thorliek rather snappishly. Now the next winter passed, and summer comes, and time wears on towards the Thing. The sons of Hoskuld got ready to go to the Thing. It was soon seen clearly enough how Olaf took the lead of the brothers. When they got to the Thing they set up three booths, and make themselves comfortable in a handsome manner.

CHAPTER XXVII

The Funeral Feast for Hoskuld

It is told how one day when people went to the law rock Olaf stood up and asked for a hearing, and told them first of the death of his father, "and there are now here many men, kinsmen and friends of his. It is the will of my brothers that I ask you to a funeral feast in memory of Hoskuld our father. All you chieftains, for most of the mightier men are such, as were bound by alliances to him, I let it be known that no one of the greater men shall go away giftless. And herewith I bid all the farmers and any who will accept—rich or poor—to a half month's feast at Hoskuldstead ten weeks before the winter." And when Olaf finished his speech good cheer was made thereto, and his bidding was looked upon as a right lordly one. And when Olaf came home to the booth he told his brothers what he had settled to do. The brothers were not much pleased, and thought that this was going in for far too much state. After the Thing the brothers rode home and the summer now wears on. Then the brothers got ready for the feast, and Olaf put forward unstintedly his third part, and the feast was furnished with the best of provisions. Great stores were laid in for this feast, for it was expected many folk would come. And when the time came it is said that most of the chief men came that were asked. There were so many that most men say that there could not be far short of nine hundred (1080). This is the most crowded burial feast that has been in Iceland, second to that which the sons of Hialti gave at the funeral of their father, at which time there were 1440 guests. But this feast was of the bravest in every way, and the brothers got great honour therefrom, Olaf being at the head of the affair throughout. Olaf took even share with his brothers in the gifts; and gifts were bestowed on all the chiefs. When most of the men had gone away Olaf went to have a talk with Thorliek his brother, and said, "So it is, kinsman, as you know, that no love has been lost between us; now I would beg for a better understanding in our brotherhood. I know you did not like when I took the heirlooms my father gave me on his dying day. Now if you think yourself wronged in this, I will do as much for gaining back your whole good-will as to give fostering to your son. For it is said that ever he is the lesser man who fosters another's child." Thorliek took this in good part, and said, as was true, that this was honourably offered. And now Olaf took home Bolli, the son of Thorliek, who at this time was three winters old. They parted now with the utmost affection, and Bolli went home to Herdholt with Olaf. Thorgerd received him well, and Bolli grew up there and was loved no less than their own children.

CHAPTER XXVIII
The Birth of Kjartan, Olaf's Son, A.D. 978

Olaf and Thorgerd had a son, and the boy was sprinkled with water and a name was given him, Olaf letting him be called Kjartan after Myrkjartan his mother's father. Bolli and Kjartan were much of an age. Olaf and Thorgerd had still more children; three sons were called Steinthor and Halldor and Helgi, and Hoskuld was the name of the youngest of Olaf's sons. The daughters of Olaf and his wife were named Bergthora, Thorgerd, and Thorbjorg. All their children were of goodly promise as they grew up. At that time Holmgang Bersi lived in Saurby at an abode called Tongue. He comes to see Olaf and asked for Halldor his son to foster. Olaf agreed to this and Halldor went home with him, being then one winter old. That summer Bersi fell ill, and lay in bed for a great part of the summer. It is told how one day, when all the men were out haymaking at Tongue and only they two, Bersi and Halldor, were left in the house, Halldor lay in his cradle and the cradle fell over under the boy and he fell out of it on to the floor, and Bersi could not get to him. Then Bersi said this ditty:

Here we both lie In helpless plight, Halldor and I, Have no power left us; Old age afflicts me, Youth afflicts you, You will get better But I shall get worse.

Later on people came in and picked Halldor up off the floor, and Bersi got better. Halldor was brought up there, and was a tall man and doughty looking. Kjartan, Olaf's son, grew up at home at Herdholt. He was of all men the goodliest of those who have been born in Iceland. He was striking of countenance and fair of feature, he had the finest eyes of any man, and was light of hue. He had a great deal of hair as fair as silk, falling in curls; he was a big man, and strong, taking after his mother's father Egil, or his uncle Thorolf. Kjartan was better proportioned than any man, so that all wondered who saw him. He was better skilled at arms than most men; he was a deft craftsman, and the best swimmer of all men. In all deeds of strength he was far before others, more gentle than any other man, and so engaging that every child loved him; he was light of heart, and free with his money. Olaf loved Kjartan best of all his children. Bolli, his foster-brother, was a great man, he came next to Kjartan in all deeds of strength and prowess; he was strong, and fair of face and courteous, and most warrior-like, and a great dandy. The foster-brothers were very fond of each other. Olaf now remained quietly in his home, and for a good many years.

CHAPTER XXIX
Olaf's Second Journey to Norway, A.D. 975

It is told how one spring Olaf broke the news to Thorgerd that he wished to go out voyaging—"And I wish you to look after our household and children." Thorgerd said she did not much care about doing that; but Olaf said he would have his way. He bought a ship that stood up in the West, at Vadill. Olaf started during the summer, and brought his ship to Hordaland. There, a short way inland, lived a man whose name was Giermund Roar, a mighty man and wealthy, and a great Viking; he was an evil man to deal with, but had now settled down in quiet at home, and was of the bodyguard of Earl Hakon. The mighty Giermund went down to his ship and soon recognised Olaf, for he had heard him spoken of before. Giermund bade Olaf come and stay with him, with as many of his men as he liked to bring. Olaf accepted his invitation, and went there with seven men. The crew of Olaf went into lodgings about Hordaland. Giermund entertained Olaf well. His house was a lofty one, and there were many men there, and plenty of amusement all the winter. And towards the end of the winter Olaf told Giermund the reason of his voyage, which was that he wished to get for himself some house-timber, and said he set great store by obtaining timber of a choice kind. Giermund said, "Earl Hakon has the best of woods, and I know quite well if you went to see him you would be made welcome to them, for the Earl receives well, men who are not half so well-bred as you, Olaf, when they go to see him." In the spring Olaf got ready to go and find Hakon Earl; and the Earl gave him exceeding good welcome, and bade Olaf stay with him as long as he liked. Olaf told the Earl the reason of his journey, "And I beg this of you, sir, that you give us permission to cut wood for house-building from your forests." The Earl answered, "You are welcome to load your ship with timber, and I will give it you. For I think it no every-day occurrence when such men as you come from Iceland to visit me." At parting the Earl gave him a gold-inlaid axe, and the best of keepsakes it was; and therewith they parted in the greatest friendship. Giermund in the meantime set stewards over his estates secretly, and made up his mind to go to Iceland in the summer in Olaf's ship. He kept this secret from every one. Olaf knew nothing about it till Giermund brought his money to Olaf's ship, and very great wealth it was. Olaf said, "You should not have gone in my ship if I had known of this before-hand, for I think there are those in Iceland for whom it would be better never to have seen you. But since you have come with so much goods, I cannot drive you out like a straying cur." Giermund said, "I shall not return for all your high words, for I mean to be your passenger." Olaf and his got on board, and put out to sea. They had a good voyage and made Broadfirth, and they put out their gangways and landed at Salmon-river-Mouth. Olaf had the wood taken out of his ship, and the ship put up in the shed his father had made. Olaf then asked Giermund to come and stay with him. That summer Olaf had a fire-hall built at Herdholt, a greater and better than had ever been seen before. Noble legends were painted on its wainscoting and in the roof, and this was so well done that the hall was thought even more beautiful when the hangings were not up. Giermund did not meddle with every-day matters, but was uncouth to most people. He was usually dressed in this way—he wore a scarlet kirtle below and a grey cloak outside, and a bearskin cap on his head, and a sword in his hand. This was a great weapon and good, with a hilt of walrus tooth, with no silver on it; the brand was sharp, and no rust would stay thereon. This sword he called Footbiter, and he never let it out of his hands. Giermund had not been there long before he fell in love with Thured, Olaf's daughter, and proposed to Olaf for her hand; but he gave him a straight refusal. Then Giermund gave some money to Thorgerd with a view to gaining the match. She took the money, for it was offered unstintedly. Then Thorgerd broached the matter to Olaf, and said she thought their daughter could not be better married, "for he is a very brave man, wealthy and high-mettled." Then Olaf answered, "I will not go against you in this any more than in other things, though I would sooner marry Thured to some one else." Thorgerd went away and thought her business had sped well, and now told Giermund the upshot of it. He thanked her for her help and her determination, and Giermund broached the wooing a second time to Olaf, and now won the day easily. After that Giermund and Thured were betrothed, and the wedding was to be held at the end of the winter at Herdholt. The wedding feast was a very crowded one, for the new hall was finished. Ulf Uggason was of the bidden guests, and he had made a poem on Olaf Hoskuldson and of the legends that were painted round the hall, and he gave it forth at the feast. This poem is called the "House Song," and is well made. Olaf rewarded him well for the poem. Olaf gave great gifts to all the chief men who came. Olaf was considered to have gained in renown by this feast.

CHAPTER XXX

About Giermund and Thured, A.D. 978

Giermund and Thured did not get on very well together, and little love was lost between them on either side. When Giermund had stayed with Olaf three winters he wished to go away, and gave out that Thured and his daughter Groa should remain behind. This little maid was by then a year old, and Giermund would not leave behind any money for them. This the mother and daughter liked very ill, and told Olaf so. Olaf said, "What is the matter now, Thorgerd? is the Eastman now not so bounteous as he was that autumn when he asked for the alliance?" They could get Olaf to do nothing, for he was an easygoing man, and said the girl should remain until she wished to go, or knew how in some way to shift for herself. At parting Olaf gave Giermund the merchant ship all fitted out. Giermund thanked him well therefor, and said it was a noble gift. Then he got on board his ship, and sailed out of the Salmon-river-Mouth by a north-east breeze, which dropped as they came out to the islands. He now lies by Oxe-isle half a month without a fair wind rising for a start. At that time Olaf had to leave home to look after his foreshore drifts. Then Thured, his daughter, called to his house-carles, and bade them come with her. She had the maid Groa with her, and they were a party of ten together. She lets run out into the water a ferry-boat that belonged to Olaf, and Thured bade them sail and row down along

Hvamfirth, and when they came out to the islands she bade them put out the cock-boat that was in the ferry. Thured got into the boat with two men, and bade the others take care of the ship she left behind until she returned. She took the little maid in her arms, and bade the men row across the current until they should reach the ship (of Giermund). She took a gimlet out of the boat's locker, and gave it to one of her companions, and bade him go to the cockle-boat belonging to the merchant ship and bore a hole in it so as to disable it if they needed it in a hurry. Then she had herself put ashore with the little maid still in her arms. This was at the hour of sunrise. She went across the gangway into the ship, where all men were asleep. She went to the hammock where Giermund slept. His sword Footbiter hung on a peg pole. Thured now sets the little maid in the hammock, and snatched off Footbiter and took it with her. Then she left the ship and rejoined her companions. Now the little maid began to cry, and with that Giermund woke up and recognised the child, and thought he knew who must be at the bottom of this. He springs up wanting to seize his sword, and misses it, as was to be expected, and then went to the gunwale, and saw that they were rowing away from the ship. Giermund called to his men, and bade them leap into the cockle-boat and row after them. They did so, but when they got a little way they found how the coal-blue sea poured into them, so they went back to the ship. Then Giermund called Thured and bade her come back and give him his sword Footbiter, "and take your little maid, and with her as much money as you like." Thured answered, "Would you rather than not have the sword back?" Giermund answered, "I would give a great deal of money before I should care to let my sword go." Thured answered, "Then you shall never have it again, for you have in many ways behaved cowardly towards me, and here we shall part for good." Then Giermund said, "Little luck will you get with the sword." Thured said she would take the risk of that. "Then I lay thereon this spell," said Giermund, "That this sword shall do to death the man in your family in who would be the greatest loss, and in a manner most ill-fated." After that Thured went home to Herdholt. Olaf had then come home, and showed his displeasure at her deed, yet all was quiet. Thured gave Bolli, her cousin, the sword Footbiter, for she loved him in no way less than her brothers. Bolli bore that sword for a long time after. After this Giermund got a favourable wind, and sailed out to sea, and came to Norway in the autumn. They sailed one night on to some hidden rocks before Stade, and then Giermund and all his crew perished. And that is the end of all there is to tell about Giermund.

CHAPTER XXXI
Thured's Second Marriage, A.D. 980

Olaf Hoskuldson now stayed at home in much honour, as has been told before. There was a man named Gudmund, who was the son of Solmund, and lived at Asbjornness north in Willowdale. He wooed Thured, and got her and a great deal of wealth with her. Thured was a wise woman, high-tempered and most stirring. Their sons were called Hall and Bard and Stein and Steingrim. Gudrun and Olof were their daughters. Thorbjorg, Olaf's daughter, was of women the most beautiful and stout of build. She was called Thorbjorg the Stout, and was married west in Waterfirth to Asgier, the son of Knott. He was a noble man. Their son was Kjartan, father of Thorvald, the father of Thord, the father of Snorri, the father of Thorvald, from whom is sprung the Waterfirth race. Afterwards, Vermund, the son of Thorgrim, had Thorbjorg for wife. Their daughter was Thorfinna, whom Thorstein Kuggason had for wife. Bergthora, Olaf's daughter, was married west in Deepfirth to Thorhall the Priest. Their son was Kjartan, father of Smith-Sturla, the foster son of Thord Gilson. Olaf Peacock had many costly cattle. He had one very good ox named Harri; it was dapple-grey of coat, and bigger than any other of his cattle. It had four horns, two great and fair ones, the third stood straight up, and a fourth stood out of its forehead, stretching down below its eyes. It was with this that he opened the ice in winter to get water. He scraped snow away to get at pasture like a horse. One very hard winter he went from Herdholt into the Broadfirth-Dales to a place that is now called Harristead. There he roamed through the winter with sixteen other cattle, and got grazing for them all. In the spring he returned to the home pastures, to the place now called Harris'-Lair in Herdholt land. When Harri was eighteen winters old his ice-breaking horn fell off, and that same autumn Olaf had him killed. The next night Olaf dreamed that a woman came to him, and she was great and wrathful to look at. She spoke and said, "Are you asleep?" He said he was awake. The woman said, "You are asleep, though it comes to the same thing as if you were awake. You have had my son slain, and let him come to my hand in a shapeless plight, and for this deed you shall see your son, blood-stained all over through my doing, and him I shall choose thereto whom I know you would like to lose least of all." After that she disappeared, and Olaf woke up and still thought he saw the features of the woman. Olaf took the dream very much to heart, and told it to his friends, but no one could read it to his liking. He thought those spoke best about this matter who said that what had appeared to him was only a dream or fancy.

CHAPTER XXXII
Of Osvif Helgeson

Osvif was the name of a man. He was the son of Helgi, who was the son of Ottar, the son of Bjorn the Eastman, who was the son of Ketill Flatnose, the son of Bjorn Buna. The mother of Osvif was named Nidbiorg. Her mother was Kadlin, the daughter of Ganging-Hrolf, the son of Ox-Thorir, who was a most renowned "Hersir" (war-lord) east in Wick. Why he was so called, was that he owned three islands with eighty oxen on each. He gave one island and its oxen to Hakon the King, and his gift was much talked about. Osvif was a great sage. He lived at Laugar in Salingsdale. The homestead of Laugar stands on the northern side of Salingsdale-river, over against Tongue. The name of his wife was Thordis, daughter of Thjodolf the Low. Ospak was the name of one of their sons. Another was named Helgi, and a third Vandrad, and a fourth Jorrad, and a fifth Thorolf. They were all doughty men for fighting. Gudrun was the name of their daughter. She was the goodliest of women who grew up in Iceland, both as to looks and wits. Gudrun was such a woman of state that at that time whatever other women wore in the way of finery of dress was looked upon as children's gewgaws beside hers. She was the most cunning and the fairest spoken of all women, and an open-handed woman withal. There was a woman living with Osvif who was named Thorhalla, and was called the Chatterer. She was some sort of relation to Osvif. She had two sons, one named Odd and the other Stein. They were muscular men, and in a great measure the hardest toilers for Osvif's household. They were talkative like their mother, but ill liked by people; yet were upheld greatly by the sons of Osvif. At Tongue there lived a man named Thorarin, son of Thorir Sæling (the Voluptuous). He was a well-off yeoman, a big man and strong. He had very good land, but less of live stock. Osvif wished to buy some of his land from him, for he had lack of land but a multitude of live stock. So this then came about that Osvif bought of the land of Thorarin all the tract from Gnupaskard along both sides of the valley to Stack-gill, and very good and fattening land it was. He had on it an out-dairy. Osvif had at all times a great many servants, and his way of living was most noble. West in Saurby is a place called Hol, there lived three kinsmen-in-law—Thorkell the Whelp and Knut, who were brothers, they were very well-born men, and their brother-in-law, who shared their household with them, who was named Thord. He was, after his mother, called Ingun's-son. The father of Thord was Glum Gierison. Thord was a handsome and valiant man, well knit, and a great man of law-suits. Thord had for wife the sister of Thorkell and Knut, who was called Aud, neither a goodly nor a bucksome woman. Thord loved her little, as he had chiefly married her for her money, for there a great wealth was stored together, and the household flourished from the time that Thord came to have hand in it with them.

CHAPTER XXXIII
Of Gest Oddleifson and Gudrun's Dreams

Gest Oddleifson lived west at Bardastrand, at Hagi. He was a great chieftain and a sage; was foreseeing in many things and in good friendship with all the great men, and many came to him for counsel. He rode every summer to the Thing, and always would put up at Hol. One time it so happened once more that Gest rode to the Thing and was a guest at Hol. He got ready to leave early in the morning, for the journey was a long one and he meant to get to Thickshaw in the evening to Armod, his brother-in-law's, who had for wife Thorunn, a sister of Gest's. Their sons were Ornolf and Haldor. Gest rode all that day from Saurby and came to the Sælingsdale spring, and tarried there for a while. Gudrun came to the spring and greeted her relative, Gest, warmly. Gest gave her a good welcome, and they began to talk together, both being wise and of ready speech. And as the day was wearing on, Gudrun said, "I wish, cousin, you would ride home with us with all your followers, for it is the wish of my father, though he gave me the honour of bearing the message, and told me to say that he would wish you to come and stay with us every time you rode to or from the west." Gest received the message well, and thought it a very manly offer, but said he must ride on now as he had purposed. Gudrun said, "I have dreamt many dreams this winter; but four of the dreams do trouble my mind much, and no man has been able to explain them as I like, and yet I ask not for any favourable interpretation of them." Gest said, "Tell me your dreams, it may be that I can make something of them." Gudrun said, "I thought I stood out of doors by a certain brook, and I had a crooked coif on my head, and I thought it misfitted me, and I wished to alter the coif, and many people told me I should not do so, but I did not listen to them, and I tore the hood from my head, and cast it into the brook, and that was the end of that dream." Then Gudrun said again, "This is the next dream. I thought I stood near some water, and I thought there was a silver ring on my arm. I thought it was my own, and that it fitted me exceeding well. I thought it was a most precious thing, and long I wished to keep it. But when I was least aware of it, the ring slipped off my arm and into the water, and nothing more did I see of it afterwards. I felt this loss much more than it was likely I should ever feel the loss of a mere keepsake. Then I awoke." Gest answered this alone: "No lesser a dream is that one." Gudrun still spoke: "This is the third dream, I thought I had a gold ring on my hand, which I thought belonged to me, and I thought my loss was now made good again. And the thought entered my mind that I would keep this ring longer than the first; but it did not seem to me that this keepsake suited me better than the former at anything like the rate that gold is more precious than silver. Then I thought I fell, and tried to steady myself with my hand, but then the gold ring struck on a certain stone and broke in two, and the two pieces bled. What I had to bear after this felt more like grief than regret for a loss. And it struck me now that there must have been some flaw in the ring, and when I looked at the pieces I thought I saw sundry more flaws in them; yet I had a feeling that if I had taken better care of it, it might still have been whole; and this dream was no longer." Gest said, "The dreams are not waning." Then said Gudrun, "This is my fourth dream. I thought I had a helm of gold upon my head, set with many precious stones. And I thought this precious thing belonged to me, but what I chiefly found fault with was that it was rather too heavy, and I could scarcely bear it, so that I carried my head on one side; yet I did not blame the helm for this, nor had I any mind to part with it. Yet the helm tumbled from my head out into Hvammfirth, and after that I awoke. Now I have told you all my dreams." Gest answered, "I clearly see what these dreams betoken; but you will find my unravelling savouring much of sameness, for I must read them all nearly in the same way. You will have four husbands, and it misdoubts me when you are married to the first it will be no love match. Inasmuch as you thought you had a great coif on your head and thought it ill-fitting, that shows you will love him but little. And whereas you took it off your head and cast it into the water, that shows that you will leave him. For that, men say, is 'cast on to the sea,' when a man loses what is his own, and gets nothing in return for it." And still Gest spake: "Your second dream was that you thought you had a silver ring on your arm, and that shows you will marry a nobleman whom you will love much, but enjoy him for but a short time, and I should not wonder if you lose him by drowning. That is all I have to tell of that dream. And in the third dream you thought you had a gold ring on your hand; that shows you will have a third husband; he will not excel the former at the rate that you deemed this metal more rare and precious than silver; but my mind forebodes me that by that time a change of faith will have come about, and your husband will have taken the faith which we are minded to think is the more exalted. And whereas you thought the ring broke in two through some misheed of yours, and blood came from the two pieces, that shows that this husband of yours will be slain, and then you will think you see for the first time clearly all the flaws of that match." Still Gest went on to say: "This is your fourth dream, that you thought you had a helm on your head, of gold set with precious stones, and that it was a heavy one for you to bear. This shows you will have a fourth husband who will be the greatest nobleman (of the four), and will bear somewhat a helm of awe over you. And whereas you thought it tumbled out into

Hvammfirth, it shows that that same firth will be in his way on the last day of his life. And now I go no further with this dream." Gudrun sat with her cheeks blood red whilst the dreams were unravelled, but said not a word till Gest came to the end of his speech. Then said Gudrun, "You would have fairer prophecies in this matter if my delivery of it into your hands had warranted; have my thanks all the same for unravelling the dreams. But it is a fearful thing to think of, if all this is to come to pass as you say." Gudrun then begged Gest would stay there the day out, and said that he and Osvif would have many wise things to say between them. He answered, "I must ride on now as I have made up my mind. But bring your father my greeting and tell him also these my words, that the day will come when there will be a shorter distance between Osvif's and my dwellings, and then we may talk at ease, if then we are allowed to converse together." Then Gudrun went home and Gest rode away. Gest met a servant of Olaf's by the home-field fence, who invited Gest to Herdholt, at the bidding of Olaf. Gest said he would go and see Olaf during the day, but would stay (the night) at Thickshaw. The servant returned home and told Olaf so. Olaf had his horse brought and rode with several men out to meet Gest. He and Gest met up at Lea-river. Olaf greeted him well and asked him in with all his followers. Gest thanked him for the invitation, and said he would ride up to the homestead and have a look and see how he was housed, but he must stay with Armod. Gest tarried but a little while, yet he saw over the homestead and admired it and said, "No money has been spared for this place." Olaf rode away with Gest to the Salmon-river. The foster-brothers had been swimming there during the day, and at this sport the sons of Olaf mostly took the lead. There

Anonymous

were many other young men from the other houses swimming too. Kjartan and Bolli leapt out of the water as the company rode down and were nearly dressed when Olaf and Gest came up to them. Gest looked at these young men for a while, and told Olaf where Kjartan was sitting as well as Bolli, and then Gest pointed his spear shaft to each one of Olaf's sons and named by name all of them that were there. But there were many other handsome young men there who had just left off swimming and sat on the river-bank with Kjartan and Bolli. Gest said he did not discover the family features of Olaf in any of these young men. Then said Olaf: "Never is there too much said about your wits, Gest, knowing, as you do, men you have never seen before. Now I wish you to tell me which of those young men will be the mightiest man." Gest replied, "That will fall out much in keeping with your own love, for Kjartan will be the most highly accounted of so long as he lives." Then Gest smote his horse and rode away. A little while after Thord the Low rode up to his side, and said, "What has now come to pass, father, that you are shedding tears?" Gest answered, "It is needless to tell it, yet I am loath to keep silence on matters that will happen in your own days. To me it will not come unawares if Bolli one day should *have* at his feet the head of Kjartan slain, and should by the deed bring about his own death, and this is an ill thing to know of such sterling men." Then they rode on to the Thing, and it was an uneventful meeting.

CHAPTER XXXIV
Gudruᶇ's First Marriage, A.D. 989

Thorvald was the name of a man, son of Haldor Garpdale's Priest. He lived at Garpsdale in Gilsfirth, a wealthy man, but not much of a hero. At the Thing he wooed Gudrun, Osvif's daughter, when she was fifteen years old. The matter was not taken up in a very adverse manner, yet Osvif said that against the match it would tell, that he and Gudrun were not of equal standing. Thorvald spoke gently, and said he was wooing a wife, not money. After that Gudrun was betrothed to Thorvald, and Osvif settled alone the marriage contract, whereby it was provided that Gudrun should alone manage their money affairs straightway when they came into one bed, and be entitled to one-half thereof as her own, whether their married life were long or short. He should also buy her jewels, so that no woman of equal wealth should have better to show. Yet he should retain his farm-stock unimpaired by such purchases. And now men ride home from the Thing. Gudrun was not asked about it, and took it much to heart; yet things went on quietly. The wedding was at Garpsdale, in Twinmonth (latter part of August to the latter part of September). Gudrun loved Thorvald but little, and was extravagant in buying finery. There was no jewel so costly in all the West-firths that Gudrun did not deem it fitting that it should be hers, and rewarded Thorvald with anger if he did not buy it for her, however dear it might be. Thord, Ingun's son, made himself very friendly with Thorvald and Gudrun, and stayed with them for long times together, and there was much talk of the love of Thord and Gudrun for each other. Once upon a time Gudrun bade Thorvald buy a gift for her, and Thorvald said she showed no moderation in her demands, and gave her a box on the ear. Then said Gudrun, "Now you have given me that which we women set great store by having to perfection—a fine colour in the cheeks—and thereby have also taught me how to leave off importuning you." That same evening Thord came there. Gudrun told him about the shameful mishandling, and asked him how she should repay it. Thord smiled, and said: "I know a very good counsel for this: make him a shirt with such a large neck-hole that you may have a good excuse for separating from him, because he has a low neck like a woman." Gudrun said nothing against this, and they dropped their talk. That same spring Gudrun separated herself from Thorvald, and she went home to Laugar. After that the money was divided between Gudrun and Thorvald, and she had half of all the wealth, which now was even greater than before (her marriage). They had lived two winters together. That same spring Ingun sold her land in Crookfirth, the estate which was afterwards called Ingunstead, and went west to Skalmness. Glum Gierison had formerly had her for wife, as has been before written. At that time Hallstein the Priest lived at Hallsteinness, on the west side of Codfirth. He was a mighty man, but middling well off as regards friends.

CHAPTER XXXV
Gudrun's Second Marriage, A.D. 991

Kotkell was the name of a man who had only come to Iceland a short time before, Grima was the name of his wife. Their sons were Hallbjorn Whetstone-eye, and Stigandi. These people were natives of Sodor. They were all wizards and the greatest of enchanters. Hallstein Godi took them in and settled them down at Urdir in Skalm-firth, and their dwelling there was none of the best liked. That summer Gest went to the Thing and went in a ship to Saurby as he was wont. He stayed as guest at Hol in Saurby. The brothers-in-law found him in horses as was their former wont. Thord Ingunson was amongst the followers of Gest on this journey and came to Laugar in Salingsdale. Gudrun Osvif's daughter rode to the Thing, and Thord Ingunson rode with her. It happened one day as they were riding over Blueshaw-heath, the weather being fine, that Gudrun said, "Is it true, Thord, that your wife Aud always goes about in breeches with gores in the seat, winding swathings round her legs almost to her feet?" Thord said, "He had not noticed that." "Well, then, there must be but little in the tale," said Gudrun, "if you have not found it out, but for what then is she called Breeches Aud?" Thord said, "I think she has been called so for but a short time." Gudrun answered, "What is of more moment to her is that she bear the name for a long time hereafter." After that people arrived at the Thing and no tidings befell there. Thord spent much time in Gest's booth and always talked to Gudrun. One day Thord Ingunson asked Gudrun what the penalty was for a woman who went about always in breeches like men. Gudrun replied, "She deserves the same penalty as a man who is dressed in a shirt with so low a neck that his naked breast be seen— separation in either case." Then Thord said, "Would you advise me to proclaim my separation from Aud here at the Thing or in the country by the counsel of many men? For I have to deal with high-tempered men who will count themselves as ill-treated in this affair." Gudrun answered after a while, "For evening waits the idler's suit." Then Thord sprang up and went to the law rock and named to him witnesses, declared his separation from Aud, and gave as his reason that she made for herself gored breeches like a man. Aud's brothers disliked this very much, but things kept quiet. Then Thord rode away from the Thing with the sons of Osvif. When Aud heard these tidings, she said, "Good! Well, that I know that I am left thus single." Then Thord rode, to divide the money, west into Saurby and twelve men with him, and it all went off easily, for Thord made no difficulties as to how the money was divided. Thord drove from the west unto Laugar a great deal of live stock. After that he wooed Gudrun and that matter was easily settled; Osvif and Gudrun said nothing against it. The wedding was to take place in the tenth week of the summer, and that was a right noble feast. Thord and Gudrun lived happily together. What alone withheld Thorkell Whelp and Knut from setting afoot a lawsuit against Thord Ingunson was, that they got no backing up to that end. The next summer the men of Hol had an out-dairy business in Hvammdale, and Aud stayed at the dairy. The men of Laugar had their out-dairy in Lambdale, which cuts westward into the mountains off Salingsdale. Aud asked the man who looked after the sheep how often he met the shepherd from Laugar. He said nearly always as was likely since there was only a neck of land between the two dairies. Then said Aud, "You shall meet the shepherd from Laugar to-day, and you can tell me who there are staying at the winter-dwelling[3] or who at the dairy, and speak in a friendly way of Thord as it behoves you to do." The boy promised to do as she told him. And in the evening when the shepherd came home Aud asked what tidings he brought. The shepherd answered, "I have heard tidings which you will think good, that now there is a broad bedroom-floor between the beds of Thord and Gudrun, for she is at the dairy and he is swinging at the rear of the hall, he and Osvif being two together alone at the winter-dwelling." "You have espied well," said she, "and see to have saddled two horses at the time when people are going to bed." The shepherd did as she bade him. A little before sunset Aud mounted, and was now indeed in breeches. The shepherd rode the other horse and could hardly keep up with her, so hard did she push on riding. She rode south over Salingsdale-heath and never stopped before she got to the home-field fence at Laugar. Then she dismounted, and bade the shepherd look after the horses whilst she went to the house. Aud went to the door and found it open, and she went into the fire-hall to the locked-bed in the wall. Thord lay asleep, the door had fallen to, but the bolt was not on, so she walked into the bedroom. Thord lay asleep on his back. Then Aud woke Thord, and he turned on his side when he saw a man had come in. Then she drew a sword and thrust it at Thord and gave him great wounds, the sword striking his right arm and wounding him on both nipples. So hard did she follow up the stroke that the sword stuck in the bolster. Then Aud went away and to her horse and leapt on to its back, and thereupon rode home. Thord tried to spring up when he got the blow, but could not, because of his loss of blood. Then Osvif awoke and asked what had happened, and Thord told that he had been wounded somewhat. Osvif asked if he knew who had done the deed on him, and got up and bound up his wounds. Thord said he was minded to think that Aud had done it. Osvif offered to ride after her, and said she must have gone on this errand with few men, and her penalty was ready-made for her. Thord said that should not be done at all, for she had only done what she ought to have done. Aud got home at sunrise, and her brothers asked her where she had been to. Aud said she had been to Laugar, and told them what tidings had befallen in her journey. They were pleased at this, and said that too little was likely to have been done by her. Thord lay wounded a long time. His chest wound healed well, but his arm grew no better for work than before (*i.e.* when it first was wounded). All was now quiet that

Anonymous

winter. But in the following spring Ingun, Thord's mother, came west from Skalmness. Thord greeted her warmly: she said she wished to place herself under his protection, and said that Kotkell and his wife and sons were giving her much trouble by stealing her goods, and through witchcraft, but had a strong support in Hallstein the Priest. Thord took this matter up swiftly, and said he should have the right of these thieves no matter how it might displease Hallstein. He got speedily ready for the journey with ten men, and Ingun went west with him. He got a ferry-boat out of Tjaldness. Then they went to Skalmness. Thord had put on board ship all the chattels his mother owned there, and the cattle were to be driven round the heads of the firths. There were twelve of them altogether in the boat, with Ingun and another woman. Thord and ten men went to Kotkell's place. The sons of Kotkell were not at home. He then summoned Kotkell and Grima and their sons for theft and witchcraft, and claimed outlawry as award. He laid the case to the Althing, and then returned to his ship. Hallbjorn and Stigandi came home when Thord had got out but a little way from land, and Kotkell told his sons what had happened there. The brothers were furious at that, and said that hitherto people had taken care not to show them in so barefaced a manner such open enmity. Then Kotkell had a great spell-working scaffold made, and they all went up on to it, and they sang hard twisted songs that were enchantments. And presently a great tempest arose. Thord, Ingun's son, and his companions, continued out at sea as he was, soon knew that the storm was raised against him. Now the ship is driven west beyond Skalmness, and Thord showed great courage with seamanship. The men who were on land saw how he threw overboard all that made up the boat's lading, saving the men; and the people who were on land expected Thord would come to shore, for they had passed the place that was the rockiest; but next there arose a breaker on a rock a little way from the shore that no man had ever known to break sea before, and smote the ship so that forthwith up turned keel uppermost. There Thord and all his followers were drowned, and the ship was broken to pieces, and the keel was washed up at a place now called Keelisle. Thord's shield was washed up on an island that has since been called Shieldisle. Thord's body and the bodies of his followers were all washed ashore, and a great howe was raised over their corpses at the place now called Howesness.

[3] i.e., at home at Laugar.

CHAPTER XXXVI
About Kotkell and Grima

These tidings spread far and wide, and were very ill-spoken of; they were accounted of as men of doomed lives, who wrought such witchcraft as that which Kotkell and his had now shown. Gudrun took the death of Thord sorely to heart, for she was now a woman not hale, and coming close to her time. After that Gudrun gave birth to a boy, who was sprinkled with water and called Thord. At that time Snorri the Priest lived at Holyfell; he was a kinsman and a friend of Osvif's, and Gudrun and her people trusted him very much. Snorri went thither (to Laugar), being asked to a feast there. Then Gudrun told her trouble to Snorri, and he said he would back up their case when it seemed good to him, but offered to Gudrun to foster her child to comfort her. This Gudrun agreed to, and said she would rely on his foresight. This Thord was surnamed the Cat, and was father of the poet Stúf. After that Gest Oddleifson went to see Hallstein, and gave him choice of two things, either that he should send away these wizards or he said that he would kill them, "and yet it comes too late." Hallstein made his choice at once, and bade them rather be off, and put up nowhere west of Daleheath, adding that it was more justly they ought to be slain. After that Kotkell and his went away with no other goods than four stud-horses. The stallion was black; he was both great and fair and very strong, and tried in horse-fighting. Nothing is told of their journey till they came to Combeness, to Thorliek, Hoskuld's son. He asked to buy the horses from them, for he said that they were exceeding fine beasts. Kotkell replied, "I'll give you the choice. Take you the horses and give me some place to dwell in here in your neighbourhood." Thorliek said, "Will the horses not be rather dear, then, for I have heard tell you are thought rather guilty in this countryside?" Kotkell answers, "In this you are hinting at the men of Laugar." Thorliek said that was true. Then Kotkell said, "Matters point quite another way, as concerning our guilt towards Gudrun and her brothers, than you have been told; people have overwhelmed us with slander for no cause at all. Take the horses, nor let these matters stand in the way. Such tales alone are told of you, moreover, as would show that we shall not be easily tripped up by the folk of this countryside, if we have your help to fall back upon." Thorliek now changed his mind in this matter, for the horses seemed fair to him, and Kotkell pleaded his case cunningly; so Thorliek took the horses, and gave them a dwelling at Ludolfstead in Salmon-river-Dale, and stocked them with farming beasts. This the men of Laugar heard, and the sons of Osvif wished to fall forthwith on Kotkell and his sons; but Osvif said, "Let us take now the counsel of Priest Snorri, and leave this business to others, for short time will pass before the neighbours of Kotkell will have brand new cases against him and his, and Thorliek, as is most fitting, will abide the greatest hurt from them. In a short while many will become his enemies from whom heretofore he has only had good will. But I shall not stop you from doing whatever hurt you please to Kotkell and his, if other men do not come forward to drive them out of the countryside or to take their lives, by the time that three winters have worn away." Gudrun and her brothers said it should be as he said. Kotkell and his did not do much in working for their livelihood, but that winter they were in no need to buy hay or food; but an unbefriended neighbourhood was theirs, though men did not see their way to disturbing their dwelling because of Thorliek.

CHAPTER XXXVII
About Hrut and Eldgrim, A.D. 995

One summer at the Thing, as Thorliek was sitting in his booth, a very big man walked into the booth. He greeted Thorliek, who took well the greeting of this man and asked his name and whence he was. He said he was called Eldgrim, and lived in Burgfirth at a place called Eldgrimstead—but that abode lies in the valley which cuts westward into the mountains between Mull and Pigtongue, and is now called Grimsdale. Thorliek said, "I have heard you spoken of as being no small man." Eldgrim said, "My errand here is that I want to buy from you the stud-horses, those valuable ones that Kotkell gave you last summer." Thorliek answered, "The horses are not for sale." Eldgrim said, "I will offer you equally many stud-horses for them and some other things thrown in, and many would say that I offer you twice as much as the horses are worth." Thorliek said, "I am no haggler, but these horses you will never have, not even though you offer three times their worth." Eldgrim said, "I take it to be no lie that you are proud and self-willed, and I should, indeed, like to see you getting a somewhat less handsome price for them than I have now offered you, and that you should have to let the horses go none the less." Thorliek got angered at these words, and said, "You need, Eldgrim, to come to closer quarters if you mean to frighten out me the horses." Eldgrim said, "You think it unlikely that you will be beaten by me, but this summer I shall go and see the horses, and we will see which of us will own them after that." Thorliek said, "Do as you like, but bring up no odds against me." Then they dropped their talk. The man who heard this said that for this sort of dealing together here were two just fitting matches for each other. After that people went home from the Thing, and nothing happened to tell tidings of. It happened one morning early that a man looked out at Hrutstead at goodman Hrut's, Herjolf's son's, and when he came in Hrut asked what news he brought. He said he had no other tidings to tell save that he saw a man riding from beyond Vadlar towards where Thorliek's horses were, and that the man got off his horse and took the horses. Hrut asked where the horses were then, and the house-carle replied, "Oh, they have stuck well to their pasture, for they stood as usual in your meadows down below the fence-wall." Hrut replied, "Verily, Thorliek, my kinsman, is not particular as to where he grazes his beasts; and I still think it more likely that it is not by his order that the horses are driven away." Then Hrut sprang up in his shirt and linen breeches, and cast over him a grey cloak and took in his hand his gold inlaid halberd that King Harald had given him. He went out quickly and saw where a man was riding after horses down below the wall. Hrut went to meet him, and saw that it was Eldgrim driving the horses. Hrut greeted him, and Eldgrim returned his greeting, but rather slowly. Hrut asked him why he was driving the horses. Eldgrim replied, "I will not hide it from you, though I know what kinship there is between you and Thorliek; but I tell you I have come after these horses, meaning that he shall never have them again. I have also kept what I promised him at the Thing, that I have not gone after the horses with any great company." Hrut said, "That is no deed of fame to you to take away the horses while Thorliek lies in his bed and sleeps; you would keep best what you agreed upon if you go and meet himself before you drive the horses out of the countryside." Eldgrim said, "Go and warn Thorliek if you wish, for you may see I have prepared myself in such a manner as that I should like it well if we were to meet together, I and Thorliek," and therewith he brandished the barbed spear he had in his hand. He had also a helmet on his head, and a sword girded on his side, and a shield on his flank, and had on a chain coat. Hrut said, "I think I must seek for something else than to go to Combeness for I am heavy of foot; but I mean not to allow Thorliek to be robbed if I have means thereto, no matter how little love there may go with our kinship." Eldgrim said, "And do you mean to take the horses away from me?" Hrut said, "I will give you other stud-horses if you will let these alone, though they may not be quite so good as these are." Eldgrim said, "You speak most kindly, Hrut, but since I have got hold of Thorliek's horses you will not pluck them out of my hands either by bribes or threats." Hrut replied, "Then I think you are making for both of us the choice that answers the worst." Eldgrim now wanted to part, and gave the whip to his horse, and when Hrut saw that, he raised up his halberd and struck Eldgrim through the back between the shoulders so that the coat of mail was torn open and the halberd flew out through the chest, and Eldgrim fell dead off his horse, as was only natural. After that Hrut covered up his body at the place called Eldgrim's-holt south of Combeness. Then Hrut rode over to Combeness and told Thorliek the tidings. Thorliek burst into a rage, and thought a great shame had been done him by this deed, while Hrut thought he had shown him great friendship thereby. Thorliek said that not only had he done this for an evil purpose, but that, moreover, no good would come in return for it. Hrut said that Thorliek must do what pleased him, and so they parted in no loving kindness. Hrut was eighty years old when he killed Eldgrim, and he was considered by that deed to have added much to his fame. Thorliek thought that Hrut was none the worthier of any good from him for being more renowned for this deed, for he held it was perfectly clear he would have himself have got the better of Eldgrim if they had had a trial of arms between them, seeing how little was needed to trip Eldgrim up. Thorliek now went to see his tenants Kotkell and Grima, and bade them do something to the shame of Hrut. They took this up gladly, and said they were quite ready to do so. Thorliek now went home. A little later they, Kotkell and Grima and their sons, started on a journey from home, and that was by night. They went to Hrut's dwelling, and made great incantations there, and when the spell-working began, those within were at a loss to make out what could be the reason of it; but sweet indeed was that singing they heard. Hrut alone knew what these goings-on meant, and bade no man look out that night, "and let every one who may keep awake, and no harm will come to us if that counsel is followed." But all the people fell asleep. Hrut watched longest, and at last he too slept. Kari was the name of a son of Hrut, and he was then twelve winters old. He was the most promising of all Hrut's sons, and Hrut loved him much. Kari hardly slept at all, for to him the play was made; he did not sleep very soundly, and at last he got up and looked out, and walked in the direction of the enchantment, and fell down dead at once. Hrut awoke in the morning, as also did his household, and missed his son, who was found dead a short way from the door. This Hrut felt as the greatest bereavement, and had a cairn raised over Kari. Then he rode to Olaf Hoskuldson and told him the tidings of what had happened there. Olaf was madly wroth at this, and said it showed great lack of forethought that they had allowed such scoundrels as Kotkell and his family to live so near to him, and said that Thorliek had shaped for himself an evil lot by dealing as he had done with Hrut, but added that more must have been done than Thorliek had ever could have wished. Olaf said too that forthwith Kotkell and his wife and sons must be slain, "late though it is now." Olaf and Hrut set out with fifteen men. But when Kotkell and his family saw the company of men riding up to their dwelling, they took to their heels up to the mountain. There Hallbjorn Whetstone-eye was caught and a bag was drawn over his head, and while some men were left to guard him others went in pursuit of Kotkell, Grima, and Stigandi up on the mountain. Kotkell and Grima were laid hands on on the neck of land between Hawkdale and Salmon-river-Dale, and were stoned to death and a heap of stones thrown up over them, and the remains are still to be seen, being called Scratch-beacon. Stigandi took to his heels south over the neck towards Hawkdale, and there got out of their sight. Hrut

Anonymous

and his sons went down to the sea with Hallbjorn, and put out a boat and rowed out from land with him, and they took the bag off his head and tied a stone round his neck. Hallbjorn set gloating glances on the land, and the manner of his look was nowise of the goodliest. Then Hallbjorn said, "It was no day of bliss when we, kinsfolk, came to this Combeness and met with Thorliek. And this spell I utter," says he, "that Thorliek shall from henceforth have but few happy days, and that all who fill his place have a troublous life there." And this spell, men deem, has taken great effect. After that they drowned him, and rowed back to land.

A little while afterwards Hrut went to find Olaf his kinsman, and told him that he would not leave matters with Thorliek as they stood, and bade him furnish him with men to go and make a house-raid on Thorliek. Olaf replied, "It is not right that you two kinsmen should be laying hands on each other; on Thorliek's behalf this has turned out a matter of most evil luck. I would sooner try and bring about peace between you, and you have often waited well and long for your good turn." Hrut said, "It is no good casting about for this; the sores between us two will never heal up; and I should like that from henceforth we should not both live in Salmon-river-Dale." Olaf replied, "It will not be easy for you to go further against Thorliek than I am willing to allow; but if you do it, it is not unlikely that dale and hill will meet."[4] Hrut thought he now saw things stuck hard and fast before him; so he went home mightily ill pleased; but all was quiet or was called so. And for that year men kept quiet at home.

[4] i.e., old age = Hrut, and youthful power=Olaf, the greatest "goði" in the countryside.

CHAPTER XXXVIII

The Death of Stigandi. Thorliek leaves Iceland

Now, to tell of Stigandi, he became an outlaw and an evil to deal with. Thord was the name of a man who lived at Hundidale; he was a rich man, but had no manly greatness. A startling thing happened that summer in Hundidale, in that the milking stock did not yield much milk, but a woman looked after the beast there. At last people found out that she grew wealthy in precious things, and that she would disappear long and often, and no one knew where she was. Thord brought pressure to bear on her for confession, and when she got frightened she said a man was wont to come and meet her, "a big one," she said, "and in my eyes very handsome." Thord then asked how soon the man would come again to meet her, and she said she thought it would be soon. After that Thord went to see Olaf, and told him that Stigandi must be about, not far away from there, and bade him bestir himself with his men and catch him. Olaf got ready at once and came to Hundidale, and the bonds-woman was fetched for Olaf to have talk of her. Olaf asked her where the lair of Stigandi was. She said she did not know. Olaf offered to pay her money if she would bring Stigandi within reach of him and his men; and on this they came to a bargain together. The next day she went out to herd her cattle, and Stigandi comes that day to meet her. She greeted him well, and offers to look through (the hair of) his head. He laid his head down on her knee, and soon went to sleep. Then she slunk away from under his head, and went to meet Olaf and his men, and told them what had happened. Then they went towards Stigandi, and took counsel between them as to how it should not fare with

Anonymous

him as his brother, that he should cast his glance on many things from which evil would befall them. They take now a bag, and draw it over his head. Stigandi woke at that, and made no struggle, for now there were many men to one. The sack had a slit in it, and Stigandi could see out through it the slope on the other side; there the lay of the land was fair, and it was covered with thick grass. But suddenly something like a whirlwind came on, and turned the sward topsy-turvy, so that the grass never grew there again. It is now called Brenna. Then they stoned Stigandi to death, and there he was buried under a heap of stones. Olaf kept his word to the bonds-woman, and gave her her freedom, and she went home to Herdholt. Hallbjorn Whetstone-eye was washed up by the surf a short time after he was drowned. It was called Knorstone where he was put in the earth, and his ghost walked about there a great deal. There was a man named Thorkell Skull who lived at Thickshaw on his father's inheritance. He was a man of very dauntless heart and mighty of muscle. One evening a cow was missing at Thickshaw, and Thorkell and his house-carle went to look for it. It was after sunset, but was bright moonlight. Thorkell said they must separate in their search, and when Thorkell was alone he thought he saw the cow on a hill-rise in front of him, but when he came up to it he saw it was Whetstone-eye and no cow. They fell upon each in mighty strength. Hallbjorn kept on the defensive, and when Thorkell least expected it he crept down into the earth out of his hands. After that Thorkell went home. The house-carle had come home already, and had found the cow. No more harm befell ever again from Hallbjorn.

Thorbjorn Skrjup was dead by then, and so was Melkorka, and they both lie in a cairn in Salmon-river-

Dale. Lambi, their son, kept house there after them. He was very warrior-like, and had a great deal of money. Lambi was more thought of by people than his father had been, chiefly because of his mother's relations; and between him and Olaf there was fond brotherhood. Now the winter next after the killing of Kotkell passed away. In the spring the brothers Olaf and Thorliek met, and Olaf asked if Thorliek was minded to keep on his house. Thorliek said he was. Olaf said, "Yet I would beg you, kinsman, to change your way of life, and go abroad; you will be thought an honourable man whereever you come; but as to Hrut, our kinsman, I know he feels how your dealings with him come home to him. And it is little to my mind that the risk of your sitting so near to each other should be run any longer. For Hrut has a strong run of luck to fall back upon, and his sons are but reckless bravos. On account of my kinship I feel I should be placed in a difficulty if you, my kinsman, should come to quarrel in full enmity." Thorliek replied, "I am not afraid of not being able to hold myself straight in the face of Hrut and his sons, and that is no reason why I should depart the country. But if you, brother, set much store by it, and feel yourself in a difficult position in this matter, then, for your words I will do this; for then I was best contented with my lot in life when I lived abroad. And I know you will not treat my son Bolli any the worse for my being nowhere near; for of all men I love him the best." Olaf said, "You have, indeed, taken an honourable course in this matter, if you do after my prayer; but as touching Bolli, I am minded to do to him henceforth as I have done hitherto, and to be to him and hold him no worse than my own sons." After that the brothers parted in great affection. Thorliek now sold his land, and spent his money on his journey abroad. He bought a ship that stood up in Daymealness; and when he was full ready he stepped on board ship with his wife and household. That ship made a good voyage, and they made Norway in the autumn. Thence he went south to Denmark, as he did not feel at home in Norway, his kinsmen and friends there being either dead or driven out of the land. After that Thorliek went to Gautland. It is said by most men that Thorliek had little to do with old age; yet he was held a man of great worth throughout life. And there we close the story of Thorliek.

CHAPTER XXXIX
Of Kjartan's Friendship for Bolli

At that time, as concerning the strife between Hrut and Thorliek, it was ever the greatest gossip throughout the Broadfirth-Dales how that Hrut had had to abide a heavy lot at the hands of Kotkell and his sons. Then Osvif spoke to Gudrun and her brothers, and bade them call to mind whether they thought now it would have been the best counsel aforetime then and there to have plunged into the danger of dealing with such "hell-men" (terrible people) as Kotkell and his were. Then said Gudrun, "He is not counsel-bereft, father, who has the help of thy counsel." Olaf now abode at his manor in much honour, and all his sons are at home there, as was Bolli, their kinsman and foster-brother. Kjartan was foremost of all the sons of Olaf. Kjartan and Bolli loved each other the most, and Kjartan went nowhere that Bolli did not follow. Often Kjartan would go to the Sælingdale-spring, and mostly it happened that Gudrun was at the spring too. Kjartan liked talking to Gudrun, for she was both a woman of wits and clever of speech. It was the talk of all folk that of all men who were growing up at the time Kjartan was the most even match for

Gudrun. Between Olaf and Osvif there was also great friendship, and often they would invite one another, and not the less frequently so when fondness was growing up between the young folk. One day when Olaf was talking to Kjartan, he said: "I do not know why it is that I always take it to heart when you go to Laugar and talk to Gudrun. It is not because I do not consider Gudrun the foremost of all other women, for she is the one among womenkind whom I look upon as a thoroughly suitable match for you. But it is my foreboding, though I will not prophesy it, that we, my kinsmen and I, and the men of Laugar will not bring altogether good luck to bear on our dealings together." Kjartan said he would do nothing against his father's will where he could help himself, but he hoped things would turn out better than he made a guess to. Kjartan holds to his usual ways as to his visits (to Laugar), and Bolli always went with him, and so the next seasons passed.

CHAPTER XL.
Kjartan and Bolli Voyage to Norway, A.D. 996

Asgeir was the name of a man, he was called Eider-drake. He lived at Asgeir's-river, in Willowdale; he was the son of Audun Skokul; he was the first of his kinsmen who came to Iceland; he took to himself Willowdale. Another son of Audun was named Thorgrim Hoaryhead; he was the father of Asmund, the father of Gretter. Asgeir Eider-drake had five children; one of his sons was called Audun, father of Asgeir, father of Audun, father of Egil, who had for wife Ulfeid, the daughter of Eyjolf the Lame; their son was Eyjolf, who was slain at the All Thing. Another of Asgeir's sons was named Thorvald; his daughter was Wala, whom Bishop Isleef had for wife; their son was Gizor, the bishop. A third son of Asgeir was named Kalf. All Asgeir's sons were hopeful men. Kalf Asgeirson was at that time out travelling, and was accounted of as the worthiest of men. One of Asgeir's daughters was named Thured; she married Thorkell Kuggi, the son of Thord Yeller; their son was Thorstein. Another of Asgeir's daughters was named Hrefna; she was the fairest woman in those northern countrysides and very winsome. Asgeir was a very mighty man. It is told how one time Kjartan Olafson went on a journey south to Burgfirth. Nothing is told of his journey before he got to Burg. There at that time lived Thorstein, Egil's son, his mother's brother. Bolli was with him, for the foster-brothers loved each other so dearly that neither thought he could enjoy himself if they were not together. Thorstein received Kjartan with loving kindness, and said he should be glad for his staying there a long rather than a short time. So Kjartan stayed awhile at Burg. That summer there was a ship standing up in Steam-river-Mouth, and this ship belonged to Kalf Asgeirson, who had been staying through the winter with Thorstein, Egil's son. Kjartan told Thorstein in secret that his chief errand to the south then was, that he wished to buy the half of Kalf's ship, "for I have set my mind on going abroad," and he asked Thorstein what sort of a man he thought Kalf was. Thorstein said he thought he was a good man and true. "I can easily understand," said Thorstein, "that you wish to see other men's ways of life, and your journey will be remarkable in one way or another, and your kinsfolk will be very anxious as to how the journey may speed for you." Kjartan said it would speed well enough. After that Kjartan bought a half share in Kalf's ship, and they made up half-shares partnership between them; Kjartan was to come on board when ten weeks of summer had passed.

Kjartan was seen off with gifts on leaving Burg, and he and Bolli then rode home. When Olaf heard of this arrangement he said he thought Kjartan had made up his mind rather suddenly, but added that he would not foreclose the matter. A little later Kjartan rode to Laugar to tell Gudrun of his proposed journey abroad. Gudrun said, "You have decided this very suddenly, Kjartan," and she let fall sundry words about this, from which Kjartan got to understand that Gudrun was displeased with it. Kjartan said, "Do not let this displease you. I will do something else that shall please you." Gudrun said, "Be then a man of your word, for I shall speedily let you know what I want." Kjartan bade her do so. Gudrun said, "Then, I wish to go out with you this summer; if that comes off, you would have made amends to me for this hasty resolve, for I do not care for Iceland." Kjartan said, "That cannot be, your brothers are unsettled yet, and your father is old, and they would be bereft of all care if you went out of the land; so you wait for me three winters." Gudrun said she would promise nothing as to that matter, and each was at variance with the other, and therewith they parted. Kjartan rode home. Olaf rode to the Thing that summer, and Kjartan rode with his father from the west out of Herdholt, and they parted at North-river-Dale. From thence Kjartan rode to his ship, and his kinsman Bolli went along with him. There were ten Icelanders altogether who went with Kjartan on this journey, and none would part with him for the sake of the love they bore him. So with this following Kjartan went to the ship, and Kalf Asgeirson greeted them warmly. Kjartan and Bolli took a great many goods with them abroad. They now got ready to start, and when the wind blew they sailed out along Burgfirth with a light and good breeze, and then out to sea. They had a good journey, and got to Norway to the northwards and came into Thrandhome, and fell in with men there and asked for tidings. They were told that change of lords over the land had befallen, in that Earl Hakon had fallen and King Olaf Tryggvason had come in, and all Norway had fallen under his power. King Olaf was ordering a change of faith in Norway, and the people took to it most unequally. Kjartan and his companions took their craft up to Nidaross. At that time many Icelanders had come to Norway who were men of high degree. There lay beside the landing-stage three ships, all owned by Icelanders. One of the ships belonged to Brand the Bounteous, son of Vermund Thorgrimson. And another ship belonged to Hallfred the Trouble-Bard. The third ship belonged to two brothers, one named Bjarni, and the other Thorhall; they were sons of Broad-river-Skeggi, out of Fleetlithe in the east. All these men had wanted to go west to Iceland that summer, but the king had forbidden all these ships to sail because the Icelanders would not take the new faith that he was preaching. All the Icelanders greeted Kjartan warmly, but especially Brand, as they had known each other already before. The Icelanders now took counsel together and came to an agreement among themselves that they would refuse this faith that the king preached, and all the men previously named bound themselves together to do this. Kjartan and his companions brought their ship up to the landing-stage and unloaded it and disposed of their goods. King Olaf was then in the town. He heard of the coming of the ship and that men of great account were on board. It happened one fair-weather day in the autumn that the men went out of the town to swim in the river Nid. Kjartan and his friends saw this. Then Kjartan said to his companions that they should also go and disport themselves that day. They did so. There was one man who was by much the best at this sport. Kjartan asked Bolli if he felt willing to try swimming against the townsman. Bolli answered, "I don't think I am a match for him." "I cannot think where your courage can now have got to," said Kjartan, "so I shall go and try." Bolli replied, "That you may do if you like." Kjartan then plunges into the river and up to this man who was the best swimmer and drags him forthwith under and keeps him down for awhile, and then lets him go up again. And when they had been up for a long while, this man suddenly clutches Kjartan and drags him under; and they keep down for such a time as Kjartan thought quite long enough, when up they come a second time. Not a word had either to say to the other. The third time they went down together, and now they keep under for much the longest time, and Kjartan now misdoubted him how this play would end, and thought he had never before found himself in such a tight place; but at last they come up and strike out for the bank. Then said the townsman, "Who is this man?" Kjartan told him his name. The townsman said, "You are very deft at swimming. Are you as good at other deeds of prowess as at this?" Kjartan answered rather coldly, "It was said when I was in Iceland that the others kept pace with this one. But now this one is not worth much." The townsman replied, "It makes some odds with whom you have had to do. But why do you not ask me anything?" Kjartan replied, "I do not want to know your name." The townsman answered, "You are not only a stalwart man, but you bear yourself very proudly as well, but none the less you shall know my name, and with whom you have been having a swimming match. Here is Olaf the king, the son of Tryggvi." Kjartan answered nothing, but turned away

Anonymous

forthwith without his cloak. He had on a kirtle of red scarlet. The king was then well-nigh dressed; he called to Kjartan and bade him not go away so soon. Kjartan turned back, but rather slowly. The king then took a very good cloak off his shoulders and gave it to Kjartan, saying he should not go back cloakless to his companions. Kjartan thanked the king for the gift, and went to his own men and showed them the cloak. His men were nowise pleased as this, for they thought Kjartan had got too much into the king's power; but matters went on quietly. The weather set in very hard that autumn, and there was a great deal of frost, the season being cold. The heathen men said it was not to be wondered at that the weather should be so bad; "it is all because of the newfangled ways of the king and this new faith that the gods are angry." The Icelanders kept all together in the town during the winter, and Kjartan took mostly the lead among them. On the weather taking a turn for the better, many people came to the town at the summons of King Olaf. Many people had become Christians in Thrandhome, yet there were a great many more who withstood the king. One day the king had a meeting out at Eyrar, and preached the new faith to men—a long harangue and telling. The people of Thrandhome had a whole host of men, and in turn offered battle to the king. The king said they must know that he had had greater things to cope with than fighting there with churls out of Thrandhome. Then the good men lost heart and gave the whole case into the king's power, and many people were baptized then and there. After that, the meeting came to an end. That same evening the king sent men to the lodgings of the Icelanders, and bade them get sure knowledge of what they were saying. They did so. They heard much noise within. Then Kjartan began to speak, and said to Bolli, "How far are you willing, kinsman, to take this new faith the king preaches?" "I certainly am not willing thereto," said Bolli, "for their faith seems to me to be most feeble." Kjartan said, "Did ye not think the king was holding out threats against those who should be unwilling to submit to his will?" Bolli answered, "It certainly seemed to me that he spoke out very clearly that they would have to take exceeding hard treatment at his hands." "I will be forced under no one's thumb," said Kjartan, "while I have power to stand up and wield my weapons. I think it most unmanly, too, to be taken like a lamb in a fold or a fox in a trap. I think that is a better thing to choose, if a man must die in any case, to do first some such deed as shall be held aloft for a long time afterwards." Bolli said, "What will you do?" "I will not hide it from you," Kjartan replied; "I will burn the king in his hall." "There is nothing cowardly in that," said Bolli; "but this is not likely to come to pass, as far as I can see. The king, I take it, is one of great good luck and his guardian spirit mighty, and, besides, he has a faithful guard watching both day and night." Kjartan said that what most men failed in was daring, however valiant they might otherwise be. Bolli said it was not so certain who would have to be taunted for want of courage in the end. But here many men joined in, saying this was but an idle talk. Now when the king's spies had overheard this, they went away and told the king all that had been said. The next morning the king wished to hold a meeting, and summoned all the Icelanders to it; and when the meeting was opened the king stood up and thanked men for coming, all those who were his friends and had taken the new faith. Then he called to him for a parley the Icelanders. The king asked them if they would

Anonymous

be baptized, but they gave little reply to that. The king said they were making for themselves the choice that would answer the worst. "But, by the way, who of you thought it the best thing to do to burn me in my hall?" Then Kjartan answered, "You no doubt think that he who did say it would not have the pluck to confess it; but here you can see him." "I can indeed see you," said the king, "man of no small counsels, but it is not fated for you to stand over my head, done to death by you; and you have done quite enough that you should be prevented making a vow to burn more kings in their houses yet, for the reason of being taught better things than you know and because I do not know whether your heart was in your speech, and that you have bravely acknowledged it, I will not take your life. It may also be that you follow the faith the better the more outspoken you are against it; and I can also see this, that on the day you let yourself be baptized of your own free will, several ships' crews will on that day also take the faith. And I think it likely to happen that your relations and friends will give much heed to what you speak to them when you return to Iceland. And it is in my mind that you, Kjartan, will have a better faith when you return from Norway than you had when you came hither. Go now in peace and safety wheresoever you like from the meeting. For the time being you shall not be tormented into Christianity, for God says that He wills that no one shall come to Him unwillingly." Good cheer was made at the king's speech, though mostly from the Christian men; but the heathen left it to Kjartan to answer as he liked. Kjartan said, "We thank you, king, that you grant safe peace unto us, and the way whereby you may most surely draw us to take the faith is, on the one hand, to forgive us great offences, and on the other to speak in this kindly manner on all matters, in spite of your this day having us and all our concerns in your power even as it pleases you. Now, as for myself, I shall receive the faith in Norway on that understanding alone that I shall give some little worship to Thor the next winter when I get back to Iceland." Then the king said and smiled, "It may be seen from the mien of Kjartan that he puts more trust in his own weapons and strength than in Thor and Odin." Then the meeting was broken up. After a while many men egged the king on to force Kjartan and his followers to receive the faith, and thought it unwise to have so many heathen men near about him. The king answered wrathfully, and said he thought there were many Christians who were not nearly so well-behaved as was Kjartan or his company either, "and for such one would have long to wait." The king caused many profitable things to be done that winter; he had a church built and the market-town greatly enlarged. This church was finished at Christmas. Then Kjartan said they should go so near the church that they might see the ceremonies of this faith the Christians followed; and many fell in, saying that would be right good pastime. Kjartan with his following and Bolli went to the church; in that train was also Hallfred and many other Icelanders. The king preached the faith before the people, and spoke both long and tellingly, and the Christians made good cheer at his speech. And when Kjartan and his company went back to their chambers, a great deal of talk arose as to how they had liked the looks of the king at this time, which Christians accounted of as the next greatest festival. "For the king said, so that we might hear, that this night was born the Lord, in whom we are now to believe, if we do as the king bids us." Kjartan says: "So greatly was I taken with the looks of the king when I saw him for the first time, that I knew at once that he was a man of the highest excellence, and that feeling has kept steadfast ever since, when I have seen him at folk-meetings, and that but by much the best, however, I liked the looks of him to-day; and I cannot help thinking that the turn of our concerns hangs altogether on our believing Him to be the true God in whom the king bids us to believe, and the king cannot by any means be more eager in wishing that I take this faith than I am to let myself be baptized. The only thing that puts off my going straightway to see the king now is that the day is far spent, and the king, I take it, is now at table; but that day will be delayed, on which we, companions, will let ourselves all be baptized." Bolli took to this kindly, and bade Kjartan alone look to their affairs. The king had heard of the talk between Kjartan and his people before the tables were cleared away, for he had his spies in every chamber of the heathens. The king was very glad at this, and said, "In Kjartan has come true the saw: 'High tides best for happy signs.'" And the first thing the next morning early, when the king went to church, Kjartan met him in the street with a great company of men. Kjartan greeted the king with great cheerfulness, and said he had a pressing errand with him. The king took his greeting well, and said he had had a thoroughly clear news as to what his errand must be, "and that matter will be easily settled by you." Kjartan begged they should not delay fetching the water, and said that a great deal would be needed. The king answered and smiled. "Yes, Kjartan," says he, "on this matter I do not think your eager-mindedness would part us, not even if you put the price higher still." After that Kjartan and Bolli were baptized and all their crew, and a multitude of other men as well. This was on the second day of Yule before

Holy Service. After that the king invited Kjartan to his Yule feast with Bolli his kinsman. It is the tale of most men that Kjartan on the day he laid aside his white baptismal-robes became a liegeman of the king's, he and Bolli both. Hallfred was not baptized that day, for he made it a point that the king himself should be his godfather, so the king put it off till the next day. Kjartan and Bolli stayed with Olaf the king the rest of the winter. The king held Kjartan before all other men for the sake of his race and manly prowess, and it is by all people said that Kjartan was so winsome that he had not a single enemy within the court. Every one said that there had never before come from Iceland such a man as Kjartan. Bolli was also one of the most stalwart of men, and was held in high esteem by all good men. The winter now passes away, and, as spring came on, men got ready for their journeys, each as he had a mind to.

CHAPTER XLI
Bolli returns to Iceland, A.D. 999

Kalf Asgeirson went to see Kjartan and asks what he was minded to do that summer. Kjartan said, "I have been thinking chiefly that we had better take our ship to England, where there is a good market for Christian men. But first I will go and see the king before I settle this, for he did not seem pleased at my going on this journey when we talked about it in the spring." Then Kalf went away and Kjartan went to speak to the king, greeting him courteously. The king received him most kindly, and asked what he and his companion (Kalf) had been talking about. Kjartan told what they had mostly in mind to do, but said that his errand to the king was to beg leave to go on this journey. "As to that matter, I will give you your choice, Kjartan. Either you will go to

Iceland this summer, and bring men to Christianity by force or by expedients; but if you think this too difficult a journey, I will not let you go away on any account, for you are much better suited to serve noble men than to turn here into a chapman." Kjartan chose rather to stay with the king than to go to Iceland and preach the faith to them there, and said he could not be contending by force against his own kindred. "Moreover, it would be more likely that my father and other chiefs, who are near kinsmen of mine, would go against thy will with all the less stubbornness the better beholden I am under your power." The king said, "This is chosen both wisely and as beseems a great man." The king gave Kjartan a whole set of new clothes, all cut out of scarlet cloth, and they suited him well; for people said that King Olaf and Kjartan were of an even height when they went under measure. King Olaf sent the court priest, named Thangbrand, to Iceland. He brought his ship to Swanfirth, and stayed with Side-Hall all the winter at Wash-river, and set forth the faith to people both with fair words and harsh punishments. Thangbrand slew two men who went most against him. Hall received the faith in the spring, and was baptized on the Saturday before Easter, with all his household; then Gizor the White let himself be baptized, so did Hjalti Skeggjason and many other chiefs, though there were many more who spoke against it; and then dealings between heathen men and Christians became scarcely free of danger. Sundry chiefs even took counsel together to slay Thangbrand, as well as such men who should stand up for him. Because of this turmoil Thangbrand ran away to Norway, and came to meet King Olaf, and told him the tidings of what had befallen in his journey, and said he thought Christianity would never thrive in Iceland. The king was very wroth at this, and said that many Icelanders would rue the day unless they came round to him. That summer Hjalti Skeggjason was made an outlaw at the Thing for blaspheming the gods. Runolf Ulfson, who lived in Dale, under Isles'-fells, the greatest of chieftains, upheld the lawsuit against him. That summer Gizor left Iceland and Hjalti with him, and they came to Norway, and went forthwith to find King Olaf. The king gave them a good welcome, and said they had taken a wise counsel; he bade them stay with him, and that offer they took with thanks. Sverling, son of Runolf of Dale, had been in Norway that winter, and was bound for Iceland in the summer. His ship was floating beside the landing stage all ready, only waiting for a wind. The king forbade him to go away, and said that no ships should go to Iceland that summer. Sverling went to the king and pleaded his case, and begged leave to go, and said it mattered a great deal to him, that they should not have to unship their cargo again. The king spake, and then he was wroth: "It is well for the son of a sacrificer to be where he likes it worst." So Sverling went no whither. That winter nothing to tell of befell. The next summer the king sent Gizor and Hjalti Skeggjason to Iceland to preach the faith anew, and kept four men back as hostages Kjartan Olafson, Halldor, the son of Gudmund the Mighty, Kolbein, son of Thord the priest of Frey, and Sverling, son of Runolf of Dale. Bolli made up his mind to journey with Gizor and Hjalti, and went to Kjartan, his kinsman, and said, "I am now ready to depart; I should wait for you through the next winter, if next summer you were more free to go away than you are now. But I cannot help thinking that the king will on no account let you go free. I also take it to be the truth that you yourself call to mind but few of the things that afford pastime in Iceland when you sit talking to Ingibjorg, the king's sister." She was at the court of King Olaf, and the most beautiful of all the women who were at that time in the land. Kjartan said, "Do not say such things, but bear my greeting to both my kinsfolk and friends."

CHAPTER XLII

Bolli makes love to Gudrun, A.D. 1000

After that Kjartan and Bolli parted, and Gizor and Hjalti sailed from Norway and had a good journey, and came to the Westmen's Isles at the time the Althing was sitting, and went from thence to the mainland, and had there meetings and parleys with their kinsmen. Thereupon they went to the Althing and preached the faith to the people in an harangue both long and telling, and then all men in Iceland received the faith. Bolli rode from the Thing to Herdholt in fellowship with his uncle Olaf, who received him with much loving-kindness. Bolli rode to Laugar to disport himself after he had been at home for a short time, and a good welcome he had there. Gudrun asked very carefully about his journey and then about Kjartan. Bolli answered right readily all Gudrun asked, and said there were no tidings to tell of his journey. "But as to what concerns Kjartan there are, in truth, the most excellent news to be told of his ways of life, for he is in the king's bodyguard, and is there taken before every other man; but I should not wonder if he did not care to have much to do with this country for the next few winters to come." Gudrun then asked if there was any other reason for it than the friendship between Kjartan and the king. Bolli then tells what sort of way people were talking about the friendship of Kjartan with Ingibjorg the king's sister, and said he could not help thinking the king would sooner marry Ingibjorg to Kjartan than let him go away if the choice lay between the two things. Gudrun said these were good tidings, "but Kjartan would be fairly matched only if he got a good wife." Then she let the talk drop all of a sudden and went away and was very red in the face; but other people doubted if she really thought these tidings as good as she gave out she thought they were. Bolli remained at home in Herdholt all that summer, and had gained much honour from his journey; all his kinsfolk and acquaintances set great store by his valiant bearing; he had, moreover, brought home with him a great deal of wealth. He would often go over to Laugar and while away time talking to Gudrun. One day Bolli asked Gudrun what she would answer if he were to ask her in marriage. Gudrun replied at once, "No need for you to bespeak such a thing, Bolli, for I cannot marry any man whilst I know Kjartan to be still alive." Bolli answered, "I think then you will have to abide husbandless for sundry winters if you are to wait for Kjartan; he might have chosen to give me some message concerning the matter if he set his heart at all greatly on it." Sundry words they gave and took, each at variance with the other. Then Bolli rode home.

CHAPTER XLIII
Kjartan comes back to Iceland, A.D. 1001

A little after this Bolli talked to his uncle Olaf, and said, "It has come to this, uncle, that I have it in mind to settle down and marry, for I am now grown up to man's estate. In this matter I should like to have the assistance of your words and your backing-up, for most of the men hereabouts are such as will set much store by your words." Olaf replied, "Such is the case with most women, I am minded to think, that they would be fully

Anonymous

well matched in you for a husband. And I take it you have not broached this matter without first having made up your mind as to where you mean to come down." Bolli said, "I shall not go beyond this countryside to woo myself a wife whilst there is such an goodly match so near at hand. My will is to woo Gudrun, Osvif's daughter, for she is now the most renowned of women." Olaf answered, "Ah, that is just a matter with which I will have nothing to do. To you it is in no way less well known, Bolli, than to me, what talk there was of the love between Kjartan and Gudrun; but if you have set your heart very much on this, I will put no hindrance in the way if you and Osvif settle the matter between you. But have you said anything to Gudrun about it?" Bolli said that he had once hinted at it, but that she had not given much heed to it, "but I think, however, that Osvif will have most to say in the matter." Olaf said Bolli could go about the business as it pleased himself. Not very long after Bolli rode from home with Olaf's sons, Halldor and Steinthor; there were twelve of them together. They rode to Laugar, and Osvif and his sons gave them a good welcome. Bolli said he wished to speak to Osvif, and he set forth his wooing, and asked for the hand of Gudrun, his daughter. Osvif answered in this wise, "As you know, Bolli, Gudrun is a widow, and has herself to answer for her, but, as for myself, I shall urge this on." Osvif now went to see Gudrun, and told her that Bolli Thorliekson had come there, "and has asked you in marriage; it is for you now to give the answer to this matter. And herein I may speedily make known my own will, which is, that Bolli will not be turned away if my counsel shall avail." Gudrun answered, "You make a swift work of looking into this matter; Bolli himself once bespoke it before me, and I rather warded it off, and the same is still uppermost in my mind." Osvif said, "Many a man will tell you that this is spoken more in overweening pride than in wise forethought if you refuse such a man as is Bolli. But as long as I am alive, I shall look out for you, my children, in all affairs which I know better how to see through things than you do." And as Osvif took such a strong view of the matter, Gudrun, as far as she was concerned, would not give an utter refusal, yet was most unwilling on all points. The sons of Osvif's urged the matter on eagerly, seeing what great avail an alliance with Bolli would be to them; so the long and short of the matter was that the betrothal took place then and there, and the wedding was to be held at the time of the winter nights.[5] Thereupon Bolli rode home and told this settlement to Olaf, who did not hide his displeasure thereat. Bolli stayed on at home till he was to go to the wedding. He asked his uncle to it, but Olaf accepted it nowise quickly, though, at last, he yielded to the prayers of Bolli. It was a noble feast this at Laugar. Bolli stayed there the winter after. There was not much love between Gudrun and Bolli so far as she was concerned. When the summer came, and ships began to go and come between Iceland and Norway, the tidings spread to Norway that Iceland was all Christian. King Olaf was very glad at that, and gave leave to go to Iceland unto all those men whom he had kept as hostages, and to fare whenever they liked. Kjartan answered, for he took the lead of all those who had been hostages, "Have great thanks, Lord King, and this will be the choice we take, to go and see Iceland this summer." Then King Olaf said, "I must not take back my word, Kjartan, yet my order pointed rather to other men than to yourself, for in my view you, Kjartan, have been more of a friend than a hostage through your stay here. My wish would be, that you should not set your heart on going to Iceland though you have noble relations there; for, I take it, you could choose for yourself such a station in life in Norway, the like of which would not be found in Iceland." Then Kjartan answered, "May our Lord reward you, sire, for all the honours you have bestowed on me since I came into your power, but I am still in hopes that you will give leave to me, no less than to the others you have kept back for a while." The king said so it should be, but avowed that it would be hard for him to get in his place any untitled man such as Kjartan was. That winter Kalf Asgeirson had been in Norway and had brought, the autumn before, west-away from England, the ship and merchandise he and Kjartan had owned. And when Kjartan had got leave for his journey to Iceland Kalf and he set themselves to get the ship ready. And when the ship was all ready Kjartan went to see Ingibjorg, the king's sister. She gave him a cheery welcome, and made room for him to sit beside her, and they fell a-talking together, and Kjartan tells Ingibjorg that he has arranged his journey to Iceland. Then Ingibjorg said, "I am minded to think, Kjartan, that you have done this of your own wilfulness rather than because you have been urged by men to go away from Norway and to Iceland." But thenceforth words between them were drowned in silence. Amidst this Ingibjorg turns to a "mead-cask" that stood near her, and takes out of it a white coif inwoven with gold and gives it to Kjartan, saying, that it was far too good for Gudrun Osvif's daughter to fold it round her head, yet "you will give her the coif as a bridal gift, for I wish the wives of the Icelanders to see as much as that she with whom you have had your talks in Norway comes of no thrall's blood." It was in a pocket of costly stuff, and was altogether a most precious thing. "Now I shall not go to see you off," said Ingibjorg. "Fare you well, and hail!" After that Kjartan stood up and embraced Ingibjorg, and people told it as a true story that they took it sorely to heart being parted. And now Kjartan went away and unto the king, and told the king he now was ready for his journey. Then the king led Kjartan to his ship and many men with him, and when they came to where the ship was floating with one of its gangways to land, the king said, "Here is a sword, Kjartan, that you shall take from me at our parting; let this weapon be always with you, for my mind tells me you will never be a 'weapon-bitten' man if you bear this sword." It was a most noble keepsake, and much ornamented. Kjartan thanked the king with fair words for all the honour and advancement he had bestowed on him while he had been in Norway. Then the king spoke, "This I will bid you, Kjartan, that you keep your faith well." After that they parted, the king and Kjartan in dear friendship, and Kjartan stepped on board his ship. The king looked after him and said, "Great is the worth of Kjartan and his kindred, but to cope with their fate is not an easy matter."

[5] Winter nights (vetrnœtr), the two last days of autumn and the first day of winter.

CHAPTER XLIV
Kjartan comes home, A.D. 1001

Now Kjartan and Kalf set sail for the main. They had a good wind, and were only a short time out at sea. They hove into White-river, in Burgfirth. The tidings spread far and wide of the coming of Kjartan. When Olaf, his father, and his other kinsfolk heard of it they were greatly rejoiced. Olaf rode at once from the west out of the Dales and south to Burgfirth, and there was a very

joyful meeting between father and son. Olaf asked
Kjartan to go and stay with him, with as many of his men
as he liked to bring. Kjartan took that well, and said that
there only of all places in Iceland he meant to abide. Olaf
now rides home to Herdholt, and Kjartan remained with
his ship during the summer. He now heard of the
marriage of Gudrun, but did not trouble himself at all
over it; but that had heretofore been a matter of anxiety
to many. Gudmund, Solmund's son, Kjartan's brother-in-
law, and Thurid, his sister, came to his ship, and Kjartan
gave them a cheery welcome. Asgeir Eider-drake came
to the ship too to meet his son Kalf, and journeying with
him was Hrefna his daughter, the fairest of women.
Kjartan bade his sister Thurid have such of his wares as
she liked, and the same Kalf said to Hrefna. Kalf now
unlocked a great chest and bade them go and have a
look at it. That day a gale sprang up, and Kjartan and Kalf
had to go out to moor their ship, and when that was
done they went home to the booths. Kalf was the first to
enter the booth, where Thurid and Hrefna had turned
out most of the things in the chest. Just then Hrefna
snatched up the coif and unfolded it, and they had much
to say as to how precious a thing it was. Then Hrefna
said she would coif herself with it, and Thurid said she
had better, and Hrefna did so. When Kalf saw that he
gave her to understand that she had done amiss, and
bade her take it off at her swiftest. "For that is the one
thing that we, Kjartan and I, do not own in common."
And as he said this Kjartan came into the booth. He had
heard their talk, and fell in at once and told them there
was nothing amiss. So Hrefna sat still with the head-
dress on. Kjartan looked at her heedfully and said, "I
think the coif becomes you very well, Hrefna," says he,
"and I think it fits the best that both together, coif and

maiden, be mine." Then Hrefna answered, "Most people take it that you are in no hurry to marry, and also that the woman you woo, you will be sure to get for wife." Kjartan said it would not matter much whom he married, but he would not stand being kept long a waiting wooer by any woman. "Now I see that this gear suits you well, and it suits well that you become my wife." Hrefna now took off the head-dress and gave it to Kjartan, who put it away in a safe place. Gudmund and Thurid asked Kjartan to come north to them for a friendly stay some time that winter, and Kjartan promised the journey. Kalf Asgeirson betook himself north with his father. Kjartan and he now divided their partnership, and that went off altogether in good-nature and friendship. Kjartan also rode from his ship westward to the Dales, and they were twelve of them together. Kjartan now came home to Herdholt, and was joyfully received by everybody. Kjartan had his goods taken to the west from the ship during the autumn. The twelve men who rode with Kjartan stayed at Herdholt all the winter. Olaf and Osvif kept to the same wont of asking each other to their house, which was that each should go to the other every other autumn. That autumn the wassail was to be at Laugar, and Olaf and all the Herdholtings were to go thither. Gudrun now spoke to Bolli, and said she did not think he had told her the truth in all things about the coming back of Kjartan. Bolli said he had told the truth about it as best he knew it. Gudrun spoke little on this matter, but it could be easily seen that she was very displeased, and most people would have it that she still was pining for Kjartan, although she tried to hide it. Now time glides on till the autumn feast was to be held at Laugar. Olaf got ready and bade Kjartan come with him. Kjartan said he would stay at home and look after the household. Olaf bade him not to show that he was angry with his kinsmen. "Call this to mind, Kjartan, that you have loved no man so much as your foster-brother Bolli, and it is my wish that you should come, for things will soon settle themselves between you, kinsmen, if you meet each other." Kjartan did as his father bade him. He took the scarlet clothes that King Olaf had given him at parting, and dressed himself gaily; he girded his sword, the king's gift, on; and he had a gilt helm on his head, and on his side a red shield with the Holy Cross painted on it in gold; he had in his hand a spear, with the socket inlaid with gold. All his men were gaily dressed. There were in all between twenty and thirty men of them. They now rode out of Herdholt and went on till they came to Laugar. There were a great many men gathered together already.

CHAPTER XLV
Kjartaŋ marries Hrefŋa, A.D. 1002

Bolli, together with the sons of Osvif, went out to meet Olaf and his company, and gave them a cheery welcome. Bolli went to Kjartan and kissed him, and Kjartan took his greeting. After that they were seen into the house, Bolli was of the merriest towards them, and Olaf responded to that most heartily, but Kjartan was rather silent. The feast went off well. Now Bolli had some stud-horses which were looked upon as the best of their kind. The stallion was great and goodly, and had never failed at fight; it was light of coat, with red ears and forelock. Three mares went with it, of the same hue as the stallion. These horses Bolli wished to give to Kjartan, but Kjartan said he was not a horsey man, and could not take the gift. Olaf bade him take the horses, "for these are most noble gifts." Kjartan gave a flat refusal. They parted after this nowise blithely, and the Herdholtings went home, and all was quiet. Kjartan was rather gloomy all the winter, and people could have but little talk of him. Olaf thought this a great misfortune. That winter after Yule Kjartan got ready to leave home, and there were twelve of them together, bound for the countrysides of the north. They now rode on their way till they came to Asbjornness, north in Willowdale, and there Kjartan was greeted with the greatest blitheness and cheerfulness. The housing there was of the noblest. Hall, the son of Gudmund, was about twenty winters old, and took much after the kindred of the men of Salmon-river-Dale; and it is all men's say, there was no more valiant-looking a man in all the north land. Hall greeted Kjartan, his uncle, with the greatest blitheness. Sports are now at once started at Asbjornness, and men were gathered together from far and near throughout the countrysides, and people came from the west from Midfirth and from Waterness and Waterdale all the way and from out of Longdale, and there was a great gathering together. It was the talk of all folk how strikingly Kjartan showed above other men. Now the sports were set going, and Hall took the lead. He asked Kjartan to join in the play, "and I wish, kinsman, you would show your courtesy in this." Kjartan said, "I have been training for sports but little of late, for there were other things to do with King Olaf, but I will not refuse you this for once." So Kjartan now got ready to play, and the strongest men there were chosen out to go against him. The game went on all day long, but no man had either strength or litheness of limb to cope with Kjartan. And in the evening when the games were ended, Hall stood up and said, "It is the wish and offer of my father concerning those men who have come from the farthest hither, that they all stay here over night and take up the pastime again to-morrow." At this message there was made a good cheer, and the offer deemed worthy of a great man. Kalf Asgeirson was there, and he and Kjartan were dearly fond of each other. His sister Hrefna was there also, and was dressed most showily. There were over a hundred (*i.e.* over 120) men in the house that night. And the next day sides were divided for the games again. Kjartan sat by and looked on at the sports. Thurid, his sister, went to talk to him, and said, "It is told me, brother, that you have been rather silent all the winter, and men say it must be because you are pining after Gudrun, and set forth as a proof thereof that no fondness now is shown between you and Bolli, such as through all time there had been between you. Do now the good and befitting thing, and don't allow yourself to take this to heart, and grudge not your kinsman a good wife. To me it seems your best counsel to marry, as you bespoke it last summer, although the match be not altogether even for you, where Hrefna is, for such a match you cannot find within this land. Asgeir, her father, is a noble and a high-born man, and he does not lack wealth wherewith to make this match fairer still; moreover, another daughter of his is married to a mighty man. You have also told me yourself that Kalf Asgeirson is the doughtiest of men, and their way of life is of the stateliest. It is my wish that you go and talk to Hrefna, and I ween you will find that there great wits and goodliness go together." Kjartan took this matter up well, and said she had ably pleaded the case. After this Kjartan and Hrefna are brought together that they may have their talk by themselves, and they talked together all day. In the evening Thurid asked Kjartan how he liked the manner in which Hrefna turned her speech. He was well pleased about it, and said he thought the woman was in all ways one of the noblest as far as he could see. The next morning men were sent to Asgeir to ask him to Asbjornness. And now they had a parley between them on this affair, and Kjartan wooed Hrefna, Asgeir's daughter. Asgeir took up the matter with a good will, for he was a wise man, and saw what an honourable offer was made to them. Kalf, too, urged the matter on very much, saying, "I will not let anything be spared (towards the dowry)." Hrefna, in her turn, did not make unwilling answers, but bade her father follow his own counsel. So now the match was covenanted and settled before witnesses. Kjartan would hear of nothing but that the wedding should be held at Herdholt, and Asgeir and Kalf had nothing to say against it. The wedding was then settled to take place at Herdholt when five weeks of summer had passed. After that Kjartan rode home with great gifts. Olaf was delighted at these tidings, for Kjartan was much merrier than before he left home. Kjartan kept fast through Lent, following therein the example of no man in this land; and it is said he was the first man who ever kept fast in this land. Men thought it so wonderful a thing that Kjartan could live so long without meat, that people came over long ways to see him. In a like manner Kjartan's other ways went beyond those of other men. Now Easter passed, and after that Kjartan and Olaf made ready a great feast. At the appointed time Asgeir and Kalf came from the north as well as Gudmund and Hall, and altogether there were sixty men. Olaf and Kjartan had already many men gathered together there. It was a most brave feast, and for a whole week the feasting went on. Kjartan made Hrefna a bridal gift of the rich head-dress, and a most famous gift was that; for no one was there so knowing

Anonymous

or so rich as ever to have seen or possessed such a treasure, for it is the saying of thoughtful men that eight ounces of gold were woven into the coif. Kjartan was so merry at the feast that he entertained every one with his talk, telling of his journey. Men did marvel much how great were the matters that entered into that tale; for he had served the noblest of lords—King Olaf Tryggvason. And when the feast was ended Kjartan gave Gudmund and Hall good gifts, as he did to all the other great men. The father and son gained great renown from this feast. Kjartan and Hrefna loved each other very dearly.

CHAPTER XLVI
Feast at Herdholt and the Loss of Kjartan's Sword, A.D. 1002

Olaf and Osvif were still friends, though there was some deal of ill-will between the younger people. That summer Olaf had his feast half a month before winter. And Osvif was also making ready a feast, to be held at "Winter-nights," and they each asked the other to their homes, with as many men as each deemed most honourable to himself. It was Osvif's turn to go first to the feast at Olaf's, and he came to Herdholt at the time appointed. In his company were Bolli and Gudrun and the sons of Osvif. In the morning one of the women on going down the hall was talking how the ladies would be shown to their seats. And just as Gudrun had come right against the bedroom wherein Kjartan was wont to rest, and where even then he was dressing and slipping on a red kirtle of scarlet, he called out to the woman who had been speaking about the seating of the women, for no one else was quicker in giving the answer, "Hrefna shall sit in the high seat and be most honoured in all things so long as I am alive." But before this Gudrun had always had the high seat at Herdholt and everywhere else. Gudrun heard this, and looked at Kjartan and flushed up, but said nothing. The next day Gudrun was talking to Hrefna, and said she ought to coif herself with the head-dress, and show people the most costly treasure that had ever come to Iceland. Kjartan was near, but not quite close, and heard what Gudrun said, and he was quicker to answer than Hrefna. "She shall not coif herself with the headgear at this feast, for I set more store by Hrefna owning the greatest of treasures than by the guests having it to feast thereon their eyes at this time." The feast at Olaf's was to last a week. The next day Gudrun spoke on the sly to Hrefna, and asked her to show her the head-dress, and Hrefna said she would. The next day they went to the out-bower where the precious things were kept, and Hrefna opened a chest and took out the pocket of costly stuff, and took from thence the coif and showed it to Gudrun. She unfolded the coif and looked at it a while, but said no word of praise or blame. After that Hrefna put it back, and they went to their places, and after that all was joy and amusement. And the day the guests should ride away Kjartan busied himself much about matters in hand, getting change of horses for those who had come from afar, and speeding each one on his journey as he needed. Kjartan had not his sword "King's-gift" with him while he was taken up with these matters, yet was he seldom wont to let it go out of his hand. After this he went to his room where the sword had been, and found it now gone. He then went and told his father of the loss. Olaf said, "We must go about this most gently. I will get men to spy into each batch of them as they ride away," and he did so. An the White had to ride with Osvif's company, and to keep an eye upon men turning aside, or baiting. They rode up

Anonymous

past Lea-shaws, and past the homesteads which are called Shaws, and stopped at one of the homesteads at Shaws, and got off their horses. Thorolf, son of Osvif, went out from the homestead with a few other men. They went out of sight amongst the brushwood, whilst the others tarried at the Shaws' homestead. An followed him all the way unto Salmon-river, where it flows out of Sælingsdale, and said he would turn back there. Thorolf said it would have done no harm though he had gone nowhere at all. The night before a little snow had fallen so that footprints could be traced. An rode back to the brushwood, and followed the footprints of Thorolf to a certain ditch or bog. He groped down with his hand, and grasped the hilt of a sword. An wished to have witnesses with him to this, and rode for Thorarin in Sælingsdale Tongue, and he went with An to take up the sword. After that An brought the sword back to Kjartan. Kjartan wrapt it in a cloth, and laid it in a chest. The place was afterwards called Sword-ditch, where An and Thorarin had found the "King's-gift." This was all kept quiet. The scabbard was never found again. Kjartan always treasured the sword less hereafter than heretofore. This affair Kjartan took much to heart, and would not let the matter rest there. Olaf said, "Do not let it pain you; true, they have done a nowise pretty trick, but you have got no harm from it. We shall not let people have this to laugh at, that we make a quarrel about such a thing, these being but friends and kinsmen on the other side." And through these reasonings of Olaf, Kjartan let matters rest in quiet. After that Olaf got ready to go to the feast at Laugar at "winter nights," and told Kjartan he must go too. Kjartan was very unwilling thereto, but promised to go at the bidding of his father. Hrefna was also to go, but she wished to leave her coif behind.

"Goodwife," Thorgerd said, "whenever will you take out such a peerless keepsake if it is to lie down in chests when you go to feasts?" Hrefna said, "Many folk say that it is not unlikely that I may come to places where I have fewer people to envy me than at Laugar." Thorgerd said, "I have no great belief in people who let such things fly here from house to house." And because Thorgerd urged it eagerly Hrefna took the coif, and Kjartan did not forbid it when he saw how the will of his mother went. After that they betake themselves to the journey and came to Laugar in the evening, and had a goodly welcome there. Thorgerd and Hrefna handed out their clothes to be taken care of. But in the morning when the women should dress themselves Hrefna looked for the coif and it was gone from where she had put it away. It was looked for far and near, and could not be found. Gudrun said it was most likely the coif had been left behind at home, or that she had packed it so carelessly that it had fallen out on the way. Hrefna now told Kjartan that the coif was lost. He answered and said it was no easy matter to try to make them take care of things, and bade her now leave matters quiet; and told his father what game was up. Olaf said, "My will is still as before, that you leave alone and let pass by this trouble and I will probe this matter to the bottom in quiet; for I would do anything that you and Bolli should not fall out. Best to bind up a whole flesh, kinsman," says he. Kjartan said, "I know well, father, that you wish the best for everybody in this affair; yet I know not whether I can put up with being thus overborne by these folk of Laugar." The day that men were to ride away from the feast Kjartan raised his voice and said, "I call on you, Cousin Bolli, to show yourself more willing henceforth than hitherto to do to us as behoves a good man and true. I

Anonymous

shall not set this matter forth in a whisper, for within the knowledge of many people it is that a loss has befallen here of a thing which we think has slipped into your own keep. This harvest, when we gave a feast at Herdholt, my sword was taken; it came back to me, but not the scabbard. Now again there has been lost here a keepsake which men will esteem a thing of price. Come what may, I will have them both back." Bolli answered, "What you put down to me, Kjartan, is not my fault, and I should have looked for anything else from you sooner than that you would charge me with theft." Kjartan says, "I must think that the people who have been putting their heads together in this affair are so near to you that it ought to be in your power to make things good if you but would. You affront us far beyond necessity, and long we have kept peaceful in face on your enmity. But now it must be made known that matters will not rest as they are now." Then Gudrun answered his speech and said, "Now you rake up a fire which it would be better should not smoke. Now, let it be granted, as you say, that there be some people here who have put their heads together with a view to the coif disappearing. I can only think that they have gone and taken what was their own. Think what you like of what has become of the head-dress, but I cannot say I dislike it though it should be bestowed in such a way as that Hrefna should have little chance to improve her apparel with it henceforth." After that they parted heavy of heart, and the Herdholtings rode home. That was the end of the feasts, yet everything was to all appearances quiet. Nothing was ever heard of the head-dress. But many people held the truth to be that Thorolf had burnt it in fire by the order of Gudrun, his sister. Early that winter Asgeir Eider-drake died. His sons inherited his estate and chattels.

CHAPTER XLVII

Kjartaŋ goes to Laugar, aŋd of the Bargaiŋ for Toŋgue, A.D. 1003

After Yule that winter Kjartan got men together, and they mustered sixty men altogether. Kjartan did not tell his father the reason of his journey, and Olaf asked but little about it. Kjartan took with him tents and stores, and rode on his way until he came to Laugar. He bade his men get off their horses, and said that some should look after the horses and some put up the tents. At that time it was the custom that outhouses were outside, and not so very far away from the dwelling-house, and so it was at Laugar. Kjartan had all the doors of the house taken, and forbade all the inmates to go outside, and for three nights he made them do their errands within the house. After that Kjartan rode home to Herdholt, and each of his followers rode to his own home. Olaf was very ill-pleased with this raid, but Thorgerd said there was no reason for blame, for the men of Laugar had deserved this, yea, and a still greater shame. Then Hrefna said, "Did you have any talk with any one at Laugar, Kjartan?" He answered, "There was but little chance of that," and said he and Bolli had exchanged only a few words. Then Hrefna smiled and said, "It was told me as truth that you and Gudrun had some talk together, and I have likewise heard how she was arrayed, that she had coifed herself with the head-dress, and it suited her exceeding well." Kjartan answered, and coloured up, and it was easy to see he was angry with her for making a mockery of this. "Nothing of what you say, Hrefna, passed before my eyes, and there was no need for Gudrun to coif herself with the head-dress to look statelier than all other women." Thereat Hrefna dropped the talk. The men of

Laugar bore this exceedingly ill, and thought it by much a greater and worse disgrace than if Kjartan had even killed a man or two of them. The sons of Osvif were the wildest over this matter, but Bolli quieted them rather. Gudrun was the fewest-spoken on the matter, yet men gathered from her words that it was uncertain whether any one took it as sorely to heart as she did. Full enmity now grows up between the men of Laugar and the Herdholtings. As the winter wore on Hrefna gave birth to a child, a boy, and he was named Asgier. Thorarin, the goodman of Tongue, let it be known that he wished to sell the land of Tongue. The reason was that he was drained of money, and that he thought ill-will was swelling too much between the people of the countryside, he himself being a friend of either side. Bolli thought he would like to buy the land and settle down on it, for the men of Laugar had little land and much cattle. Bolli and Gudrun rode to Tongue at the advice of Osvif; they thought it a very handy chance to be able to secure this land so near to themselves, and Osvif bade them not to let a small matter stand in the way of a covenant. Then they (Bolli and Gudrun) bespoke the purchase with Thorarin, and came to terms as to what the price should be, and also as to the kind wherein it should be paid, and the bargain was settled with Thorarin. But the buying was not done in the presence of witnesses, for there were not so many men there at the time as were lawfully necessary. Bolli and Gudrun rode home after that. But when Kjartan Olafson hears of these tidings he rides off with twelve men, and came to Tongue early one day. Thorarin greeted him well, and asked him to stay there. Kjartan said he must ride back again in the morning, but would tarry there for some time. Thorarin asked his errand, and Kjartan said, "My errand here is to speak about a certain sale of land that you and Bolli have agreed upon, for it is very much against my wishes if you sell this land to Bolli and Gudrun." Thorarin said that to do otherwise would be unbecoming to him, "For the price that Bolli has offered for the land is liberal, and is to be paid up speedily." Kjartan said, "You shall come in for no loss even if Bolli does not buy your land; for I will buy it at the same price, and it will not be of much avail to you to speak against what I have made up my mind to have done. Indeed it will soon be found out that I shall want to have the most to say within this countryside, being more ready, however, to do the will of others than that of the men of Laugar." Thorarin answered, "Mighty to me will be the master's word in this matter, but it would be most to my mind that this bargain should be left alone as I and Bolli have settled it." Kjartan said, "I do not call that a sale of land which is not bound by witnesses. Now you do one of two things, either sell me the lands on the same terms as you agreed upon with the others, or live on your land yourself." Thorarin chooses to sell him the land, and witnesses were forthwith taken to the sale, and after the purchase Kjartan rode home. That same evening this was told at Laugar. Then Gudrun said, "It seems to me, Bolli, that Kjartan has given you two choices somewhat harder than those he gave Thorarin—that you must either leave the countryside with little honour, or show yourself at some meeting with him a good deal less slow than you have been heretofore." Bolli did not answer, but went forthwith away from this talk. All was quiet now throughout what was left of Lent. The third day after Easter Kjartan rode from home with one other man, on the beach, for a follower. They came to Tongue in the day. Kjartan wished Thorarin to ride with them to

Saurby to gather in debts due to him, for Kjartan had much money-at-call in these parts. But Thorarin had ridden to another place. Kjartan stopped there awhile, and waited for him. That same day Thorhalla the Chatterbox was come there. She asked Kjartan where he was minded to go. He said he was going west to Saurby. She asked, "Which road will you take?" Kjartan replied, "I am going by Sælingsdale to the west, and by Swinedale from the west." She asked how long he would be. Kjartan answered, "Most likely I shall be riding from the west next Thursday (the fifth day of the week)." "Would you do an errand for me?" said Thorhalla. "I have a kinsman west at Whitedale and Saurby; he has promised me half a mark's worth of homespun, and I would like you to claim it for me, and bring it with you from the west." Kjartan promised to do this. After this Thorarin came home, and betook himself to the journey with them. They rode westward over Sælingsdale heath, and came to Hol in the evening to the brothers and sister there. There Kjartan got the best of welcomes, for between him and them there was the greatest friendship. Thorhalla the Chatterbox came home to Laugar that evening. The sons of Osvif asked her who she had met during the day. She said she had met Kjartan Olafson. They asked where he was going. She answered, telling them all she knew about it, "And never has he looked braver than now, and it is not wonderful at all that such men should look upon everything as low beside themselves;" and Thorhalla still went on, "and it was clear to me that Kjartan liked to talk of nothing so well as of his land bargain with Thorarin." Gudrun spoke, "Kjartan may well do things as boldly as it pleases him, for it is proven that for whatever insult he may pay others, there is none who dares even to shoot a shaft at him." Present at this talk of Gudrun and Thorhalla were both Bolli and the sons of Osvif. Ospak and his brothers said but little, but what there was, rather stinging for Kjartan, as was always their way. Bolli behaved as if he did not hear, as he always did when Kjartan was spoken ill of, for his wont was either to hold his peace, or to gainsay them.

CHAPTER XLVIII
The Men of Laugar and Gudrun plan an Ambush for Kjartan, A.D. 1003

Kjartan spent the fourth day after Easter at Hol, and there was the greatest merriment and gaiety. The night after An was very ill at ease in his sleep, so they waked him. They asked him what he had dreamt. He answered, "A woman came to me most evil-looking and pulled me forth unto the bedside. She had in one hand a short sword, and in the other a trough; she drove the sword into my breast and cut open all the belly, and took out all my inwards and put brushwood in their place. After that she went outside." Kjartan and the others laughed very much at this dream, and said he should be called An "brushwood belly," and they caught hold of him and said they wished to feel if he had the brushwood in his stomach. Then Aud said, "There is no need to mock so much at this; and my counsel is that Kjartan do one of two things: either tarry here longer, or, if he will ride away, then let him ride with more followers hence than hither he did." Kjartan said, "You may hold An 'brushwood belly' a man very sage as he sits and talks to you all day, since you think that whatever he dreams must be a very vision, but go I must, as I have already made up my mind to, in spite of this dream." Kjartan got ready to go on the fifth day in Easter week; and at the advice of Aud, so did Thorkell Whelp and Knut his brother. They rode on the way with Kjartan a band of twelve together. Kjartan came to Whitedale and fetched the homespun for Thorhalla Chatterbox as he had said he would. After that he rode south through Swinedale. It is told how at Laugar in Sælingsdale Gudrun was early afoot directly after sunrise. She went to where her brothers were sleeping. She roused Ospak and he woke up at once, and then too the other brothers. And when Ospak saw that there was his sister, he asked her what she wanted that she was up so early. Gudrun said she wanted to know what they would be doing that day. Ospak said he would keep at rest, "for there is little work to do." Gudrun said, "You would have the right sort of temper if you were the daughters of some peasant, letting neither good nor bad be done by you. Why, after all the disgrace and shame that Kjartan has done to you, you none the less lie quietly sleeping, though he rides past this place with but one other man. Such men indeed are richly endowed with the memory of swine. I think it is past hoping that you will ever have courage enough to go and seek out Kjartan in his home, if you dare not meet him now that he rides with but one other man or two; but here you sit at home and bear yourselves as if you were hopeful men; yea, in sooth there are too many of you." Ospak said she did not mince matters and it was hard to gainsay her, and he sprang up forthwith and dressed, as did also each of the brothers one after the other. Then they got ready to lay an ambush for Kjartan. Then Gudrun called on Bolli to bestir him with them. Bolli said it behoved him not for the sake of his kinship with Kjartan, set forth how lovingly Olaf had brought him up. Gudrun answered, "Therein you speak the truth, but you will not have the good luck always to do what pleases all men, and if you cut yourself out of this journey, our married life must be at an end." And through Gudrun's harping on the matter Bolli's mind swelled at all the enmity and guilts that lay at the door of Kjartan, and speedily he donned his weapons, and they grew a band of nine together. There were the five sons of Osvif— Ospak, Helgi, Vandrad, Torrad, and Thorolf. Bolli was the sixth and Gudlaug, the son of Osvif's sister, the hopefullest of men, the seventh. There were also Odd and Stein, sons of Thorhalla Chatterbox. They rode to Swinedale and took up their stand beside the gill which is called Goat-gill.[6] They bound up their horses and sat down. Bolli was silent all day, and lay up on the top of the gill bank. Now when Kjartan and his followers were come south past Narrowsound, where the dale begins to widen out, Kjartan said that Thorkell and the others had better turn back. Thorkell said they would ride to the end of the dale. Then when they came south past the out-dairies called Northdairies Kjartan spake to the brothers and bade them not to ride any farther. "Thorolf the thief," he said, "shall not have that matter to laugh at that I dare not ride on my way with few men." Thorkell Whelp said, "We will yield to you in not following you any farther; but we should rue it indeed not to be near if you should stand in need of men to-day." Then Kjartan said, "Never will Bolli, my kinsman, join hands with plotters against my life. But if the sons of Osvif lie in wait for me, there is no knowing which side will live to tell the tale, even though I may have some odds to deal with." Thereupon the brothers rode back to the west.

[6] Gill=gorge, deep watercourse.

CHAPTER XLIX

The Death of Kjartan

Now Kjartan rode south through the dale, he and they three together, himself, An the Black, and Thorarin. Thorkell was the name of a man who lived at Goat-peaks in Swinedale, where now there is waste land. He had been seeing after his horses that day, and a shepherd of his with him. They saw the two parties, the men of Laugar in ambush and Kjartan and his where they were riding down the dale three together. Then the shepherd said they had better turn to meet Kjartan and his; it would be, quoth he, a great good hap to them if they could stave off so great a trouble as now both sides were steering into. Thorkell said, "Hold your tongue at once. Do you think, fool as you are, you will ever give life to a man to whom fate has ordained death? And, truth to tell, I would spare neither of them from having now as evil dealings together as they like. It seems to me a better plan for us to get to a place where we stand in danger of nothing, and from where we can have a good look at their meeting, so as to have some fun over their play. For all men make a marvel thereof, how Kjartan is of all men the best skilled at arms. I think he will want it now, for we two know how overwhelming the odds are." And so it had to be as Thorkell wished. Kjartan and his followers now rode on to Goat-gill. On the other hand the sons of Osvif misdoubt them why Bolli should have sought out a place for himself from where he might well be seen by men riding from the west. So they now put their heads together, and, being of one mind that Bolli was playing them false, they go for him up unto the brink and took to wrestling and horse-playing with him, and took him by the feet and dragged him down over the brink. But Kjartan and his followers came up apace as they were riding fast, and when they came to the south side of the gill they saw the ambush and knew the men. Kjartan at once sprung off his horse and turned upon the sons of Osvif. There stood near by a great stone, against which Kjartan ordered they should wait the onset (he and his). Before they met Kjartan flung his spear, and it struck through Thorolf's shield above the handle, so that therewith the shield was pressed against him, the spear piercing the shield and the arm above the elbow, where it sundered the main muscle, Thorolf dropping the shield, and his arm being of no avail to him through the day. Thereupon Kjartan drew his sword, but he held not the "King's-gift." The sons of Thorhalla went at Thorarin, for that was the task allotted to them. That outset was a hard one, for Thorarin was mightily strong, and it was hard to tell which would outlast the other. Osvif's sons and Gudlaug set on Kjartan, they being five together, and Kjartan and An but two. An warded himself valiantly, and would ever be going in front of Kjartan. Bolli stood aloof with Footbiter. Kjartan smote hard, but his sword was of little avail (and bent so), he often had to straighten it under his foot. In this attack both the sons of Osvif and An were wounded, but Kjartan had no wound as yet. Kjartan fought so swiftly and dauntlessly that Osvif's sons recoiled and turned to where An was. At that moment An fell, having fought for some time, with his inwards coming out. In this attack Kjartan cut off one leg of Gudlaug above the knee, and that hurt was enough to cause death. Then the four sons of Osvif made an onset on Kjartan, but he warded himself so bravely that in no way did he give them the chance of any advantage. Then spake Kjartan, "Kinsman Bolli, why did you leave home if you meant quietly to stand by? Now the choice lies before you, to help one side or the other, and try now how Footbiter will do." Bolli made as if he did not hear. And when Ospak saw that they would no how bear Kjartan over, he egged on Bolli in every way, and said he surely would not wish that shame to follow after him, to have promised them his aid in this fight and not to grant it now. "Why, heavy enough in dealings with us was Kjartan then, when by none so big a deed as this we had offended him; but if Kjartan is now to get away from us, then for you, Bolli, as even for us, the way to exceeding hardships will be equally short." Then Bolli drew Footbiter, and now turned upon Kjartan. Then Kjartan said to Bolli, "Surely thou art minded now, my kinsman, to do a dastard's deed; but oh, my kinsman, I am much more fain to take my death from you than to cause the same to you myself." Then Kjartan flung away his weapons and would defend himself no longer; yet he was but slightly wounded, though very tired with fighting. Bolli gave no answer to Kjartan's words, but all the same he dealt him his death-wound. And straightway Bolli sat down under the shoulders of him, and Kjartan breathed his last in the lap of Bolli. Bolli rued at once his deed, and declared the manslaughter due to his hand. Bolli sent the sons of Osvif into the countryside, but he stayed behind together with Thorarin by the dead bodies. And when the sons of Osvif came to Laugar they told the tidings. Gudrun gave out her pleasure thereat, and then the arm of Thorolf was bound up; it healed slowly, and was never after any use to him. The body of Kjartan was brought home to Tongue, but Bolli rode home to Laugar. Gudrun went to meet him, and asked what time of day it was. Bolli said it was near noontide. Then spake Gudrun, "Harm spurs on to hard deeds (work); I have spun yarn for twelve ells of homespun, and you have killed Kjartan." Bolli replied," unhappy deed might well go late from my mind even if you did not remind me of it." Gudrun said "Such things I do not count among mishaps. It seemed to me you stood in higher station during the year Kjartan was in Norway than now, when he trod you under foot when he came back to Iceland. But I count that last which to me is dearest, that Hrefna will not go laughing to her bed to-night." Then Bolli said and right wroth he was, "I think it is quite uncertain that she will turn paler at these tidings than you do; and I have my doubts as to whether you would not have been less startled if I had been lying behind on the field of battle, and Kjartan had told the tidings." Gudrun saw that Bolli was wroth, and spake, "Do not upbraid me with such things, for I am very grateful to you for your deed; for now I think I know that you will not do anything against my mind." After that Osvif's sons went and hid in an underground chamber, which had been made for them in secret, but Thorhalla's sons were sent west to Holy-Fell to tell Snorri Godi the Priest these tidings, and therewith the message that they bade him send them speedily all availing strength against Olaf and those men to whom it came to follow up the blood-suit after Kjartan. At Sælingsdale Tongue it happened, the night after the day on which the fight befell, that An sat up, he who they had all thought was dead. Those who waked the bodies were very much afraid, and thought this a wondrous marvel. Then An spake to them, "I beg you, in God's name, not to be afraid of me, for I have had both my life and my wits all unto the hour when on me fell the heaviness of a swoon. Then I dreamed of the same woman as before, and methought she now took the brushwood out of my belly and put my own inwards in instead, and the change seemed good to me." Then the wounds that An had were bound up and he became a hale man, and was ever afterwards called An Brushwood-belly. But now when Olaf Hoskuld's son heard these tidings he took the slaying of Kjartan most sorely to heart, though he bore it like a brave man. His sons wanted to set on Bolli forthwith and kill him. Olaf said, "Far be it from me, for my son is none the more atoned to me though Bolli be slain; moreover, I loved Kjartan before all men, but as to Bolli, I could not bear any harm befalling him. But I see a more befitting business for you to do. Go ye and meet the sons of Thorhalla, who are now sent to Holy-Fell with the errand of summoning up a band against us. I shall be well pleased for you to put them to any penalty you like." Then Olaf's sons swiftly turn to journeying, and went on board a ferry-boat that Olaf owned, being seven of them together, and rowed out down Hvamsfirth, pushing on their journey at their lustiest. They had but little wind, but fair what there was, and they rowed with the sail until they came under Scoreisle, where they tarried for some while and asked about the journeyings of men thereabouts. A little while after they saw a ship coming from the west across the firth, and soon they saw who the men were, for there were the sons of Thorhalla, and Halldor and his followers boarded them straightway. They met with no resistance, for the sons of Olaf leapt forthwith on board their ships and set upon them. Stein and his brother were laid hands on and beheaded overboard. The sons of Olaf now turn back, and their journey was deemed to have sped most briskly.

CHAPTER L

The End of Hrefna. The Peace Settled, A.D. 1003

Olaf went to meet Kjartan's body. He sent men south to Burg to tell Thorstein Egilson these tidings, and also that he would have his help for the blood-suit; and if any great men should band themselves together against him with the sons of Osvif, he said he wanted to have the whole matter in his own hands. The same message he sent north to Willowdale, to Gudmund, his son-in-law, and to the sons of Asgeir; with the further information that he had charged as guilty of the slaying of Kjartan all the men who had taken part in the ambush, except Ospak, son of Osvif, for he was already under outlawry because of a woman who was called Aldis, the daughter of Holmganga-Ljot of Ingjaldsand. Their son was Ulf, who later became a marshal to King Harold Sigurdsson, and had for wife Jorunn, the daughter of Thorberg. Their son was Jon, father of Erlend the Laggard, the father of Archbishop Egstein. Olaf had proclaimed that the blood-suit should be taken into court at Thorness Thing. He had Kjartan's body brought home, and a tent was rigged over it, for there was as yet no church built in the Dales. But when Olaf heard that Thorstein had bestirred him swiftly and raised up a band of great many men, and that the Willowdale men had done likewise, he had men gathered together throughout all the Dales, and a great multitude they were. The whole of this band Olaf sent to Laugar, with this order: "It is my will that you guard Bolli if he stand in need thereof, and do it no less faithfully than if you were following me; for my mind misgives me that the men from beyond this countryside, whom, coming soon, we shall be having on our hands, will deem that they have somewhat of a loss to make up with Bolli.

Anonymous

And when he had put the matter in order in this manner, Thorstein, with his following, and also the Willowdale men, came on, all wild with rage. Hall Gudmund's son and Kalf Asgeirson egged them on most to go and force Bolli to let search be made for the sons of Osvif till they should be found, for they could be gone nowhere out of the countryside. But because Olaf set himself so much against their making a raid on Laugar, messages of peace were borne between the two parties, and Bolli was most willing, and bade Olaf settle all terms on his behalf, and Osvif said it was not in his power to speak against this, for no help had come to him from Snorri the Priest. A peace meeting, therefore, took place at Lea-Shaws, and the whole case was laid freely in Olaf's hand. For the slaughter of Kjartan there were to come such fines and penalties as Olaf liked. Then the peace meeting came to an end. Bolli, by the counsel of Olaf, did not go to this meeting. The award should be made known at Thorness Thing. Now the Mere-men and Willowdale men rode to Herdholt. Thorstein Kuggison begged for Asgeir, son of Kjartan, to foster, as a comfort to Hrefna. Hrefna went north with her brothers, and was much weighed down with grief, nevertheless she bore her sorrow with dignity, and was easy of speech with every man. Hrefna took no other husband after Kjartan. She lived but a little while after coming to the north; and the tale goes that she died of a broken heart.

CHAPTER LI
Osvif's Sons are Banished

Kjartan's body lay in state for a week in Herdholt. Thorstein Egilson had had a church built at Burg. He took the body of Kjartan home with him, and Kjartan was buried at Burg. The church was newly consecrated, and as yet hung in white. Now time wore on towards the Thorness Thing, and the award was given against Osvif's sons, who were all banished the country. Money was given to pay the cost of their going into exile, but they were forbidden to come back to Iceland so long as any of Olaf's sons, or Asgeir, Kjartan's son, should be alive. For Gudlaug, the son of Osvif's sister, no weregild (atonement) should be paid, because of his having set out against, and laid ambush for, Kjartan, neither should Thorolf have any compensation for the wounds he had got. Olaf would not let Bolli be prosecuted, and bade him ransom himself with a money fine. This Halldor and Stein, and all the sons of Olaf, liked mightily ill, and said it would go hard with Bolli if he was allowed to stay in the same countryside as themselves. Olaf saw that would work well enough as long as he was on his legs. There was a ship in Bjornhaven which belonged to Audun Cable-hound. He was at the Thing, and said, "As matters stand, the guilt of these men will be no less in Norway, so long as any of Kjartan's friends are alive." Then Osvif said, "You, Cable-hound, will be no soothsayer in this matter, for my sons will be highly accounted of among men of high degree, whilst you, Cable-hound, will pass, this summer, into the power of trolls." Audun Cable-hound went out a voyage that summer and the ship was wrecked amongst the Faroe Isles and every man's child on board perished, and Osvif's prophecy was thought to have come thoroughly home. The sons of Osvif went abroad that summer, and none ever came back again. In such a manner the blood-suit came to an end that Olaf was held to have shown himself all the greater a man, because where it was due, in the case of the sons of Osvif, to wit, he drove matters home to the very bone, but spared Bolli for the sake of their kinship. Olaf thanked men well for the help they had afforded him. By Olaf's counsel Bolli bought the land at Tongue. It is told that Olaf lived three winters after Kjartan was slain. After he was dead his sons shared the inheritance he left behind. Halldor took over the manor of Herdholt. Thorgerd, their mother, lived with Halldor; she was most hatefully-minded towards Bolli, and thought the reward he paid for his fostering a bitter one.

CHAPTER LII
The Killing of Thorkell of Goat's Peak

In the spring Bolli and Gudrun set up householding at Sælingsdale-Tongue, and it soon became a stately one. Bolli and Gudrun begat a son. To that boy a name was given, and he was called Thorleik; he was early a very fine lad, and a right nimble one. Halldor Olafson lived at Herdholt, as has before been written, and he was in most matters at the head of his brothers. The spring that Kjartan was slain Thorgerd Egil's daughter placed a lad, as kin to her, with Thorkell of Goat-Peaks, and the lad herded sheep there through the summer. Like other people he was much grieved over Kjartan's death. He could never speak of Kjartan if Thorkell was near, for he always spoke ill of him, and said he had been a "white" man and of no heart; he often mimicked how Kjartan had taken his death-wound. The lad took this very ill, and went to Herdholt and told Halldor and Thorgerd and begged them to take him in. Thorgerd bade him remain in his service till the winter. The lad said he had no strength to bear being there any longer. "And you would not ask this of me if you knew what heart-burn I suffer from all this." Then Thorgerd's heart turned at the tale of his grief, and she said that as far as she was concerned, she would make a place for him there. Halldor said, "Give no heed to this lad, he is not worth taking in earnest." Then Thorgerd answered, "The lad is of little account," says she, "but Thorkell has behaved evilly in every way in this matter, for he knew of the ambush the men of Laugar laid for Kjartan, and would not warn him, but made fun and sport of their dealings together, and has since said many unfriendly things about the matter; but it seems a matter far beyond you brothers ever to seek revenge where odds are against you, now that you cannot pay out for their doings such scoundrels as Thorkell is." Halldor answered little to that, but bade Thorgerd do what she liked about the lad's service. A few days after Halldor rode from home, he and sundry other men together. He went to Goat-Peaks, and surrounded Thorkell's house. Thorkell was led out and slain, and he met his death with the utmost cowardice. Halldor allowed no plunder, and they went home when this was done. Thorgerd was well pleased over this deed, and thought this reminder better than none. That summer all was quiet, so to speak, and yet there was the greatest ill-will between the sons of Olaf and Bolli. The brothers bore themselves in the most unyielding manner towards Bolli, while he gave in to his kinsmen in all matters as long as he did not lower himself in any way by so doing, for he was a very proud man. Bolli had many followers and lived richly, for there was no lack of money. Steinthor, Olaf's son, lived in Danastead in Salmon-river-Dale. He had for wife Thurid, Asgeir's daughter, who had before been married to Thorkell Kuggi. Their son was Steinthor, who was called "Stone-grig."

CHAPTER LIII

Thorgerd's Egging, A.D. 1007

The next winter after the death of Olaf Hoskuldson, Thorgerd, Egil's daughter, sent word to her son Steinthor that he should come and meet her. When the mother and son met she told him she wished to go up west to Saurby, and see her friend Aud. She told Halldor to come too. They were five together, and Halldor followed his mother. They went on till they came to a place in front of the homestead of Sælingsdale Tongue. Then Thorgerd turned her horse towards the house and asked, "What is this place called?" Halldor answered, "You ask this, mother, not because you don't know it. This place is called Tongue." "Who lives here?" said she. He answered, "You know that, mother." Thorgerd said and snorted, "I know that well enough," she said. "Here lives Bolli, the slayer of your brother, and marvellously unlike your noble kindred you turn out in that you will not avenge such a brother as Kjartan was; never would Egil, your mother's father, have behaved in such a manner; and a piteous thing it is to have dolts for sons; indeed, I think it would have suited you better if you had been your father's daughter and had married. For here, Halldor, it comes to the old saw: 'No stock without a duffer,' and this is the ill-luck of Olaf I see most clearly, how he blundered in begetting his sons. This I would bring home to you, Halldor," says she, "because you look upon yourself as being the foremost among your brothers. Now we will turn back again, for all my errand here was to put you in mind of this, lest you should have forgotten it already." Then Halldor answered, "We shall not put it down as your fault, mother, if this should slip out of our minds." By way of answer Halldor had few words to say about this, but his heart swelled with wrath towards Bolli. The winter now passed and summer came, and time glided on towards the Thing. Halldor and his brothers made it known that they will ride to the Thing. They rode with a great company, and set up the booth Olaf had owned. The Thing was quiet, and no tidings to tell of it. There were at the Thing from the north the Willowdale men, the sons of Gudmund Solmundson. Bardi Gudmundson was then eighteen winters old; he was a great and strong man. The sons of Olaf asked Bardi, their nephew, to go home with them, and added many pressing words to the invitation. Hall, the son of Gudmund, was not in Iceland then. Bardi took up their bidding gladly, for there was much love between those kinsmen. Bardi rode west from the Thing with the sons of Olaf. They came home to Herdholt, and Bardi tarried the rest of the summer time.

CHAPTER LIV

Halldor prepares to avenge Kjartan

Now Halldor told Bardi in secret that the brothers had made up their minds to set on Bolli, for they could no longer withstand the taunts of their mother. "And we will not conceal from you, kinsman Bardi, that what mostly lay behind the invitation to you was this, that we wished to have your help and fellowship." Then Bardi answered, "That will be a matter ill spoken of, to break the peace on one's own kinsmen, and on the other hand it seems to me nowise an easy thing to set on Bolli. He has many men about him and is himself the best of fighters, and is not at a loss for wise counsel with Gudrun and Osvif at his side. Taking all these matters together they seem to me nowise easy to overcome."

Halldor said, "There are things we stand more in need of than to make the most of the difficulties of this affair. Nor have I broached it till I knew that it must come to pass, that we make earnest of wreaking revenge on Bolli. And I hope, kinsman, you will not withdraw from doing this journey with us." Bardi answered, "I know you do not think it likely that I will draw back, neither do I desire to do so if I see that I cannot get you to give it up yourselves." "There you do your share in the matter honourably," said Halldor, "as was to be looked for from you." Bardi said they must set about it with care. Halldor said he had heard that Bolli had sent his house-carles from home, some north to Ramfirth to meet a ship and some out to Middlefell strand. "It is also told me that Bolli is staying at the out-dairy in Sælingsdale with no more than the house-carles who are doing the haymaking. And it seems to me we shall never have a better chance of seeking a meeting with Bolli than now." So this then Halldor and Bardi settled between them. There was a man named Thorstein the Black, a wise man and wealthy; he lived at Hundidale in the Broadfirth-Dales; he had long been a friend of Olaf Peacock's. A sister of Thorstein was called Solveig; she was married to a man who was named Helgi, who was son of Hardbein. Helgi was a very tall and strong man, and a great sailor; he had lately come to Iceland, and was staying with his brother-in-law Thorstein. Halldor sent word to Thorstein the Black and Helgi his brother-in-law, and when they were come to Herdholt Halldor told them what he was about, and how he meant to carry it out, and asked them to join in the journey with him. Thorstein showed an utter dislike of this undertaking, saying, "It is the most heinous thing that you kinsmen should go on killing each other off like that; and now there are but few men left in your family equal to Bolli." But though Thorstein spoke in this wise it went for nought. Halldor sent word to Lambi, his father's brother, and when he came and met Halldor he told him what he was about, and Lambi urged hard that this should be carried out. Goodwife Thorgerd also egged them on eagerly to make an earnest of their journey, and said she should never look upon Kjartan as avenged until Bolli paid for him with his life. After this they got ready for the journey. In this raid there were the four sons of Olaf and the fifth was Bardi. There were the sons of Olaf, Halldor, Steinthor, Helgi, and Hoskuld, but Bardi was Gudmund's son. Lambi was the sixth, the seventh was Thorstein, and the eighth Helgi, his brother-in-law, the ninth An Brushwood-belly. Thorgerd betook herself also to the raid with them; but they set themselves against it, and said that such were no journeys for women. She said she would go indeed, "For so much I know of you, my sons, that whetting is what you want." They said she must have her own way.

CHAPTER LV
The Death of Bolli

After that they rode away from home out of Herdholt, the nine of them together, Thorgerd making the tenth. They rode up along the foreshore and so to Lea-shaws during the early part of the night. They did not stop before they got to Sælingsdale in the early morning tide. There was a thick wood in the valley at that time. Bolli was there in the out-dairy, as Halldor had heard. The dairy stood near the river at the place now called Bolli's-tofts. Above the dairy there is a large hill-rise stretching all the way down to Stack-gill. Between the mountain slope above and the hill-rise there is a wide meadow called Barni; it was there Bolli's house-carles were working. Halldor and his companions rode across Ran-meads unto Oxgrove, and thence above Hammer-Meadow, which was right against the dairy. They knew there were many men at the dairy, so they got off their horses with a view to biding the time when the men should leave the dairy for their work. Bolli's shepherd went early that morning after the flocks up into the mountain side, and from there he saw the men in the wood as well as the horses tied up, and misdoubted that those who went on the sly in this manner would be no men of peace. So forthwith he makes for the dairy by the straightest cut in order to tell Bolli that men were come there. Halldor was a man of keen sight. He saw how that a man was running down the mountain side and making for the dairy. He said to his companions that "That must surely be Bolli's shepherd, and he must have seen our coming; so we must go and meet him, and let him take no news to the dairy." They did as he bade them. An Brushwood-belly went the fastest of them and overtook the man, picked him up, and flung him down. Such was that fall that the lad's back-bone was broken. After that they rode to the dairy. Now the dairy was divided into two parts, the sleeping-room and the byre. Bolli had been early afoot in the morning ordering the men to their work, and had lain down again to sleep when the house-carles went away. In the dairy therefore there were left the two, Gudrun and Bolli. They awoke with the din when they got off their horses, and they also heard them talking as to who should first go on to the dairy to set on Bolli. Bolli knew the voice of Halldor, as well as that of sundry more of his followers. Bolli spoke to Gudrun, and bade her leave the dairy and go away, and said that their meeting would not be such as would afford her much pastime. Gudrun said she thought such things alone would befall there worthy of tidings as she might be allowed to look upon, and held that she would be of no hurt to Bolli by taking her stand near to him. Bolli said that in this matter he would have his way, and so it was that Gudrun went out of the dairy; she went down over the brink to a brook that ran there, and began to wash some linen. Bolli was now alone in the dairy; he took his weapon, set his helm on his head, held a shield before him, and had his sword, Footbiter, in his hand: he had no mail coat. Halldor and his followers were talking to each other outside as to how they should set to work, for no one was very eager to go into the dairy. Then said An Brushwood-belly, "There are men here in this train nearer in kinship to Kjartan than I am, but not one there will be in whose mind abides more steadfastly than in mine the event when Kjartan lost his life. When I was being brought more dead than alive home to Tongue, and Kjartan lay slain, my one thought was that I would gladly do Bolli some harm whenever I should get the chance. So I shall be the first to go into the dairy." Then Thorstein the Black answered, "Most valiantly is that spoken; but it would be wiser not to plunge headlong beyond heed, so let us go warily now, for Bolli will not be standing quiet when he is beset; and however underhanded he may be where he is, you may make up your mind for a brisk defence on his part, strong and skilled at arms as he is. He also has a sword that for a weapon is a trusty one." Then An went into the dairy hard and swift, and held his shield over his head, turning forward the narrower part of it. Bolli dealt him a blow with Footbiter, and cut off the tail-end of the shield, and clove An through the head down to the shoulder, and forthwith he gat his death. Then Lambi went in; he held his shield before him, and a drawn sword in his hand. In the nick of time Bolli pulled Footbiter out of the wound, whereat his shield veered aside so as to lay him open to attack. So Lambi made a thrust at him in the thigh, and a great wound that was. Bolli hewed in return, and struck Lambi's shoulder, and the sword flew down along the side of him, and he was rendered forthwith unfit to fight, and never after that time for the rest of his life was his arm any more use to him. At this brunt Helgi, the son of Hardbien, rushed in with a spear, the head of which was an ell long, and the shaft bound with iron. When Bolli saw that he cast away his sword, and took his shield in both hands, and went towards the dairy door to meet Helgi. Helgi thrust at Bolli with the spear right through the shield and through him. Now Bolli leaned up against the dairy wall, and the men rushed into the dairy, Halldor and his brothers, to wit, and Thorgerd went into the dairy as well. Then spoke Bolli, "Now it is safe, brothers, to come nearer than hitherto you have done," and said he weened that defence now would be but short. Thorgerd answered his speech, and said there was no need to shrink from dealing unflinchingly with Bolli, and bade them "walk between head and trunk." Bolli stood still against the dairy wall, and held tight to him his kirtle lest his inside should come out. Then Steinthor Olafson leapt at Bolli, and hewed at his neck with a large axe just above his shoulders, and forthwith his head flew off. Thorgerd bade him "hale enjoy hands," and said that Gudrun would have now a while a red hair to trim for Bolli. After that they went out of the dairy. Gudrun now came up from the brook, and spoke to Halldor, and asked for tidings of what had befallen in their dealings with Bolli. They told her all that had happened. Gudrun was dressed in a kirtle of "rám"-stuff,[7] and a tight-fitting woven bodice, a high bent coif on her head, and she had tied a scarf round her with dark-blue stripes, and fringed at the ends. Helgi Hardbienson went up to Gudrun, and caught hold of the scarf end, and wiped the blood off the spear with it, the same spear with which he had thrust Bolli through. Gudrun glanced at him and smiled slightly. Then Halldor said, "That was blackguardly and gruesomely done." Helgi bade him not be angry about it, "For I am minded to think that under this scarf end abides undoer of my life." Then they took their horses and rode away. Gudrun went along with them talking with them for a while, and then she turned back.

[7] Unknown what stuff.

CHAPTER LVI

Bolli Bollison is born, A.D. 1008

The followers of Halldor now fell a-talking how that Gudrun must think but little of the slaying of Bolli, since she had seen them off chatting and talked to them altogether as if they had done nothing that she might take to heart. Then Halldor answered, "That is not my feeling, that Gudrun thinks little of Bolli's death; I think the reason of her seeing us off with a chat was far rather, that she wanted to gain a thorough knowledge as to who the men were who had partaken in this journey. Nor is it too much said of Gudrun that in all mettle of mind and heart she is far above other women. Indeed, it is only what might be looked for that Gudrun should take sorely to heart the death of Bolli, for, truth to tell, in such men as was Bolli there is the greatest loss, though we kinsmen, bore not about the good luck to live in peace together." After that they rode home to Herdholt. These tidings spread quickly far and wide and were thought startling, and at Bolli's death there was

Anonymous

the greatest grief. Gudrun sent straightway men to Snorri the Priest, for Osvif and she thought that all their trust was where Snorri was. Snorri started quickly at the bidding of Gudrun and came to Tongue with sixty men, and a great ease to Gudrun's heart his coming was. He offered her to try to bring about a peaceful settlement, but Gudrun was but little minded on behalf of Thorleik to agree to taking money for the slaughter of Bolli. "It seems to me, Snorri, that the best help you can afford me," she said, "is to exchange dwellings with me, so that I be not next-door neighbour to the Herdholtings." At that time Snorri had great quarrels with the dwellers at Eyr, but said he would do this for the sake of his friendship with Gudrun. "Yet, Gudrun, you will have to stay on this year at Tongue." Snorri then made ready to go away, and Gudrun gave him honourable gifts. And now Snorri rides away, and things went pretty quietly on that year. The next winter after the killing of Bolli Gudrun gave birth to a child; it was a male, and he was named Bolli. He was at an early age both big and goodly, and Gudrun loved him very much. Now as the winter passed by and the spring came the bargain took place which had been bespoken in that Snorri and Gudrun changed lands. Snorri went to Tongue and lived there for the rest of his life, and Gudrun went to Holyfell, she and Osvif, and there they set up a stately house. There Thorleik and Bolli, the sons of Gudrun, grew up. Thorleik was four years old at the time when Bolli his father was slain.

CHAPTER LVII
About Thorgils Hallason, A.D. 1018

There was a man named Thorgils Hallason; he was known by his mother's name, as she lived longer than his father, whose name was Snorri, son of Alf o' Dales. Halla, Thorgil's mother, was daughter of Gest Oddliefson. Thorgils lived in Horddale at a place called Tongue. Thorgils was a man great and goodly of body, the greatest swaggerer, and was spoken of as one of no fairness in dealings with men. Between him and Snorri the Priest there was often little love lost, for Snorri found Thorgils both meddlesome and flaunting of demeanour. Thorgils would get up many errands on which to go west into the countryside, and always came to Holyfell offering Gudrun to look after her affairs, but she only took the matter quietly and made but little of it all. Thorgils asked for her son Thorleik to go home with him, and he stayed for the most part at Tongue and learnt law from Thorgils, for he was a man most skilled in law-craft. At that time Thorkell Eyjolfson was busy in trading journeys; he was a most renowned man, and of high birth, and withal a great friend of Snorri the Priest. He would always be staying with Thorstein Kuggison, his kinsman, when he was out here (in Iceland). Now, one time when Thorkell had a ship standing up in Vadil, on Bardistrand, it befell, in Burgfirth, that the son of Eid of Ridge was killed by the sons of Helga from Kropp. Grim was the name of the man who had done the manslaughter, and that of his brother was Nial, who was drowned in White-river; a little later on Grim was outlawed to the woods because of the manslaughter, and he lay out in the mountains whilst he was under the award of outlawry. He was a great man and strong. Eid was then very old when this happened, so the case was not followed up. People blamed Thorkell very much that he did not see matters righted. The next spring when Thorkell had got his ship ready he went south across Broadfirth-country, and got a horse there and rode alone, not stopping in his journey till he got as far as Ridge, to Eid, his kinsman. Eid took him in joyfully. Thorkell told him his errand, how that he would go and find Grim his outlaw, and asked Eid if he knew at all where his lair was. Eid answered, "I am nowise eager for this; it seems to me you have much to risk as to how the journey may speed, seeing that you will have to deal with a man of Hel's strength, such as Grim. But if you will go, then start with many men, so that you may have it all your own way." "That to me is no prowess," said Thorkell, "to draw together a great company against one man. But what I wish is, that you would lend me the sword Skofnung, for then I ween I shall be able to overcome a mere runagate, be he never so mighty a man of his hands." "You must have your way in this," said Eid, "but it will not come to me unawares, if, some day, you should come to rue this wilfulness. But inasmuch as you will have it that you are doing this for my sake, what you ask for shall not be withheld, for I think Skofnung well bestowed if you bear it. But the nature of the sword is such that the sun must not shine upon its hilt, nor must it be drawn if a woman should be near. If a man be wounded by the sword the hurt may not be healed, unless the healing-stone that goes with the sword be rubbed thereon." Thorkell said he would pay careful heed to this, and takes over the sword, asking Eid to point out to him the way to where Grim might have his lair. Eid said he was most minded to think that Grim had his lair north on Twodays-Heath by the Fishwaters. Then Thorkell rode northward upon the heath the way which Eid did point out to him, and when he had got a long way onward over the heath he saw near some great water a hut, and makes his way for it.

CHAPTER LVIII

Thorkell and Grim, and their Voyage Abroad

Thorkell now comes to the hut, he sees where a man is sitting by the water at the mouth of a brook, where he was line-fishing, and had a cloak over his head. Thorkell leapt off his horse and tied it up under the wall of the hut. Then he walks down to the water to where the man was sitting. Grim saw the shadow of a man cast on the water, and springs up at once. By then Thorkell had got very nearly close up to him, and strikes at him. The blow caught him on his arm just above the wolf-joint (the wrist), but that was not a great wound. Grim sprang forthwith upon Thorkell, and they seized each other wrestling-wise, and speedily the odds of strength told, and Thorkell fell and Grim on the top of him. Then Grim asked who this man might be. Thorkell said that did not at all matter to him. Grim said, "Now things have befallen otherwise than you must have thought they would, for now your life will be in my power." Thorkell said he would not pray for peace for himself, "for lucklessly I have taken this in hand." Grim said he had had enough mishaps for him to give this one the slip, "for to you some other fate is ordained than that of dying at this our meeting, and I shall give you your life, while you repay me in whatever kind you please." Now they both stand up and walk home to the hut. Thorkell sees that Grim was growing faint from loss of blood, so he took Skofnung's-stone and rubbed it on, and ties it to the arm of Grim, and it took forthwith all smarting pain and swelling out of the wound. They stayed there that night. In the morning Thorkell got ready to go away, and asked if Grim would go with him. He said that sure enough that was his will. Thorkell turns straightway westward without going to meet Eid, nor halted he till he came to Sælingsdale Tongue. Snorri the Priest welcomes him with great blitheness. Thorkell told him that his journey had sped lucklessly. Snorri said it had turned out well, "for Grim looks to me a man endowed with good luck, and my will is that you make matters up with him handsomely. But now, my friend, I would like to counsel you to leave off trade-journeyings, and to settle down and marry, and become a chief as befits your high birth." Thorkell answered, "Often your counsels have stood me in good stead," and he asked if Snorri had bethought him of the woman he should woo. Snorri answers, "You must woo the woman who is the best match for you, and that woman is Gudrun, Osvif's daughter." Thorkell said it was true that a marriage with her would be an honourable one. "But," says he, "I think her fierce heart and reckless-mindedness weigh heavily, for she will want to have her husband, Bolli, avenged. Besides, it is said that on this matter there is some understanding between her and Thorgils Hallason, and it may be that this will not be altogether to his liking. Otherwise, Gudrun pleases me well." Snorri said, "I will undertake to see that no harm shall come to you from Thorgils; but as to the revenge for Bolli, I am rather in hopes that concerning that matter some change will have befallen before these seasons (this year) are out." Thorkell answered, "It may be that these be no empty words you are speaking now. But as to the revenge of Bolli, that does not seem to me more likely to happen now than it did a while ago, unless into that strife some of the greater men may be drawn." Snorri said, "I should be well pleased to see you go abroad once more this summer, to let us see then what happens." Thorkell said so it should be, and they parted, leaving matters where they now stood. Thorkell went west over Broadfirth-country to his ship. He took Grim with him abroad. They had a good summer-voyage, and came to the south of Norway. Then Thorkell said to Grim, "You know how the case stands, and what things happened to bring about our acquaintance, so I need say nothing about that matter; but I would fain that it should turn out better than at one time it seemed likely it would. I have found you a valiant man, and for that reason I will so part from you, as if I had never borne you any grudge. I will give you as much merchandise as you need in order to be able to join the guild of good merchants. But do not settle down here in the north of this land, for many of Eid's kinsmen are about on trading journeys who bear you heavy ill-will." Grim thanked him for these words, and said he could never have thought of asking for as much as he offered. At parting Thorkell gave to Grim a goodly deal of merchandise, and many men said that this deed bore the stamp of a great man. After that Grim went east in the Wick, settled there, and was looked upon as a mighty man of his ways; and therewith comes to an end what there is to be told about Grim. Thorkell was in Norway through the winter, and was thought a man of much account; he was exceeding wealthy in chattels. Now this matter must be left for a while, and the story must be taken up out in Iceland, so let us hear what matters befell there for tidings to be told of whilst Thorkell was abroad.

CHAPTER LIX
Gudrun demands Revenge for Bolli, A.D. 1019

In "Twinmonth" that summer Gudrun, Osvif's daughter, went from home up into the Dales. She rode to Thickshaw; and at this time Thorleik was sometimes at

Thickshaw with the sons of Armod Halldor and Ornolf, and sometimes Tongue with Thorgils. The same night Gudrun sent a man to Snorri Godi saying that she wished to meet him without fail the next day. Snorri got ready at once and rode with one other man until he came to Hawkdale-river; on the northern side of that river stands a crag by the river called Head, within the land of Lea-Shaw. At this spot Gudrun had bespoken that she and Snorri should meet. They both came there at one and the same time. With Gudrun there was only one man, and he was Bolli, son of Bolli; he was now twelve years old, but fulfilled of strength and wits was he, so much so, that many were they who were no whit more powerful at the time of ripe manhood; and now he carried Footbiter. Snorri and Gudrun now fell to talking together; but Bolli and Snorri's follower sat on the crag and watched people travelling up and down the countryside. When Snorri and Gudrun had asked each other for news, Snorri inquired on what errand he was called, and what had come to pass lately that she sent him word so hurriedly. Gudrun said, "Truth to tell, to me is ever fresh the event which I am about to bring up, and yet it befell twelve years ago; for it is about the revenge of Bolli I wish to speak, and it ought not to take you unawares. I have called it to your mind from time to time. I must also bring this home to you that to this end you have promised me some help if I but waited patiently, but now I think it past hope that you will give any heed to our case. I have now waited as long as my temper would hold out, and I must have whole-hearted counsel from you as to where this revenge is to be brought home." Snorri asked what she chiefly had in her mind's eye. Gudrun said, "It is my wish that all Olaf's sons should not go scatheless." Snorri said he must forbid any onset on the men who were not only of the greatest account in the countryside, but also closely akin to those who stand nearest to back up the revenge; and it is high time already that these family feuds come to an end. Gudrun said, "Then Lambi shall be set upon and slain; for then he, who is the most eager of them for evil, would be put out of the way." Snorri said, "Lambi is guilty enough that he should be slain; but I do not think Bolli any the more revenged for that; for when at length peace should come to be settled, no such disparity between them would be acknowledged as ought to be due to Bolli when the manslaughters of both should come up for award." Gudrun spoke, "It may be that we shall not get our right out of the men of Salmon-river-Dale, but some one shall pay dear for it, whatever dale he may dwell in. So we shall turn upon Thorstein the Black, for no one has taken a worse share in these matters than he." Snorri spake, "Thorstein's guilt against you is the same as that of the other men who joined in the raid against Bolli, but did not wound him. But you leave such men to sit by in quiet on whom it seems to me revenge wrought would be revenge indeed, and who, moreover, did take the life of Bolli, such as was Helgi Hardbienson." Gudrun said, "That is true, but I cannot be sure that, in that case, all these men against whom I have been stirring up enmity will sit quietly by doing nothing." Snorri said, "I see a good way to hinder that. Lambi and Thorstein shall join the train of your sons, and that is a fitting ransom for those fellows, Lambi and Thorstein; but if they will not do this, then I shall not plead for them to be let off, whatever penalty you may be pleased to put upon them." Gudrun spake: "How shall we set about getting these men that you have named to go on this journey?" Snorri spake: "That is the business of them who are to be at the head of the journey." Gudrun spake: "In this we must have your foresight as to who shall rule the journey and be the leader." Then Snorri smiled and said, "You have chosen your own men for it." Gudrun replied, "You are speaking of Thorgils." Snorri said so it was. Gudrun spake: "I have talked the matter over already with Thorgils, but now it is as good as all over, for he gave me the one choice, which I would not even look at. He did not back out of undertaking to avenge Bolli, if he could have me in marriage in return; but that is past all hope, so I cannot ask him to go this journey." Snorri spoke: "On this I will give you a counsel, for I do not begrudge Thorgils this journey. You shall promise marriage to him, yet you shall do it in language of this double meaning, that of men in this land you will marry none other but Thorgils, and that shall be holden to, for Thorkell Eyjolfson is not, for the time being, in this land, but it is he whom I have in my mind's eye for this marriage." Gudrun spake: "He will see through this trick." Snorri answered, "Indeed he will not see through it, for Thorgils is better known for foolhardiness than wits. Make the covenant with but few men for witnesses, and let Halldor, his foster-brother, be there, but not Ornolf, for he has more wits, and lay the blame on me if this will not work out." After that they parted their talk and each bade the other farewell, Snorri riding home, and Gudrun unto Thickshaw. The next morning Gudrun rode from Thickshaw and her sons with her, and when they ride west along Shawstrand they see that men are riding after them. They ride on quickly and catch them up swiftly, and lo, there was Thorgils Hallason. They greeted each other well, and now ride on in the day all together, out to Holyfell.

CHAPTER LX
The Egging of Gudrun

A few nights after Gudrun had come home she called her sons to her to have a talk with them in her orchard; and when they were come there they saw how there were lying out some linen clothes, a shirt and linen breeches, and they were much stained with blood. Then spake Gudrun: "These same clothes you see here cry to you for your father's revenge. I will not say many words on this matter, for it is past hope that you will heed an egging-on by words alone if you bring not home to your minds such hints and reminders as these." The brothers were much startled as this, and at what Gudrun had to say; but yet this way they made answer that they had been too young to seek for revenge without a leader; they knew not, they felt, how to frame a counsel for themselves or others either. "But we might well bear in mind what we have lost." Gudrun said, "They would be likely to give more thought to horse-fights or sports." After that they went away. The next night the brothers could not sleep. Thorgils got aware of this, and asked them what was the matter. They told him all the talk they had had with their mother, and this withal that they could no longer bear their grief or their mother's taunts. "We will seek revenge," said Bolli, "now that we brothers have come to so ripe an age that men will be much after us if we do not take the matter in hand." The next day Gudrun and Thorgils had a talk together, and Gudrun started speaking in this wise: "I am given to think, Thorgils, that my sons brook it ill to sit thus quietly on any longer without seeking revenge for their father's death. But what mostly has delayed the matter hitherto is that up to now I deemed Thorleik and Bolli too young to be busy in taking men's lives. But need enough there has been to call this to mind a good long time before this. Thorgils answered, "There is no use in your talking this matter over with me, because you have given a flat denial to 'walking with me' (marrying me). But I am in just the same frame of mind as I have been before, when we have had talks about this matter. If I can marry you, I shall not think twice about killing either or both of the two who had most to do with the murder of Bolli." Gudrun spoke: "I am given to think that to Thorleik no man seems as well fitted as you to be the leader if anything is to be done in the way of deeds of hardihood. Nor is it a matter to be hidden from you that the lads are minded to go for Helgi Hardbienson the 'Bareserk,' who sits at home in his house in Skorridale misdoubting himself of nothing." Thorgils spake: "I never care whether he is called Helgi or by any other name, for neither in Helgi nor in any one else do I deem I have an over-match in strength to deal with. As far as I am concerned, the last word on this matter is now spoken if you promise before witnesses to marry me when, together with your sons, I have wreaked the revenge." Gudrun said she would fulfil all she should agree to, even though such agreement were come to before few men to witness it. "And," said she, "this then we shall settle to have done." Gudrun bade be called thither Halldor, Thorgils' foster-brother, and her own sons. Thorgils bade that Ornolf should also be with them. Gudrun said there was no need of that, "For I am more doubtful of Ornolf's faithfulness to you than I think you are yourself." Thorgils told her to do as she liked. Now the brothers come and meet Gudrun and Thorgils, Halldor being also at the parley with them. Gudrun now sets forth to them that "Thorgils has said he will be the leader in this raid against Helgi Hardbienson, together with my sons, for revenge of Bolli, and Thorgils has bargained in return for this undertaking to get me for wife. Now I avow, with you to witness, that I promise this to Thorgils, that of men in this land I shall marry none but him, and I do not purpose to go and marry in any other land." Thorgils thought that this was binding enough, and did not see through it. And now they broke up their talk. This counsel is now fully settled that Thorgils must betake himself to this journey. He gets ready to leave Holyfell, and with him the sons of Gudrun, and they rode up into the Dales and first to the homestead at Tongue.

CHAPTER LXI

Of Thorstein the Black and Lambi

The next Lord's day a leet was held, and Thorgils rode thither with his company, Snorri Godi was not at the leet, but there was a great many people together. During the day Thorgils fetched up Thorstein the Black for a talk with him, and said, "As you know, you were one in the onset by the sons of Olaf when Bolli was slain, and you have made no atonement for your guilt to his sons. Now although a long time is gone since those things befell, I think their mind has not given the slip to the men who were in that raid. Now, these brothers look in this light upon the matter, that it beseem them least, by reason of kinship, to seek revenge on the sons of Olaf; and so the brothers purpose to turn for revenge upon Helgi Hardbienson, for he gave Bolli his death-wound. So we ask this of you, Thorstein, that you join in this journey with the brothers, and thus purchase for yourself peace and good-will." Thorstein replied, "It beseems me not at all to deal in treason with Helgi, my brother-in-law, and I would far rather purchase my peace with as much money as it would be to their honour to take." Thorgils said, "I think it is but little to the mind of the brothers to do aught herein for their own gain; so you need not hide it away from yourself, Thorstein, that at your hands there lie two choices: either to betake yourself to this journey, or to undergo the harshest of treatments from them as soon as they may bring it about; and my will is, that you take this choice in spite of the ties that bind you to Helgi; for when men find themselves in such straits, each must look after himself." Thorstein spake: "Will the same choice be given to more of the men who are charged with guilt by the sons of Bolli?" Thorgils answered, "The same choice will be put to Lambi." Thorstein said he would think better of it if he was not left the only one in this plight. After that Thorgils called Lambi to come and meet him, and bade Thorstein listen to their talk. He said, "I wish to talk over with you, Lambi, the same matter that I have set forth to Thorstein; to wit, what amends you are willing to make to the sons of Bolli for the charges of guilt which they have against you? For it has been told me as true that you wrought wounds on Bolli; but besides that, you are heavily guilt-beset, in that you urged it hard that Bolli should be slain; yet, next to the sons of Olaf, you were entitled to some excuse in the matter." Then Lambi asked what he would be asked to do. Thorgils said the same choice would be put to him as to Thorstein, "to join with the brothers in this journey." Lambi said, "This I think an evil price of peace and a dastardly one, and I have no mind for this journey." Then said Thorstein, "It is not the only thing open to view, Lambi, to cut so quickly away from this journey; for in this matter great men are concerned, men of much worth, moreover, who deem that they have long had to put up with an unfair lot in life. It is also told me of Bolli's sons that they are likely to grow into men of high mettle, and that they are exceeding masterful; but the wrong they have to wreak is great. We cannot think of escaping from making some amends after such awful deeds. I shall be the most open to people's reproaches for this by reason of my alliance with Helgi. But I think most people are given to 'setting all aside for life,' and the trouble on hand that presses hardest must first be thrust out of the way." Lambi said, "It is easy to see what you urge to be done, Thorstein; and I think it well befitting that you have your own way in this matter, if you think that is the only way you see open, for ours has been a long partnership in great troubles. But I will have this understood if I do go into this business, that my kinsmen, the sons of Olaf, shall be left in peace if the revenge on Helgi shall be carried out." Thorgils agreed to this on behalf of the brothers. So now it was settled that Lambi and Thorstein should betake themselves to the journey with Thorgils; and they bespoke it between them that they should come early on the third day (Tuesday)[8] to Tongue, in Hord-Dale. After that they parted. Thorgils rode home that evening to Tongue. Now passes on the time within which it was bespoken they should come to Tongue. In the morning of the third day (Tuesday), before sunrise, Thorstein and Lambi came to Tongue, and Thorgils gave them a cheerful welcome.

[8] The agreement was made on a Sunday.

CHAPTER LXII
Thorgils and his Followers leave Home

Thorgils got himself ready to leave home, and they all rode up along Hord-Dale, ten of them together. There Thorgils Hallason was the leader of the band. In

Anonymous

that train the sons of Bolli, Thorleik and Bolli, and Thord the Cat, their brother, was the fourth, the fifth was Thorstein the Black, the sixth Lambi, the seventh and eighth Haldor and Ornolf, the ninth Svein, and the tenth Hunbogi. Those last were the sons of Alf o' Dales. They rode on their way up to Sweeping-Pass, and across Long-waterdale, and then right across Burgfirth. They rode across North-river at Isleford, but across White-river at Bankford, a short way down from the homestead of By. Then they rode over Reekdale, and over the neck of land to Skorradale, and so up through the wood in the neighbourhood of the farmstead of Water-Nook, where they got off their horses, as it was very late in the evening. The homestead of Water-Nook stands a short way from the lake on the south side of the river. Thorgils said to his followers that they must tarry there over night, "and I will go to the house and spy and see if Helgi be at home. I am told Helgi has at most times very few men with him, but that he is of all men the wariest of himself, and sleeps on a strongly made lock-bed." Thorgils' followers bade him follow his own foresight. Thorgils now changed his clothes, and took off his blue cloak, and slipped on a grey foul-weather overall. He went home to the house. When he was come near to the home-field fence he saw a man coming to meet him, and when they met Thorgils said, "You will think my questions strange, comrade, but whose am I come to in this countryside, and what is the name of this dwelling, and who lives here?" The man answered, "You must be indeed a wondrous fool and wit-bereft if you have not heard Helgi Hardbienson spoken of, the bravest of warriors, and a great man withal." Thorgils next asked how far Helgi took kindly to unknown people coming to see him, such as were in great need of help. He replied,

"In that matter, if truth is told, only good can be said of Helgi, for he is the most large-hearted of men, not only in giving harbour to comers, but also in all his high conduct otherwise." "Is Helgi at home now?" asked Thorgils; "I should like to ask him to take me in." The other then asks what matters he had on his hands. Thorgils answered, "I was outlawed this summer at the Thing, and I want to seek for myself the help of some such man as is a mighty one of his hands and ways, and I will in return offer my fellowship and service. So now you take me home to the house to see Helgi." "I can do that very well, to show you home," he said, "for you will be welcome to quarters for the night, but you will not see Helgi, for he is not at home." Then Thorgils asked where he was. The man answered, "He is at his out-dairy called Sarp." Thorgils asked where that was, and what men were with him. He said his son Hardbien was there, and two other men, both outlaws, whom he had taken in to shelter. Thorgils bade him show the nearest way to the dairy, "for I want to meet Helgi at once, when I can get to him and plead my errand to him." The house-carle did so and showed him the way, and after that they parted. Thorgils returned to the wood to his companions, and told them what he had found out about Helgi. "We must tarry here through the night, and not go to the dairy till to-morrow morning." They did as he ordained, and in the morning Thorgils and his band rode up through the wood till they were within a short way from the dairy. Then Thorgils bade them get off their horses and eat their morning meal, and so they did, and kept them for a while.

Anonymous

CHAPTER LXIII

The Description of his Enemies brought to Helgi

Now we must tell what happened at the dairy where Helgi was, and with him the men that were named before. In the morning Helgi told his shepherd to go through the woods in the neighbourhood of the dairy and look out for people passing, and take heed of whatever else he saw, to tell news of, "for my dreams have gone heavily to-night." The lad went even as Helgi told him. He was away awhile, and when he came back Helgi asked what he had seen to tell tidings of. He answered, "I have seen what I think is stuff for tidings." Helgi asked what that was. He said he had seen men, "and none so few either, and I think they must have come from beyond this countryside." Helgi spoke: "Where were they when you saw them, and what were they doing, or did you take heed of the manner of raiment, or their looks?" He answered, "I was not so much taken aback at the sight as not to mind those matters, for I knew you would ask about them." He also said they were but short away from the dairy, and were eating their morning meal. Helgi asked if they sat in a ring or side by side in a line. He said they sat in a ring, on their saddles. Helgi said, "Tell me now of their looks, and I will see if I can guess from what they looked like who the men may be." The lad said, "There sat a man in a stained saddle, in a blue cloak. He was great of growth, and valiant-looking; he was bald in front and somewhat 'tooth-bare.'" Helgi said, "I know that man clearly from your tale. There you have seen Thorgils Hallason, from west out of Hord-Dale. I wonder what he wants with us, the hero." The lad spoke: "Next to him sat a man in a gilded saddle; he had on a scarlet kirtle, and a gold ring on his arm, and a gold-embroidered fillet was tied round his head. This man had yellow hair, waving down over his shoulders; he was fair of hue, with a knot on his nose, which was somewhat turned up at the tip, with very fine eyes—blue-eyed and swift-eyed, and with a glance somewhat restless, broad-browed and full-cheeked; he had his hair cut across his forehead. He was well grown as to breadth of shoulders and depth of chest. He had very beautiful hands, and strong-looking arms. All his bearing was courteous, and, in a word, I have never seen a man so altogether doughty-looking. He was a young-looking man too, for his lips had grown no beard, but it seemed to me he was aged by grief." Then Helgi answers: "You have paid a careful heed, indeed, to this man, and of much account he must needs be; yet this man, I think, I have never seen, so I must make a guess at it who he is. There, I think, must have been Bolli Bollison, for I am told he has in him the makings of a man." Then the lad went on: "Next there sat a man on an enamelled saddle in a yellow green kirtle; he had a great finger ring on his hand. This man was most goodly to behold, and must still be young of age; his hair was auburn and most comely, and in every way he was most courtly." Helgi answers, "I think I know who this man is, of whom you have now been telling. He must be Thorleik Bollison, and a sharp and mindful man you are." The lad said again, "Next sat a young man; he was in a blue kirtle and black breeches, and his tunic tucked into them. This man was straight-faced, light of hair, with a goodly-featured face, slender and graceful." Helgi answered, "I know that man, for I must have seen him, though at a time when he was quite young; for it must be Thord Thordson, fosterling of Snorri the Priest. And a very courtly band they have, the Westfirthers. What is there yet to tell?" Then the lad said, "There sat a man on a Scotch saddle, hoary of beard and very sallow of hue, with black curly hair, somewhat unsightly and yet warrior like; he had on a grey pleated cape." Helgi said, "I clearly see who that man is; there is Lambi, the son of Thorbjorn, from Salmon-river-Dale; but I cannot think why he should be in the train of these brothers." The lad spake: "There sat a man on a pommelled saddle, and had on a blue cloak for an overall, with a silver ring on his arm; he was a farmer-looking sort of man and past the prime of life, with dark auburn long curly hair, and scars about his face." "Now the tale grows worse by much," said Helgi, "for there you must have seen Thorstein the Black, my brother-in-law; and a wondrous thing indeed I deem it, that he should be in this journey, nor would I ever offer him such a home-raid. But what more is there still to tell?" He answered, "Next there sat two men like each other to look upon, and might have been of middle age; most brisk they looked, red of hair, freckled of face, yet goodly to behold." Helgi said, "I can clearly understand who those men are. There are the sons of Armod, foster-brothers of Thorgils, Halldor and Ornolf. And a very trustworthy fellow you are. But have you now told the tale of all the men you saw?" He answered, "I have but little to add now. Next there sat a man and looked out of the circle; he was in a plate-corselet and had a steel cap on his head, with a brim a hand's breadth wide; he bore a shining axe on his shoulder, the edge of which must have measured an ell in length. This man was dark of hue, black-eyed, and most viking like." Helgi answered, "I clearly know this man from your tale. There has been Hunbogi the Strong, son of Alf o' Dales. But what I find so hard to make out is, what they want journeying with such a very picked company." The lad spoke again: "And still there sat a man next to this strong-looking one, dark auburn of hair, thick-faced and red-faced, heavy of brow, of a tall middle size." Helgi said, "You need not tell the tale further, there must have been Svein, son of Alf o' Dales, brother of Hunbogi. Now it would be as well not to stand shiftless in the face of these men; for near to my mind's foreboding it is, that they are minded to have a meeting with me or ever they leave this countryside; moreover, in this train there are men who would hold that it would have been but due and meet, though this our meeting should have taken a good long time before this. Now all the women who are in the dairy slip on quickly men's dress and take the horses that are about the dairy and ride as quickly as possible to the winter dwelling; it may be that those who are besetting us about will not know whether men or women be riding there; they need give us only a short respite till we bring men together here, and then it is not so certain on which side the outlook will be most hopeful." The women now rode off, four together. Thorgils misdoubts him lest news of their coming may have reached Helgi, and so bade the others take their horses and ride after them at their swiftest, and so they did, but before they mounted a man came riding up to them openly in all men's sight. He was small of growth and all on the alert, wondrously swift of glance and had a lively horse. This man greeted Thorgils in a familiar manner, and Thorgils asked him his name and family and also whence he had come. He said his name was Hrapp, and he was from Broadfirth on his mother's side. "And then I grew up, and I bear the name of Fight-Hrapp, with the name follows that I am nowise an easy one to deal with, albeit I am small of growth; but I am a southlander on my father's side, and have tarried in the south for some winters. Now this is a lucky chance, Thorgils, I have happened of you here, for I was minded to come and see you anyhow, even though I should find it a business somewhat hard to follow up. I have a trouble on hand; I have fallen out with my master, and have had from him a treatment none of the best; but it goes with the name, that I will stand no man such shameful mishandling, so I made an outset at him, but I guess I wounded him little or not at all, for I did not wait long enough to see for myself, but thought myself safe when I got on to the back of this nag, which I took from the goodman." Hrapp says much, but asks for few things; yet soon he got to know that they were minded to set on Helgi, and that pleased him very much, and he said they would not have to look for him behind.

CHAPTER LXIV
The Death of Helgi, A.D. 1019

Thorgils and his followers, as soon as they were on horseback, set off at a hard ride, and rode now out of the wood. They saw four men riding away from the dairy, and they rode very fast too. Seeing this, some of Thorgils' companions said they had better ride after them at their swiftest. Then said Thorleik Bollison, "We will just go to the dairy and see what men are there, for I think it less likely that these be Helgi and his followers. It seems to me that those are only women." A good many of them gainsaid this. Thorgils said that Thorleik should rule in the matter, for he knew that he was a very far-sighted man. They now turned to the dairy. Hrapp rode first, shaking the spear-stick he carried in his hand, and thrusting it forward in front of himself, and saying now was high time to try one's self. Helgi and his followers were not aware of anything till Thorgils and his company had surrounded the dairy. Helgi and his men shut the door, and seized their weapons. Hrapp leapt forthwith upon the roof of the dairy, and asked if old Reynard was in. Helgi answered, "You will come to take for granted that he who is here within is somewhat hurtful, and will know how to bite near the warren." And forthwith Helgi thrust his spear out through the window and through Hrapp, so that he fell dead to earth from the spear. Thorgils bade the others go heedfully and beware of mishaps, "for we have plenty of means wherewith to get the dairy into our power, and to overcome Helgi, placed as he is now, for I am given to think that here but few men are gathered together." The dairy was rigged over one roof-beam, resting on two gables so that the ends of the beam stuck out beyond each gable; there was a single turf thatch on the house, which had not yet grown together. Then Thorgils told some of his men to go to the beam ends, and pull them so hard that either the beam should break or else the rafters should slip in off it, but others were to guard the door lest those within should try and get out. Five they were, Helgi and his within the dairy—Hardbien, his son, to wit, he was twelve years old—his shepherd and two other men, who had come to him that summer, being outlaws—one called Thorgils, and the other Eyolf. Thorstein the Black and Svein, son of Alf o' Dales, stood before the door. The rest of the company were tearing the roof off the dairy. Hunbogi the Strong and the sons of Armod took one end of the beam, Thorgils, Lambi, and Gudrun's sons the other end. They now pull hard at the beam till it broke asunder in the middle; just at this Hardbien thrust a halberd out through where the door was broken, and the thrust struck the steel cap of Thorstein the Black and stuck in his forehead, and that was a very great wound.

Anonymous

Then Thorstein said, as was true, that there were men before them. Next Helgi leapt so boldly out of the door so that those nearest shrunk aback. Thorgils was standing near, and struck after him with a sword, and caught him on the shoulder and made a great wound. Helgi turned to meet him, and had a wood-axe in his hand, and said, "Still the old one will dare to look at and face weapons," and therewith he flung the axe at Thorgils, and the axe struck his foot, and a great wound that was. And when Bolli saw this he leapt forward at Helgi with Footbiter in his hand, and thrust Helgi through with it, and that was his death-blow. Helgi's followers leapt out of the dairy forthwith, and Hardbien with them. Thorleik Bollison turned against Eyolf, who was a strong man. Thorleik struck him with his sword, and it caught him on the leg above the knee and cut off his leg, and he fell to earth dead. Hunbogi the Strong went to meet Thorgils, and dealt a blow at him with an axe, and it struck the back of him, and cut him asunder in the middle. Thord Cat was standing near where Hardbien leapt out, and was going to set upon him straightway, but Bolli rushed forward when he saw it, and bade no harm be done to Hardbien. "No man shall do a dastard's work here, and Hardbien shall have life and limbs spared." Helgi had another son named Skorri. He was brought up at Gugland in Reekdale the southernmost.

CHAPTER LXV
Of Gudrun's Deceit

After these deeds Thorgils and his band rode away over the neck to Reekdale, where they declared these manslaughters on their hands. Then they rode the same way eastward as they had ridden from the west, and did not stop their journey till they came to Hord-

Dale. They now told the tidings of what had happened in their journey, which became most famous, for it was thought a great deed to have felled such a hero as was Helgi. Thorgils thanked his men well for the journey, and the sons of Bolli did the same. And now the men part who had been in Thorgils' train; Lambi rode west to Salmon-river-Dale, and came first to Herdholt and told his kinsmen most carefully the tidings of what had happened in Skorradale. They were very ill-pleased with his journey and laid heavy reproaches upon him, saying he had shown himself much more of the stock of Thorbjorn "Skrjup" than of that of Myrkjartan, the Irish king. Lambi was very angry at their talk, and said they knew but little of good manners in overwhelming him with reproaches, "for I have dragged you out of death," says he. After that they exchanged but few words, for both sides were yet more fulfilled of ill-will than before. Lambi now rode home to his manor. Thorgils Hallason rode out to Holyfell, and with him the sons of Gudrun and his foster-brothers Halldor and Ornolf. They came late in the evening to Holyfell, when all men were in bed. Gudrun rose up and bade the household get up and wait upon them. She went into the guest-chamber and greeted Thorgils and all the others, and asked for tidings. Thorgils returned Gudrun's greeting; he had laid aside his cloak and his weapons as well, and sat then up against the pillars. Thorgils had on a red-brown kirtle, and had round his waist a broad silver belt. Gudrun sat down on the bench by him. Then Thorgils said this stave—

"To Helgi's home a raid we led, Gave ravens corpse-repast to swallow, We dyed shield-wands[9] with blood all red, As Thorleik's lead our band did follow. And at our hands there perished three Keen helmet-stems,[10] accounted truly As worthies of the folk—and we Claim Bolli now's avenged full duly."

Gudrun asked them most carefully for the tidings of what had happened on their journey. Thorgils told her all she wished. Gudrun said the journey had been most stirringly carried out, and bade them have her thanks for it. After that food was set before them, and after they had eaten they were shown to bed, and slept the rest of the night. The next day Thorgils went to talk to Gudrun, and said, "Now the matter stands thus, as you know, Gudrun, that I have brought to an end the journey you bade me undertake, and I must claim that, in a full manly wise, that matter has been turned out of hand; you will also call to mind what you promised me in return, and I think I am now entitled to that prize." Then Gudrun said, "It is not such a long time since we last talked together that I should have forgotten what we said, and my only aim is to hold to all I agreed to as concerning you. Or what does your mind tell you as to how matters were bespoken between us?" Thorgils said she must remember that, and Gudrun answered, "I think I said that of men within this land I would marry none but you; or have you aught to say against that?" Thorgils said she was right. "That is well then," said Gudrun, "that our memory should be one and the same on this matter. And I will not put it off from you any longer, that I am minded to think that it is not fated to me to be your wife. Yet I deem that I fulfil to you all uttered words, though I marry Thorkell Eyjolfson, who at present is not in this land." Then Thorgils said, and flushed up very much, "Clearly I do see from whence that chill wave comes running, and from thence cold counsels have always come to me. I know that this is the counsel of Snorri the Priest." Thorgils sprang up from this talk and was very angry, and went to his followers and said he would ride away. Thorleik disliked very much that things should have taken such a turn as to go against Thorgils' will; but Bolli was at one with his mother's will herein. Gudrun said she would give Thorgils some good gifts and soften him by that means, but Thorleik said that would be of no use, "for Thorgils is far too high-mettled a man to stoop to trifles in a matter of this sort." Gudrun said in that case he must console himself as best he could at home. After this Thorgils rode from Holyfell with his foster-brothers. He got home to Tongue to his manor mightily ill at ease over his lot.

[9] Shield-wands = swords.

[10] Helmet-stems, those who upbear the helmet = men, specially warriors.

CHAPTER LXVI
Osvif and Gest die

That winter Osvif fell ill and died, and a great loss that was deemed, for he had been the greatest of sages. Osvif was buried at Holyfell, for Gudrun had had a church built there. That same winter Gest Oddliefson fell ill, and as the sickness grew heavy on him, he called to him Thord the Low, his son, and said, "My mind forebodes me that this sickness will put an end to our living together. I wish my body to be carried to Holyfell, for that will be the greatest place about these countrysides, for I have often seen a light burning there." Thereupon Gest died. The winter had been very cold, and there was much ice about, and Broadfirth was laid under ice so far out that no ship could get over it from Bardistrand. Gest's body lay in state two nights at Hegi, and that very night there sprang up such a gale that all the ice was drawn away from the land, and the next day the weather was fair and still. Then Thord took a ship and put Gest's body on board, and went south across Broadfirth that day, and came in the evening to Holyfell. Thord had a good welcome there, and stayed there through the night. In the morning Gest's body was buried, and he and Osvif rested in one grave. So Gest's soothsaying was fulfilled, in that now it was shorter between them than at the time when one dwelt at Bardistrand and the other in Sælingsdale. Thord the Low then went home as soon as he was ready. That next night a wild storm arose, and drove the ice on to the land again, where it held on long through the winter, so that there was no going about in boats. Men thought this most marvellous, that the weather had allowed Gest's body to be taken across when there was no crossing before nor afterwards during the winter.

CHAPTER LXVII
The Death of Thorgils Hallason, A.D. 1020

Thorarin was the name of a man who lived at Longdale: he was a chieftain, but not a mighty one. His son was named Audgisl, and was a nimble sort of a man. Thorgils Hallason took the chieftainship from them both, father and son. Audgisl went to see Snorri Godi, and told him of this unfairness and asked him to help. Snorri answered only by fair words, and belittled the whole affair; but answered, "Now that Halla's-grig is getting too forward and swaggering. Will Thorgils then happen on no man that will not give in to him in everything? No doubt he is a big man and doughty, but men as good as he is have also been sent to Hel." And when Audgisl went away Snorri gave him an inlaid axe. The next spring Thorgils Hallason and Thorstein the Black went south to Burgfirth, and offered atonement to the sons of Helgi and his other kinsmen, and they came to terms of peace on the matter, and fair honour was done (to Helgi's side). Thorstein paid two parts of the atonement for the manslaughter, and the third part Thorgils was to pay, payment being due at the Thing. In the summer Thorgils rode to the Thing, but when he and his men came to the lava field by Thingvellir, they saw a woman coming to meet them, and a mighty big one she was. Thorgils rode up to her, but she turned aside, and said this—

"Take care If you go forward, And be wary Of Snorri's wiles, No one can escape, For so wise is Snorri."

And after that she went her way. Then Thorgils said, "It has seldom happened so before, when luck was with me, that you were leaving the Thing when I was riding to it." He now rode to the Thing and to his own booth. And through the early part the Thing was quiet. It happened one day during the Thing that folk's clothes were hung out to dry. Thorgils had a blue hooded cloak, which was spread out on the booth wall, and men heard the cloak say thus—

"Hanging wet on the wall, A hooded cloak knows a braid (trick); I do not say he does not know two, He has been lately washed."

This was thought a most marvellous thing. The next day Thorgils went west over the river to pay the money to the sons of Helgi. He sat down on the lava above the booths, and with him was his foster-brother Halldor and sundry more of them were there together. The sons of Helgi came to the meeting. Thorgils now began to count out the money. Audgisl Thorarinson came near, and when Thorgils had counted ten Audgisl struck at him, and all thought they heard the head say eleven as it flew off the neck. Audgisl ran to the booth of the Waterfirthers and Halldor rushed after him and struck him his death-blow in the door of the booth. These tidings came to the booth of Snorri Godi how Thorgils was slain. Snorri said, "You must be mistaken; it must be that Thorgils Hallason has slain some one." The man replied, "Why, the head flew off his trunk." "Then perhaps it is time," said Snorri. This manslaughter was peacefully atoned, as is told in the Saga of Thorgils Hallason.

CHAPTER LXVIII
Gudrun's Marriage with Thorkell Eyjolfson

The same summer that Thorgils Hallason was killed a ship came to Bjorn's-haven. It belonged to Thorkell Eyjolfson. He was by then such a rich man that he had two merchant ships on voyages. The other ship came to Ramfirth to Board-Eyr; they were both laden with timber. When Snorri heard of the coming of Thorkell he rode at once to where the ship was. Thorkell gave him a most blithe welcome; he had a great deal of drink with him in his ship, and right unstintedly it was served, and many things they found to talk about. Snorri asked tidings of Norway, and Thorkell told him everything well and truthfully. Snorri told in return the tidings of all that had happened here while Thorkell had been away. "Now it seems to me," said Snorri, "you had better follow the counsel I set forth to you before you went abroad, and should give up voyaging about and settle down in quiet, and get for yourself the same woman to wife of whom we spoke then." Thorkell replied, "I understand what you are driving at; everything we bespoke then is still uppermost in my mind, for indeed I begrudge me not the noblest of matches could it but be brought about." Snorri spake, "I am most willing and ready to back that matter up on your behalf, seeing that now we are rid of both the things that seemed to you the most troublesome to overcome, if you were to get Gudrun for wife at all, in that Bolli is revenged and Thorgils is out of the way." Thorkell said, "Your counsels go very deep, Snorri, and into this affair I go heart and soul." Snorri stayed in the ship several nights, and then they took a ten-oared boat that floated alongside of the merchant ship and got ready with five-and-twenty men, and went to Holyfell. Gudrun gave an exceeding affectionate welcome to Snorri, and a most goodly cheer they had; and when they had been there one night Snorri called Gudrun to talk to him, and spake, "Matters have come to this, that I have undertaken this journey for my friend Thorkell, Eyjolf's son, and he has now come here, as you see, and his errand hither is to set forth the wooing of you. Thorkell is a man of noble degree. You know yourself all about his race and doings in life, nor is he short of wealth either. To my mind, he is now the one man west about here who is most likely to become a chieftain, if to that end he will put himself forward. Thorkell is held in great esteem when he is out there, but by much is he more honoured when he is in Norway in the train of titled men." Then answers Gudrun: "My sons Thorleik and Bolli must have most to say in this matter; but you, Snorri, are the third man on whom I shall most rely for counsels in matters by which I set a great store, for you have long been a wholesome guide to me." Snorri said he deemed it a clear case that Thorkell must not be turned off. Thereupon Snorri had the sons of Gudrun called in, and sets forth the matter to them, laying down how great an help Thorkell might afford them by reason of his wealth and wise foresight; and smoothly he framed his speech on this matter. Then Bolli answered: "My mother will know how most clearly to see through this matter, and herein I shall be of one mind with her own will. But, to be sure, we shall deem it wise to set much store by your pleading this matter, Snorri, for you have done to us mightily well in many things." Then Gudrun spake: "In this matter we will lean most on Snorri's foresight, for to us your counsels have been wholesome." Snorri urged the matter on by every word he spoke, and the counsel taken was, that Gudrun and Thorkell should be joined in marriage. Snorri offered to have the wedding at his house; and Thorkell, liking that well, said: "I am not short of means, and I am ready to furnish them in whatever measure you please." Then Gudrun spake: "It is my wish that the feast be held here at Holyfell. I do not blench at standing the cost of it, nor shall I call upon Thorkell or any one else to trouble themselves about this matter." "Often, indeed, you show, Gudrun," said Snorri, "that you are the most high-mettled of women." So this was now settled that the wedding should take place when it lacked six weeks of summer. At matters thus settled Snorri and Thorkell went away, Snorri going home and Thorkell to his ship, and he spent the summer, turn and turn about, at Tongue or at his ship. Time now wore on towards the wedding feast. Gudrun made great preparation with much ingatherings. Snorri came to the feast together with Thorkell, and they brought with them well-nigh sixty men, and a very picked company that was, for most of the men were in dyed raiments. Gudrun had well-nigh a hundred and twenty first-bidden guests. The brothers Bolli and Thorleik, with the first-bidden guests, went to meet Snorri and his train; and to him and his fellowship was given a right cheery welcome, and their horses are taken in hand, as well as their clothes. They were shown into the guest-chamber, and Thorkell and Snorri and their followers took seats on the bench that was the upper one, and Gudrun's guests sat on the lower.

CHAPTER LXIX

The Quarrel about Gunnar at the Feast

That autumn Gunnar, the slayer of Thridrandi, had been sent to Gudrun for "trust and keep," and she had taken him in, his name being kept secret. Gunnar was outlawed because of the slaying of Thridrandi, Geitir's son, as is told in the Niard-wickers' Saga. He went about much "with a hidden head," for that many great men had their eyes upon him. The first evening of the feast, when men went to wash, a big man was standing by the water; he was broad of shoulder and wide of chest, and this man had a hat on his head. Thorkell asked who he was. He named himself as it seemed best to him. Thorkell says: "I think you are not speaking the truth; going by what the tale tells you would seem more like to Gunnar, the slayer of Thridrandi. And if you are so great a hero as other men say, you will not keep hidden your name." Then said Gunnar: "You speak most eagerly on this matter; and, truth to tell, I think I have no need to hide myself from you. You have rightly named your man; but then, what have you chiefly bethought yourself of having done to me?" Thorkell said he would like that he should soon know it, and spake to his men, ordering them to lay hands on him. Gudrun sat on the dais at the upper end of the hall, together with other women all becoifed with white linen, and when she got aware of this she rises up from the bridal bench and calls on her men to lend Gunnar help, and told them to give quarter to no man who should show any doubtful behaviour. Gudrun had the greatest number of followers, and what never was meant to happen seemed like to befall. Snorri Godi went between both sides and bade them allay this storm. "The one thing clearly to be done by you, Thorkell, is not to push things on so hotly; and now you can see what a stirring woman Gudrun is, as she overrules both of us together." Thorkell said he had promised his namesake, Thorleik Geitir's son, that he would kill Gunnar if he came into the countrysides of the west. "And he is my greatest friend," Snorri spake. "You are much more in duty bound to act as we wish; and for yourself, it is a matter of the greatest importance, for you will never find such another woman as Gudrun, however far you may seek." And because of Snorri's reasoning, and seeing that he spoke the truth, Thorkell quieted down, and Gunnar was sent away that evening. The feast now went forward well and bravely, and when it was over the guests got ready to go away. Thorkell gave to Snorri very rich gifts, and the same to all the chief men. Snorri asked Bolli Bollison to go home with him, and to live with him as long as he liked. Bolli accepted this with thanks, and rides home to Tongue. Thorkell now settled down at Holyfell, and took in hand the affairs of the household, and it was soon seen that he was no worse a hand at that than at trade-voyaging. He had the hall pulled down in the autumn and a new one built, which was finished when the winter set in, and was both large and lofty. Between Gudrun and Thorkell dear love now grew up, and so the winter passed on. In the spring Gudrun asked how Thorkell was minded to look out for Gunnar the slayer of Thridrandi. He said that Gudrun had better take the management of that matter, "for you have taken it so hard in hand, that you will put up with nothing but that he be sent away with honour." Gudrun said he guessed aright: "I wish you to give him a ship, and therewithal such things as he cannot do without." Thorkell said and smiled, "You think nothing small on most matters, Gudrun, and would be ill served if you had a mean-minded man for a husband; nor has that ever been your heart's aim. Well, this shall be done after your own will"—and carried out it was. Gunnar took the gifts most gratefully. "I shall never be so 'long-armed' as to be able to repay all this great honour you are doing to me," he said. Gunnar now went abroad and came to Norway, and then went to his own estates. Gunnar was exceeding wealthy, most great-hearted, and a good and true man withal.

CHAPTER LXX
Thorleik goes to Norway

Thorkell Eyjolfson became a great chieftain; he laid himself out much for friendships and honours. He was a masterful man within his own countryside, and busied himself much about law-suits; yet of his pleadings at court there is no tale to tell here. Thorkell was the richest man in Broadfirth during his lifetime next after Snorri. Thorkell kept his house in good order. He had all the houses at Holyfell rebuilt large and strong. He also had the ground of a church marked out, and gave it out that he had made up his mind to go abroad and fetch timber for the building of his church. Thorkell and Gudrun had a son who was called Gellir; he looked early most likely to turn out well. Bolli Bollison spent his time turn and turn about at Tongue or Holyfell, and Snorri was very fond of him. Thorleik his brother lived at Holyfell. These brothers were both tall and most doughty looking, Bolli being the foremost in all things. Thorkell was kind to his stepsons, and Gudrun loved Bolli most of all her children. He was now sixteen, and

Thorleik twenty years old. So, once on a time, Thorleik came to talk to his stepfather and his mother, and said he wished to go abroad. "I am quite tired of sitting at home like a woman, and I wish that means to travel should be furnished to me." Thorkell said, "I do not think I have done against you two brothers in anything since our alliance began. Now, I think it is the most natural thing that you should yearn to get to know the customs of other men, for I know you will be counted a brisk man wheresoever you may come among doughty men." Thorleik said he did not want much money, "for it is uncertain how I may look after matters, being young and in many ways of an unsettled mind." Thorkell bade him have as much as he wanted. After that Thorkell bought for Thorleik a share in a ship that stood up in Daymeal-Ness, and saw him off to his ship, and fitted him well out with all things from home. Thorleik journeyed abroad that summer. The ship arrived in Norway. The lord over the land then was King Olaf the Holy. Thorleik went forthwith to see King Olaf, who gave him a good welcome; he knew Thorleik from his kindred, and so asked him to stay with him. Thorleik accepted with thanks, and stayed with the king that winter and became one of his guard, and the king held him in honour. Thorleik was thought the briskest of men, and he stayed on with King Olaf for several months. Now we must tell of Bolli Bollison. The spring when he was eighteen years old he spoke to his stepfather and his mother, and said that he wished they would hand him out his father's portion. Gudrun asked him what he had set his mind on doing, since he asked them to give him this money. Bolli answered, "It is my wish that a woman be wooed on my behalf, and I wish," said Bolli, "that you, Thorkell, be my spokesman and carry this through." Thorkell asked what woman it was Bolli wished to woo. Bolli answered, "The woman's name is Thordis, and she is the daughter of Snorri the Priest; she is the woman I have most at heart to marry; I shall be in no hurry to marry if I do not get this one for wife. And I set a very great store by this matter being carried out." Thorkell answered, "My help is quite welcome to you, my son, if you think that if I follow up this matter much weight lies thereon. I think the matter will be easily got over with Snorri, for he will know well enough how to see that a fair offer is made him by such as you." Gudrun said, "I will say at once, Thorkell, that I will let spare nothing so that Bolli may but have the match that pleases him, and that for two reasons, first, that I love him most, and then he has been the most whole-hearted of my children in doing my will." Thorkell gave it out that he was minded to furnish Bolli off handsomely. "It is what for many reasons is due to him, and I know, withal, that in Bolli a good husband will be purchased." A little while after Thorkell and Bolli went with a good many followers to Tongue. Snorri gave to them a kind and blithe welcome, and they were treated to the very best of cheers at Snorri's hands. Thordis, the daughter of Snorri, was at home with her father; she was a woman both goodly and of great parts. When they had been a few nights at Tongue Thorkell broached the wooing, bespeaking on behalf of Bolli an alliance with Snorri by marriage with Thordis, his daughter. Snorri answers, "It is well you come here on this errand; it is what I might have looked for from you. I will answer the matter well, for I think Bolli one of the most hopeful of men, and that woman I deem well given in marriage who is given in marriage to him. It will, however, tell most in this matter, how far this is to Thordis' own mind; for she shall marry such a man only on whom she sets her heart." This matter coming before Thordis she answered suchwise as that therein she would lean on the foresight of her father, saying she would sooner marry Bolli, a man from within her own countryside, than a stranger from farther away. And when Snorri found that it was not against her wish to go with Bolli, the affair was settled and the betrothal took place. Snorri was to have the feast at his house about the middle of summer. With that Thorkell and Bolli rode home to Holyfell, and Bolli now stayed at home till the time of the wedding-feast. Then Thorkell and Bolli array themselves to leave home, and with them all the men who were set apart therefor, and a crowded company and the bravest band that was. They then rode on their way and came to Tongue, and had a right hearty welcome there. There were great numbers there, and the feast was of the noblest, and when the feast comes to an end the guests get ready to depart. Snorri gave honourable gifts to Thorkell, yea and to both of them, him and Gudrun, and the same to his other friends and relations. And now each one of those who had gone to the feast rode to his own home. Bolli abode at Tongue, and between him and Thordis dear love sprang speedily up. Snorri did all he could to entertain Bolli well, and to him he was even kinder than to his own children. Bolli received all this gratefully, and remained at Tongue that year in great favour. The next summer a ship came to White-river. One-half of the ship belonged to Thorleik Bollison and the other half of it belonged to some Norwegian man. When Bolli heard of the coming of his brother he rode south to Burgfirth and to the ship. The brothers greeted each other joyfully. Bolli stayed there for several nights, and then both brothers ride together west to Holyfell; Thorkell takes them in with the greatest blitheness, as did also Gudrun, and they invited Thorleik to stay with them for the winter, and that he took with thanks. Thorleik tarried at Holyfell awhile, and then he rode to White-river and lets his ship be beached and his goods be brought to the West. Thorleik had had good luck with him both as to wealth and honours, for that he had become the henchman of that noblest of lords, King Olaf. He now stayed at Holyfell through the winter, while Bolli tarried at Tongue.

CHAPTER LXXI
The Peace between the Sons of Bolli and the Sons of Olaf, A.D. 1026

That winter the brothers would always be meeting, having talks together, and took no pleasure in games or any other pastime; and one time, when Thorleik was at Tongue, the brothers talked day and night together. Snorri then thought he knew that they must be taking counsel together on some very great matter, so he went and joined the talk of the brothers. They greeted him well, but dropped their talk forthwith. He took their greeting well; and presently Snorri spoke: "What are you taking counsels about so that ye heed neither sleep nor meat?" Bolli answers: "This is no framing of counsels, for that talk is one of but little mark which we talk together." Now Snorri found that they wanted to hide from him all that was in their minds, yet misdoubted him, that they must be talking chiefly of things from which great troubles might arise, in case they should be carried out. He (Snorri) spoke to them: "This I misdoubt me now, that it be neither a vain thing nor a matter of jest you are talking about for such long hours together, and I hold you quite excused, even if such should be the case. Now, be so good as to tell it me and not to hide it away from me. We shall not, when gathered all together, be worse able to take counsel in this matter, for that I shall nowhere stand in the way of anything going forward whereby your honour grows the greater." Thorleik thought Snorri had taken up their case in a kindly manner, and told him in a few words their wishes, and how they had made up their minds to set on the sons of Olaf, and to put them to sore penalties; they said that now they lacked of nothing to bring the sons of Olaf to terms of equality, since Thorleik was a liegeman of King Olaf, and Bolli was the son-in-law of such a chief as Snorri was. Snorri answered in this way: "For the slaying of Bolli enough has come in return, in that the life of Helgi Hardbeinson was paid therefor; the troubles of men have been far too great already, and it is high time that now at last they be put a stop to." Bolli said, "What now, Snorri? are you less keen now to stand by us than you gave out but a little while ago? Thorleik would not have told you our mind as yet if he had first taken counsel with me thereon. And when you claim that Helgi's life has come in revenge for Bolli, it is a matter well known to men that a money fine was paid for the slaying of Helgi, while my father is still unatoned for." When Snorri saw he could not reason them into a change of mind, he offered them to try to bring about a peaceful atonement between them and the sons of Olaf, rather than that any more manslaughters should befall; and the brothers agreed to this. Then Snorri rode with some men to Herdholt. Halldor gave him a good welcome, and asked him to stay there, but Snorri said he must ride back that night. "But I have an urgent errand with you." So they fell to talking together, and Snorri made known his errand, saying it had come to his knowledge that Thorleik and Bolli would put up with it no longer that their father should be unatoned at the hands of the sons of Olaf. "And now I would endeavour to bring about peace, and see if an end cannot be put to the evil luck that besets you kinsmen." Halldor did not flatly refuse to deal further with the case. "I know only too well that Thorgils Hallason and Bolli's sons were minded to fall on me and my brothers, until you turned elsewhere their vengeance, so that thence-forward it seemed to them best to slay Helgi Hardbeinson. In these matters you have taken a good part, whatever your counsels may have been like in regard to earlier dealings between us kinsmen." Snorri said, "I set a great store by my errand turning out well and that it might be brought about which I have most at heart, that a sound peace should be settled between you kinsmen; for I know the minds of the men who have to deal with you in this case so well, that they will keep faithfully to whatever terms of peace they agree to." Halldor said, "I will undertake this, if it be the wish of my brothers, to pay money for the slaying of Bolli, such as shall be awarded by the umpires chosen, but I bargain that there be no outlawing of anybody concerned, nor forfeiture of my chieftainship or estate; the same claim I make in respect of the estates my brothers are possessed of, and I make a point of their being left free owners thereof whatever be the close of this case, each side to choose their own umpire." Snorri answered, "This is offered well and frankly, and the brothers will take this choice if they are willing to set any store by my counsel." Thereupon Snorri rode home and told the brothers the outcome of his errand, and that he would keep altogether aloof from their case if they would not agree to this. Bolli bade him have his own way, "And I wish that you, Snorri, be umpire on our behalf." Then Snorri sent to Halldor to say that peaceful settlement was agreed to, and he bade them choose an umpire against himself. Halldor chose on his behalf Steinthor Thorlakson of Eyr. The peace meeting should be at Drangar on Shawstrand, when four weeks of summer were passed. Thorleik Bollison rode to Holyfell, and nothing to tell tidings of befell that winter, and when time wore unto the hour bespoken for the meeting, Snorri the Priest came there with the sons of Bolli, fifteen together in all; Steinthor and his came with the same number of men to the meeting. Snorri and Steinthor talked together and came to an agreement about these matters. After that they gave out the award, but it is not told how much money they awarded; this, however, is told, that the money was readily paid and the peace well holden to. At the Thorness Thing the fines were paid out; Halldor gave Bolli a good sword, and Steinthor Olafson gave Thorleik a shield, which was also a good gift. Then the Thing was broken up, and both sides were thought to have gained in esteem from these affairs.

CHAPTER LXXII
Bolli and Thorleik go abroad, A. D. 1029

After the peace between Bolli and Thorleik and the sons of Olaf had been settled and Thorleik had been one winter in Iceland, Bolli made it known that he was minded to go abroad. Snorri, dissuading him, said, "To us it seems there is a great risk to be run as to how you may speed; but if you wish to have in hand more than you have now, I will get you a manor and stock it for you; therewithal I shall hand over to you chieftainship over men and uphold you for honours in all things; and that, I know, will be easy, seeing that most men bear you good-will." Bolli said, "I have long had it in my mind to go for once into southern lands; for a man is deemed to grow benighted if he learns to know nothing farther afield than what is to be seen here in Iceland." And when Snorri saw that Bolli had set his mind on this, and that it would come to nought to try to stop him, he bade him take as much money as he liked for his journey. Bolli was all for having plenty of money, "for I will not," he said, "be beholden to any man either here or in any foreign land." Then Bolli rode south to Burgfirth to White-river and bought half of a ship from the owners, so that he and his brother became joint owners of the same ship. Bolli then rides west again to his home. He and Thordis had one daughter whose name was Herdis, and that maiden Gudrun asked to bring up. She was one year old when she went to Holyfell. Thordis also spent a great deal of her time there, for Gudrun was very fond of her.

CHAPTER LXXIII
Bolli's Voyage

Now the brothers went both to their ship. Bolli took a great deal of money abroad with him. They now arrayed the ship, and when everything was ready they put out to sea. The winds did not speed them fast, and they were a long time out at sea, but got to Norway in the autumn, and made Thrandheim in the north. Olaf, the king, was in the east part of the land, in the Wick, where he had made ingatherings for a stay through the winter. And when the brothers heard that the king would not come north to Thrandheim that autumn, Thorleik said he would go east along the land to meet King Olaf. Bolli said, "I have little wish to drift about between market towns in autumn days; to me that is too much of worry and restraint. I will rather stay for the winter in this town. I am told the king will come north in the spring, and if he does not then I shall not set my face against our going to meet him." Bolli has his way in the matter, and they put up their ship and got their winter quarters. It was soon seen that Bolli was a very pushing man, and would be the first among other men; and in that he had his way, for a bounteous man was he, and so got speedily to be highly thought of in Norway. Bolli kept a suite about him during the winter at Thrandheim, and it was easily seen, when he went to the guild meeting-places, that his men were both better arrayed as to raiment and weapons than other townspeople. He alone also paid for all his suite when they sat drinking in guild halls, and on a par with this were his openhandedness and lordly ways in other matters. Now the brothers stay in the town through the winter. That winter the king sat east in Sarpsborg, and news spread from the east that the king was not likely to come north. Early in the spring the brothers got their ship ready and went east along the land. The journey sped well for them, and they got east to Sarpsborg, and went forthwith to meet King Olaf. The king gave a good welcome to Thorleik, his henchman, and his followers. Then the king asked who was that man of stately gait in the train of Thorleik; and Thorleik answered, "He is my brother, and is named Bolli." "He looks, indeed, a man of high mettle," said the king. Thereupon the king asks the brothers to come and stay with him, and that offer they took with thanks, and spend the spring with the king. The king was as kind to Thorleik as he had been before, yet he held Bolli by much in greater esteem, for he deemed him even peerless among men. And as the spring went on, the brothers took counsel together about their journeys. And Thorleik asked Bolli if he was minded to go back to Iceland during the summer, "or will you stay on longer here in

Norway?" Bolli answered, "I do not mean to do either. And sooth to say, when I left Iceland, my thought was settled on this, that people should not be asking for news of me from the house next door; and now I wish, brother, that you take over our ship." Thorleik took it much to heart that they should have to part. "But you, Bolli, will have your way in this as in other things." Their matter thus bespoken they laid before the king, and he answered thus: "Will you not tarry with us any longer, Bolli?" said the king. "I should have liked it best for you to stay with me for a while, for I shall grant you the same title that I granted to Thorleik, your brother." Then Bolli answered: "I should be only too glad to bind myself to be your henchman, but I must go first whither I am already bent, and have long been eager to go, but this choice I will gladly take if it be fated to me to come back." "You will have your way as to your journeyings, Bolli," says the king, "for you Icelanders are self-willed in most matters. But with this word I must close, that I think you, Bolli, the man of greatest mark that has ever come from Iceland in my days." And when Bolli had got the king's leave he made ready for his journey, and went on board a round ship that was bound south for Denmark. He also took a great deal of money with him, and sundry of his followers bore him company. He and King Olaf parted in great friendship, and the king gave Bolli some handsome gifts at parting. Thorleik remained behind with King Olaf, but Bolli went on his way till he came south to Denmark. That winter he tarried in Denmark, and had great honour there of mighty men; nor did he bear himself there in any way less lordly than while he was in Norway. When Bolli had been a winter in Denmark he started on his journey out into foreign countries, and did not halt in his journey till he came to

Micklegarth (Constantinople). He was there only a short time before he got himself into the Varangian Guard, and, from what we have heard, no Northman had ever gone to take war-pay from the Garth king before Bolli, Bolli's son. He tarried in Micklegarth very many winters, and was thought to be the most valiant in all deeds that try a man, and always went next to those in the forefront. The Varangians accounted Bolli most highly of whilst he was with them in Micklegarth.

CHAPTER LXXIV

Thorkell Eyjolfson goes to Norway

Now the tale is to be taken up again where Thorkell Eyjolfson sits at home in lordly way. His and Gudrun's son, Gellir, grew up there at home, and was early both a manly fellow and winning. It is said how once upon a time Thorkell told Gudrun a dream he had had. "I dreamed," he said, "that I had so great a beard that it spread out over the whole of Broadfirth." Thorkell bade her read his dream. Gudrun said, "What do you think this dream betokens?" He said, "To me it seems clear that in it is hinted that my power will stand wide about the whole of Broadfirth." Gudrun said, "Maybe that such is the meaning of it, but I rather should think that thereby is betokened that you will dip your beard down into Broadfirth." That same summer Thorkell runs out his ship and gets it ready for Norway. His son, Gellir, was then twelve winters old, and he went abroad with his father. Thorkell makes it known that he means to fetch timber to build his church with, and sails forthwith into the main sea when he was ready. He had an easy voyage of it, but not a very short one, and they hove into Norway northwardly. King Olaf then had his seat in Thrandheim, and Thorkell sought forthwith a meeting with King Olaf, and his son Gellir with him. They had there a good welcome. So highly was Thorkell accounted of that winter by the king, that all folk tell that the king gave him not less than one hundred marks of refined silver. The king gave to Gellir at Yule a cloak, the most precious and excellent of gifts. That winter King Olaf had a church built in the town of timber, and it was a very great minster, all materials thereto being chosen of the best. In the spring the timber which the king gave to Thorkell was brought on board ship, and large was that timber and good in kind, for Thorkell looked closely after it. Now it happened one morning early that the king went out with but few men, and saw a man up on the church which then was being built in the town. He wondered much at this, for it was a good deal earlier than the smiths were wont to be up. Then the king recognised the man, and, lo! there was Thorkell Eyjolfson taking the measure of all the largest timber, crossbeams, sills, and pillars. The king turned at once thither, and said: "What now, Thorkell, do you mean after these measurements to shape the church timber which you are taking to Iceland?" "Yes, in truth, sire," said Thorkell. Then said King Olaf, "Cut two ells off every main beam, and that church will yet be the largest built in Iceland." Thorkell answered, "Keep your timber yourself if you think you have given me too much, or your hand itches to take it back, but not an ell's length shall I cut off it. I shall both know how to go about and how to carry out getting other timber for me." Then says the king most calmly, "So it is, Thorkell, that you are not only a man of much account, but you are also now making yourself too big, for, to be sure, it is too overweening for the son of a mere peasant to try to vie with us. But it is not true that I begrudge you the timber, if only it be fated to you to build a church therewith; for it will never be large enough for all your pride to find room to lie inside it. But near it comes to the foreboding of my mind, that the timber will be of little use to men, and that it will be far from you ever to get any work by man done with this timber." After that they ceased talking, and the king turned away, and it was marked by people that it misliked him how Thorkell accounted as of nought what he said. Yet the king himself did not let people get the wind of it, and he and Thorkell parted in great good-will. Thorkell got on board his ship and put to sea. They had a good wind, and were not long out about the main. Thorkell brought his ship to Ramfirth, and rode soon from his ship home to Holyfell, where all folk were glad to see him. In this journey Thorkell had gained much honour. He had his ship hauled ashore and made snug, and the timber for the church he gave to a caretaker, where it was safely bestowed, for it could not be brought from the north this autumn, as he was at all time full of business. Thorkell now sits at home at his manor throughout the winter. He had Yule-drinking at Holyfell, and to it there came a crowd of people; and altogether he kept up a great state that winter. Nor did Gudrun stop him therein; for she said the use of money was that people should increase their state therewith; moreover, whatever Gudrun must needs be supplied with for all purposes of high-minded display, that (she said) would be readily forthcoming (from her husband). Thorkell shared that winter amongst his friends many precious things he had brought with him out to Iceland.

CHAPTER LXXV

Thorkell and Thorstein and Halldor Olafson, A.D. 1026

That winter after Yule Thorkell got ready to go from home north to Ramfirth to bring his timber from the north. He rode first up into the Dales and then to Lea-shaws to Thorstein, his kinsman, where he gathered together men and horses. He afterwards went north to Ramfirth and stayed there awhile, taken up with the business of his journey, and gathered to him horses from about the firth, for he did not want to make more than one journey of it, if that could be managed. But this did not speed swiftly, and Thorkell was busy at this work even into Lent. At last he got under way with the work, and had the wood dragged from the north by more than twenty horses, and had the timber stacked on Lea-Eyr, meaning later on to bring it in a boat out to Holyfell. Thorstein owned a large ferry-boat, and this boat Thorkell was minded to use for his homeward voyage. Thorkell stayed at Lea-shaws through Lent, for there was dear friendship between these kinsmen. Thorstein said one day to Thorkell, they had better go to Herdholt, "for I want to make a bid for some land from Halldor, he having but little money since he paid the brothers the weregild for their father, and the land being just what I want most." Thorkell bade him do as he liked; so they left home a party of twenty men together. They come to Herdholt, and Halldor gave them good welcome, and was most free of talk with them. There were few men at home, for Halldor had sent his men north to Steingrims-firth, as a whale had come ashore there in which he owned a share. Beiner the Strong was at home, the only man now left alive of those who had been there with Olaf, the father of Halldor. Halldor had said to Beiner at

Anonymous

once when he saw Thorstein and Thorkell riding up, "I can easily see what the errand of these kinsmen is—they are going to make me a bid for my land, and if that is the case they will call me aside for a talk; I guess they will seat themselves each on either side of me; so, then, if they should give me any trouble you must not be slower to set on Thorstein than I on Thorkell. You have long been true to us kinsfolk. I have also sent to the nearest homesteads for men, and at just the same moment I should like these two things to happen: the coming in of the men summoned, and the breaking up of our talk." Now as the day wore on, Thorstein hinted to Halldor that they should all go aside and have some talk together, "for we have an errand with you." Halldor said it suited him well. Thorstein told his followers they need not come with them, but Beiner went with them none the less, for he thought things came to pass very much after what Halldor had guessed they would. They went very far out into the field. Halldor had on a pinned-up cloak with a long pin brooch, as was the fashion then. Halldor sat down on the field, but on either side of him each of these kinsmen, so near that they sat well-nigh on his cloak; but Beiner stood over them with a big axe in his hand. Then said Thorstein, "My errand here is that I wish to buy land from you, and I bring it before you now because my kinsman Thorkell is with me; I should think that this would suit us both well, for I hear that you are short of money, while your land is costly to husband. I will give you in return an estate that will beseem you, and into the bargain as much as we shall agree upon." In the beginning Halldor took the matter as if it were not so very far from his mind, and they exchanged words concerning the terms of the purchase; and when they felt that he was not so far from coming to terms,

Thorkell joined eagerly in the talk, and tried to bring the bargain to a point. Then Halldor began to draw back rather, but they pressed him all the more; yet at last it came to this, that he was the further from the bargain the closer they pressed him. Then said Thorkell, "Do you not see, kinsman Thorstein, how this is going? Halldor has delayed the matter for us all day long, and we have sat here listening to his fooling and wiles. Now if you want to buy the land we must come to closer quarters." Thorstein then said he must know what he had to look forward to, and bade Halldor now come out of the shadow as to whether he was willing to come to the bargain. Halldor answered, "I do not think I need keep you in the dark as to this point, that you will have to go home to-night without any bargain struck." Then said Thorstein, "Nor do I think it needful to delay making known to you what we have in our mind to do; for we, deeming that we shall get the better of you by reason of the odds on our side, have bethought us of two choices for you: one choice is, that you do this matter willingly and take in return our friendship; but the other, clearly a worse one, is, that you now stretch out your hand against your own will and sell me the land of Herdholt." But when Thorstein spoke in this outrageous manner, Halldor leapt up so suddenly that the brooch was torn from his cloak, and said, "Something else will happen before I utter that which is not my will." "What is that?" said Thorstein. "A pole-axe will stand on your head from one of the worst of men, and thus cast down your insolence and unfairness." Thorkell answered, "That is an evil prophecy, and I hope it will not be fulfilled; and now I think there is ample cause why you, Halldor, should give up your land and have nothing for it." Then Halldor answered, "Sooner you will be embracing the sea-tangle in Broadfirth than I sell my land against my own will." Halldor went home after that, and the men he had sent for came crowding up to the place. Thorstein was of the wrothest, and wanted forthwith to make an onset on Halldor. Thorkell bade him not to do so, "for that is the greatest enormity at such a season as this; but when this season wears off, I shall not stand in the way of his and ours clashing together." Halldor said he was given to think he would not fail in being ready for them. After that they rode away and talked much together of this their journey; and Thorstein, speaking thereof, said that, truth to tell, their journey was most wretched. "But why, kinsman Thorkell, were you so afraid of falling on Halldor and putting him to some shame?" Thorkell answered, "Did you not see Beiner, who stood over you with the axe reared aloft? Why, it was an utter folly, for forthwith on seeing me likely to do anything, he would have driven that axe into your head." They rode now home to Lea-shaws; and Lent wears and Passion Week sets in.

CHAPTER LXXVI
The Drowning of Thorkell, A.D. 1026

On Maundy Thursday, early in the morning, Thorkell got ready for his journey. Thorstein set himself much against it: "For the weather looks to me uncertain," said he. Thorkell said the weather would do all right. "And you must not hinder me now, kinsman, for I wish to be home before Easter." So now Thorkell ran out the ferry-boat, and loaded it. But Thorstein carried the lading ashore from out the boat as fast as Thorkell and his followers put it on board. Then Thorkell said, "Give over now, kinsman, and do not hinder our journey this time; you must not have your own way in this."

Thorstein said, "He of us two will now follow the counsel that will answer the worst, for this journey will cause the happening of great matters." Thorkell now bade them farewell till their next meeting, and Thorstein went home, and was exceedingly downcast. He went to the guest-house, and bade them lay a pillow under his head, the which was done. The servant-maid saw how the tears ran down upon the pillow from his eyes. And shortly afterwards a roaring blast struck the house, and Thorstein said, "There, we now can hear roaring the slayer of kinsman Thorkell." Now to tell of the journey of Thorkell and his company: they sail this day out, down Broadfirth, and were ten on board. The wind began to blow very high, and rose to full gale before it blew over. They pushed on their way briskly, for the men were most plucky. Thorkell had with him the sword Skofnung, which was laid in the locker. Thorkell and his party sailed till they came to Bjorn's isle, and people could watch them journey from both shores. But when they had come thus far, suddenly a squall caught the sail and overwhelmed the boat. There Thorkell was drowned and all the men who were with him. The timber drifted ashore wide about the islands, the corner-staves (pillars) drove ashore in the island called Staff-isle. Skofnung stuck fast to the timbers of the boat, and was found in Skofnungs-isle. That same evening that Thorkell and his followers were drowned, it happened at Holyfell that Gudrun went to the church, when other people had gone to bed, and when she stepped into the lich-gate she saw a ghost standing before her. He bowed over her and said, "Great tidings, Gudrun." She said, "Hold then your peace about them, wretch." Gudrun went on to the church, as she had meant to do, and when she got up to the church she thought she saw that Thorkell and his companions were come home and stood before the door of the church, and she saw that water was running off their clothes. Gudrun did not speak to them, but went into the church, and stayed there as long as it seemed good to her. After that she went to the guest-room, for she thought Thorkell and his followers must have gone there; but when she came into the chamber, there was no one there. Then Gudrun was struck with wonder at the whole affair. On Good Friday Gudrun sent her men to find out matters concerning the journeying of Thorkell and his company, some up to Shawstrand and some out to the islands. By then the flotsam had already come to land wide about the islands and on both shores of the firth. The Saturday before Easter the tidings got known and great news they were thought to be, for Thorkell had been a great chieftain. Thorkell was eight-and-forty years old when he was drowned, and that was four winters before Olaf the Holy fell. Gudrun took much to heart the death of Thorkell, yet bore her bereavement bravely. Only very little of the church timber could ever be gathered in. Gellir was now fourteen years old, and with his mother he took over the business of the household and the chieftainship. It was soon seen that he was made to be a leader of men. Gudrun now became a very religious woman. She was the first woman in Iceland who knew the Psalter by heart. She would spend long time in the church at nights saying her prayers, and Herdis, Bolli's daughter, always went with her at night. Gudrun loved Herdis very much. It is told that one night the maiden Herdis dreamed that a woman came to her who was dressed in a woven cloak, and coifed in a head cloth, but she did not think the woman winning to look at. She spoke, "Tell your grandmother that I am displeased with her, for she creeps about over me every night, and lets fall down upon me drops so hot that I am burning all over from them. My reason for letting you know this is, that I like you somewhat better, though there is something uncanny hovering about you too. However, I could get on with you if I did not feel there was so much more amiss with Gudrun." Then Herdis awoke and told Gudrun her dream. Gudrun thought the apparition was of good omen. Next morning Gudrun had planks taken up from the church floor where she was wont to kneel on the hassock, and she had the earth dug up, and they found blue and evil-looking bones, a round brooch, and a wizard's wand, and men thought they knew then that a tomb of some sorceress must have been there; so the bones were taken to a place far away where people were least likely to be passing.

CHAPTER LXXVII
The Return of Bolli, A.D. 1030

When four winters were passed from the drowning of Thorkell Eyjolfson a ship came into Islefirth belonging to Bolli Bollison, most of the crew of which were Norwegians. Bolli brought out with him much wealth, and many precious things that lords abroad had given him. Bolli was so great a man for show when he came back from this journey that he would wear no clothes but of scarlet and fur, and all his weapons were bedight with gold: he was called Bolli the Grand. He made it known to his shipmasters that he was going west to his own countrysides, and he left his ship and goods in the hands of his crew. Bolli rode from the ship with twelve men, and all his followers were dressed in scarlet, and rode on gilt saddles, and all were they a trusty band, though Bolli was peerless among them. He had on the clothes of fur which the Garth-king had given him, he had over all a scarlet cape; and he had Footbiter girt on him, the hilt of which was dight with gold, and the grip woven with gold; he had a gilded helmet on his head, and a red shield on his flank, with a knight painted on it in gold. He had a dagger in his hand, as is the custom in foreign lands; and whenever they took quarters the women paid heed to nothing but gazing at Bolli and his grandeur, and that of his followers. In this state Bolli rode into the western parts all the way till he came to Holyfell with his following. Gudrun was very glad to see her son. Bolli did not stay there long till he rode up to Sælingsdale Tongue to see Snorri, his father-in-law, and his wife Thordis, and their meeting was exceeding joyful. Snorri asked Bolli to stay with him with as many of his men as he liked. Bolli accepted the invitation gratefully, and was with Snorri all the winter, with the men who had ridden from the north with him. Bolli got great renown from this journey. Snorri made it no less his business now to treat Bolli with every kindness than when he was with him before.

CHAPTER LXXVIII
The Death of Snorri, and the End, A.D. 1031

When Bolli had been one winter in Iceland Snorri the Priest fell ill. That illness did not gain quickly on him, and Snorri lay very long abed. But when the illness gained on him, he called to himself all his kinsfolk and affinity, and said to Bolli, "It is my wish that you shall take over the manor here and the chieftainship after my day, for I grudge honours to you no more than to my own sons, nor is there within this land now the one of my sons who I think will be the greatest man among them, Halldor to wit." Thereupon Snorri breathed his last, being seventy-seven years old. That was one winter after the fall of St. Olaf, so said Ari the Priest "Deep-in-lore." Snorri was buried at Tongue. Bolli and Thordis took over the manor of Tongue as Snorri had willed it, and Snorri's sons put up with it with a good will. Bolli grew a man of great account, and was much beloved. Herdis, Bolli's daughter, grew up at Holyfell, and was the goodliest of all women. Orm, the son of Hermund, the son of Illugi, asked her in marriage, and she was given in wedlock to him; their son was Kodran, who had for wife Gudrun, the daughter of Sigmund. The son of Kodran was Hermund, who had for wife Ulfeid, the daughter of Runolf, who was the son of Bishop Kelill; their sons were Kelill, who was Abbot of Holyfell, and Reinn and Kodran and Styrmir; their daughter was Thorvor, whom Skeggi, Bard's son, had for wife, and from whom is come the stock of the Shaw-men. Ospak was the name of the son of Bolli and Thordis. The daughter of Ospak was Gudrun, whom Thorarin, Brand's son, had to wife. Their son was Brand, who founded the benefice of Housefell. Gellir, Thorleik's son, took to him a wife, and married Valgerd, daughter of Thorgils Arison of Reekness. Gellir went abroad, and took service with King Magnus the Good, and had given him by the king twelve ounces of gold and many goods besides. The sons of Gellir were Thorkell and Thorgils, and a son of Thorgils was Ari the "Deep-in-lore." The son of Ari was named Thorgils, and his son was Ari the Strong. Now Gudrun began to grow very old, and lived in such sorrow and grief as has lately been told. She was the first nun and recluse in Iceland, and by all folk it is said that Gudrun was the noblest of women of equal birth with her in this land. It is told how once upon a time Bolli came to Holyfell, for Gudrun was always very pleased when he came to see her, and how he sat by his mother for a long time, and they talked of many things. Then Bolli said, "Will you tell me, mother, what I want very much to know? Who is the man you have loved the most?" Gudrun answered, "Thorkell was the mightiest man and the greatest chief, but no man was more shapely or better endowed all round than Bolli. Thord, son of Ingun, was the wisest of them all, and the greatest lawyer; Thorvald I take no account of." Then said Bolli, "I clearly understand that what you tell me shows how each of your husbands was endowed, but you have not told me yet whom you loved the best. Now there is no need for you to keep that hidden any longer." Gudrun answered, "You press me hard, my son, for this, but if I must needs tell it to any one, you are the one I should first choose thereto." Bolli bade her do so. Then Gudrun said, "To him I was worst whom I loved best." "Now," answered Bolli, "I think the whole truth is told," and said she had done well to tell him what he so much had yearned to know. Gudrun grew to be a very old woman, and some say she lost her sight. Gudrun died at Holyfell, and there she rests. Gellir, Thorkell's son, lived at Holyfell to old age, and many things of much account are told of him; he also comes into many Sagas, though but little be told of him here. He built a church at Holyfell, a very stately one, as Arnor, the Earls' poet, says in the funeral song which he wrote about Gellir, wherein he uses clear words about that matter. When Gellir was somewhat sunk into his latter age, he prepared himself for a journey away from Iceland. He went to Norway, but did not stay there long, and then left straightway that land and "walked" south to Rome to "see the holy apostle Peter." He was very long over this journey; and then journeying from the south he came into Denmark, and there he fell ill and lay in bed a very long time, and received all the last rites of the church, whereupon he died, and he rests at Roskild. Gellir had taken Skofnung with him, the sword that had been taken out of the barrow of Holy Kraki, and never after could it be got back. When the death of Gellir was known in Iceland, Thorkell, his son, took over his father's inheritance at Holyfell. Thorgils, another of Gellir's sons, was drowned in Broadfirth at an early age, with all hands on board. Thorkell Gellirson was a most learned man, and was said to be of all men the best stocked of lore. Here is the end of the Saga of the men of Salmon-river-Dale.

NOTE

These lines may be thus interpreted:—

"Hangs a wet hood on the wall; It knoweth of a trick; Though it be at most times 'dry,' I hide not now it knoweth two."

The ditty points to the fact that Snorri had given Audgisl Thorarinson a "chased axe" (one trick), and that, at Snorri's secret behest, Audgisl was now on the eve of taking the hood-owner's (Thorgils Hallason's) life (two). This, the hood says, it knows, though at most times it is 'dry.' 'Dry' here seems clearly to stand in the sense of 'clear of,' 'free from,' *expers, immunis*; practically, *ignorant*. At most times the hood is ignorant of such 'tricks' threatening Thorgils' life, though now it knows of one, even two. With this use of 'ðurr,' *cf.* Sturlunga[2] ii. 227_{37}—"Um sum illvirki þeirra er þat sumum mönnum eigi tvímælis-laust, hvárt þér munið þurt hafa um setið allar vitundir" = "As to some misdeeds of theirs, it is to some men (a matter) not free from double speech whether you will have sat (by) 'dry' of all knowledge (*i.e.* complicity) therein," *i.e.*, concerning certain of their misdeeds some persons will have their doubts as to whether you be 'clear of' all complicity therein.

Of course it is Thorgils' 'Fylgja' (Fetch) that speaks through the cloak.

See all available titles at
https://www.facebook.com/nebula.literature

Nebula books are organized and designed by Lu Evans, a writer who has a great passion for Fantastic Literature.

Lu Evans is an American citizen raised in Brazil where she got a Bachelor degree in Journalism and started writing fantastic literature in Portuguese.

Her first book in English is a science fiction titled **HILI** and released in 2017. But she started as a writer a long time ago.

In 2007, she published her first book in Portuguese, **TEATRO DE LU EVANS** (Theater of Lu Evans), that reunites 20 theater plays for children that she wrote between the 90's and the first decade of 2000. This book was re-edited and republished in 2015.

ZYLGOR is a fantasy series published between 2014 and 2018 and is divided into four volumes: A PRINCESA DAS ÁGUAS (The Princes of the Waters), 2014. O PRÍNCIPE FLAMEJANTE (The Flaming Prince), 2016. A PRINCESA DOS VENTOS (The Princess of the Winds), 2017. O SENHOR DOS ABISMOS (The Lord of the Abyss), published in 2018. This series is currently been translated into English.

Lu Evans is co-author (being Graci Rocha the other author) of the dystopian novel **SOMNIIS**, 2017, that will be published in English soon.

Her books have received excellent reviews from Brazilian booktubers and bloggers, and favorable reviews from the readers.

Her literary works can be found at
Amazon.com

Anonymous

CPSIA information can be obtained
at www.ICGtesting.com
Printed in the USA
LVHW031627270319
612035LV00002B/295